AFTERBURN

A KENZIE GILMORE THRILLER
BOOK 1

BIBA PEARCE

LIQUID MIND PUBLISHING

Copyright © 2021 by Biba Pearce. All rights reserved. No part of this publication may be copied, reproduced in any format, by any means, electronic or otherwise, without prior consent from the copyright owner and publisher of this book.

Liquid Mind Publishing

This is a work of fiction. All characters, names, places and events are the product of the author's imagination or used fictitiously.

ALSO BY BIBA PEARCE

The Kenzie Gilmore Series

Afterburn

Dead Heat

Heatwave

Burnout

Deep Heat

Fever Pitch

Storm Surge (Coming Soon)

Detective Rob Miller Mysteries

The Thames Path Killer

The West London Murders

The Bisley Wood Murders

The Box Hill Killer

Follow the link for your free **copy of** *Hard Line: A Kenzie Gilmore Prequel.*

https://liquidmind.media/biba-pearce-sign-up-1/

1

It was the yellow dress that caught his eye. It was so out of place amongst the murky greens and muddy browns of the swamp. A daffodil amongst the reeds. Reid Garrett angled his airboat towards it and accelerated. He flew over the sawgrass, the sudden wind providing a welcome relief to the immense heat of the day. He'd been out here for hours, watching, waiting, hoping to catch a glimpse of the killer dumping bodies in the Glades.

So far, nothing—until now.

He didn't want it to be another one, but as he got closer, there was no denying it. It was a human form. Female, long legs, dark hair entangled in the reeds.

Shit.

He cut the engine and the airboat glided to a stop. The sudden silence that followed the loud jet engine was deafening. Water lapped against the hull as he peered over the side. She'd been mutilated by alligators or the elements, or both. An arm missing, along with a chunk of her leg. No blood though. The decomp and the water had seen to that.

Nothing lasted long out here. The heat and humidity got to work almost instantly. He guessed three or four days, by the looks of her.

A relatively short time compared to the others.

The first body, found by a park ranger, had been unrecognizable. At first, he'd thought it was an animal. A deer or large raccoon maybe, unlucky enough to wander into the path of a hungry gator. He was still talking about it four months later, to anyone who would listen. Her name was Sarah Randall, an 18-year-old student from Tallahassee. She'd been in South Beach for spring break. Her friends had reported her missing when she didn't come back after a night out.

She'd met a man at the bar. He seemed nice. No, they didn't get a good look at him. Dark hair, though, and a good physique. Or so they thought. They were pretty drunk at the time.

The second victim, a few months later, was a real estate agent from Orlando. She was here on a girls' weekend. Some fun in the Miami sun before starting her new job. Her name was Miranda. Pretty, nice smile. People wanted to buy houses from her. It had taken them a week to ID her, she was so badly decomposed. Her dental records had been most helpful in the end. That smile had been expensive.

Reid had both their names and faces burned into his memory. He looked down at the slender figure floating amongst the sawgrass. Now he had another girl to add to the ghosts in his head.

Someone was dumping bodies in his backyard, and he didn't appreciate it. He'd moved out here to forget, but he only seemed to be remembering.

There was a rustle in the vegetation behind him and a silver flash of a tail. The gators weren't done with her yet. If they didn't get her out of the water soon, there wouldn't be anything left to look at.

He reached for his cell phone and dialed 911.

This part of the Everglades was so remote that recovering the body would be difficult. As expected, it took police divers three hours to get there, wading through the murky water, accompanied by sharpshooters armed with AR-15s to ward off lethal predators. The gators weren't the only thing that could kill you around here.

The CSI guys didn't even try. "No point," said the police diver in charge. "She was probably dumped somewhere else anyway."

Reid watched them turn her over and load her onto a stretcher. Once they got her to firmer ground, they'd bag her and take her to the morgue. He stared at her face, swollen and disfigured. They all looked like that afterwards, the ones found in the water, anyway. Sometimes it was so bad their own family members couldn't recognize them.

He'd snapped a couple of shots of her lying in the water before they'd pulled her out. The "After" photo.

The "Before" photo was usually taken from the victim's social media account. Happy, carefree pictures. Reckless smiles, unguarded expressions. No idea of what was coming.

He used to put both up on the board in the incident room. A reminder of *who* they used to be. A person, not a victim. That was someone else's job now.

Reid was lying in his hammock on the deck when the two detectives arrived. Jonny Silva and a female officer he hadn't met.

"How are you doing, Reid?" Jonny didn't quite look him in the eye. After what had happened last year, Reid didn't blame him. He could barely look himself in the eye.

"I'm good," he lied. "How are things at Miami PD?"

"Not so good. This freaking drug war's got everyone on edge. We're short staffed, the case load is piling up, and now we've got this crazy lunatic raping and dumping young women in the Glades."

"Not much has changed, then?"

"Pretty much." He waved a hand around. "Nice place you got here. I haven't been out this way before."

"I like it."

It was an airboat tour company that went bust. The rustic

wooden cabin was built on decking that extended over the water. There were two adjoining huts, one he'd converted into a bedroom, the other a bathroom, but the biggest alteration had been knocking out the front wall and installing glass sliding doors to the deck. He kept them wide open most days to let in the breeze.

He was close enough to civilization to have electricity and running water, but that was about it. There was no air conditioning, no Wi-Fi, the thatched roof leaked, and in the rainy months he was inundated with mosquitos. The nearest grocery store was in Homestead, a couple miles away, but there was a bar close by called Smiley Jim's, next to the low budget Gator Inn, and a fishing store that sold bait and tackle.

"Don't you get lonely out here by yourself?" asked the female detective. She was young, early twenties, with a fresh-faced enthusiasm and wide eyes that took in everything. Hard to believe he used to be like that, once upon a time.

"This is Detective Ryan," said Jonny, hastily. "Joined homicide after you left."

Reid nodded a greeting. "I enjoy the solitude."

"It's an honor to meet you, Sergeant Garrett. I've heard about you." She flushed. "I mean, the guys on the team talk."

"I'm not a sergeant anymore." But he acknowledged her compliment with a small inclination of his head. He'd had a good run at Miami PD before it had all gone to hell. If he hadn't left, if the undercover operation hadn't imploded like it did, he'd have made Lieutenant by now. But there was no point in lamenting over the past. What was done was done, and he couldn't go back. No matter how much he wished it. For him, it was over, but most of his team were still there, scattered around the department.

"Who's running the investigation?" he asked.

"Ortega, if you can call it running. The team's split down the middle. We're too busy doing damage control from last week's gang shooting to concentrate on this. The captain's on the warpath." He shook his head. "To be honest, Reid, we miss having you around."

It sounded like mayhem.

"What do you want from me?" He honed in on why they were here. The last thing he needed was a stroll down memory lane—or to be reminded of the politics in the force. The city had to be cleaned up, the gangs brought under control. Residents were looking to the authorities to restore order, and happy residents meant more votes at election time. The women found out in the Glades were not a priority.

"The Lieutenant thought you might have some insight into the dead girl."

He couldn't resist a grin. Lieutenant Pérez knew him too well. He'd known Reid wouldn't leave this alone. Not when the victims were popping up in his neck of the woods.

"Perhaps you could start with how you came to discover the body?" Detective Ryan asked.

"I was out on my boat," he said. He'd bought the airboat from the tourist operator along with the property. It was the best way to explore the waterways, especially the more remote parts. "I go out most mornings, weather permitting. I thought I'd check out the cypress swamps, and there she was. Floating face down, in that yellow dress." He shook his head at the memory. "I knew it was another one of his victims."

"The Swamp Strangler," muttered Ryan.

Reid clenched his jaw. Damn reporters and their catchy titles. All they cared about was selling newspapers. He doubted they even paused to consider the effect their words might have on the victims or their families.

"You're right about that," Jonny piped up. "This one was strangled like the others. From what we can see, it's the same MO."

"Was she also sexually assaulted?" Reid narrowed his eyes.

"We don't know yet. The autopsy is scheduled for this afternoon." Jonny gave him a hard look. "But if it's the same guy, then yeah."

The previous two victims had been brutally raped before being strangled. Reid closed his eyes, unable to think about what the poor woman had been through before he'd found her.

"What kind of man does this?" whispered Ryan, hollow-eyed.

It was a question he'd asked himself a thousand times.

"One that's not right in the head," Jonny retorted.

"Or someone who's got something against women," Reid said. "A deep-seated hatred born out of abuse or mistreatment, or an earlier trauma."

"I can't even imagine—" she began.

"It's best not to," cut in Reid.

Her phone rang. She turned away to answer it. "Detective Ryan."

Jonny walked onto the deck and gazed out over the water. The sun had set, taking the heat of the day with it. A welcome breeze blew off the wetlands, rustling the long grass. There was a splash as something slid into the water, the snap of a breaking twig.

"How are we going to catch this guy, Reid?" He turned to look at his former boss. "We have no DNA, no fibers, no nothing."

"Have you looked for a link between the girls?" Reid thought back to what he'd do, how he'd handle it. "How is he targeting them?"

"They don't appear to have anything in common," Jonny said. "Other than they were both from out of town. Sarah was from Tallahassee, Miranda was from Orlando. They didn't know each other … their families didn't know each other … they stayed at different hotels." He shrugged helplessly.

"You're kidding me!" Ryan's high-pitched voice made them turn around.

"Oh, my God." She flushed pink with excitement.

Jonny mouthed, "What?"

Ryan ended the call, her eyes gleaming. "We've just got an ID on the third victim. You're never going to believe this. It's Natalia Cruz."

Both men stared at her.

"You know, the reality TV star. Her father owns half the state of Florida. She's married to DJ Snake."

More blank stares.

"God, you two are hopeless." She threw her hands in the air. "Natalia is a celebrity. Her wedding was the society event of the year. It was in all the papers."

"The pharmaceutical billionaire?" Reid seemed to remember reading something about a high society wedding.

"Yes, that's Rhys Arnold. Natalia is his daughter. She took her mother's name after the divorce."

"Rhys Arnold. Sweet Jesus." Jonny ran a hand through his hair. "That means the press will be all over this. The Captain is going to go ape-shit."

Reid knew he was worried about the pressure that was sure to rain down from above. The case nobody cared about had suddenly become mainstream news. From what he'd read, Rhys Arnold wasn't the type of man you ignored. He wouldn't let this lie.

"The killer signed his own death warrant when he killed Natalia Cruz," he said grimly. "Whether he knew who she was or not, he's about to become the most hunted man in Florida."

2

"Holy crap, Keith, it's Natalia Cruz." Kenzie barged into her editor's office at the Miami Herald without knocking.

"Who is?" He gave her a blank stare. "Haven't you heard of knocking?"

"The girl they pulled out of the swamp yesterday. It's Natalia Freakin' Cruz."

His eyes widened. "You're shitting me."

"I swear. I just got off the phone with my police contact." She sank down in the chair opposite his desk. "Keith, this is huge. Do you know who her father is?"

He gave her a look. What newsman worth his salt didn't know who Rhys Arnold was?

"Apparently he plays golf with the Chief of Police and the case has been made a top priority. My source said they're forming a special task force to find this guy."

"Money talks," murmured Keith.

"I want it, Keith," she stated. "I've got an in at Miami PD and I've met the victim. I did a piece on her husband, DJ Snake, when I first joined the *Herald*."

"That was eons ago, and you're on the news blog until Congressman Leonard's lawsuit against us is over."

"To hell with the blog, this is a serial killer case. They don't come along every day. This is what I do best, Keith. You know that."

He was already shaking his head. "You should have thought of that before you accused Ray Leonard of cavorting with prostitutes and taking drugs on Salvatore Del Gatto's super-yacht."

"He was." She gave him a hard look.

"That's not the point." He sighed. "You're lucky you still have a job. If he'd had it his way, you'd have been fired on the spot."

"For telling the truth?" She gave an unladylike snort. "I thought that's what we're supposed to do, Keith? Or has that concept somehow gotten lost amongst the bullshit?"

"We can't operate if we're bankrupt, Kenzie. It's as simple as that. This lawsuit is costing a goddamn fortune. He's suing for—and I quote—'character assassination.' According to him, your article was a politically motivated plot to destroy his reputation."

"He didn't need me to do that," she muttered with a thin smile. "But it wasn't politically motivated. You know I don't give a damn about politics."

He sighed. "I know. I kinda wish you did, then you might be more sensitive to it. You're a great reporter, Kenzie, one of the best, but you're a loose cannon. You're off the crime beat until you can prove you won't cause havoc."

"I promise I won't insult any more politicians," she said. "Besides, it was you who put me on that case to begin with. Did you really expect me to sugarcoat it?"

He fell silent, studying her from across his cluttered desk. It had been like that ever since Kenzie could remember. Mountains of paperwork competed for space with used coffee cups, old newspapers, and an assortment of pens, pencils, and Post-it Notes. It was amazing he knew where anything was.

"Clayton's covering the story."

"But I covered the first two murders," she argued. "It makes sense for me to do it. Our readers will expect continuity. And like I said, I know the victim's husband. He's a private guy, he's not going to let Clayton in."

"But he'll let you in?" Keith arched his eyebrows.

"Yes, I think he will. My article kickstarted his career. He was an up-and-coming nobody when I met him. After the profile piece, he got that deal with Blue Note Records, and the rest is history." She waved her hand around. "He owes me."

Keith pursed his lips. Nearly a full minute ticked by.

"If, and I mean if, I give you this story, you have to promise you won't make any more waves. The paper can't cope with another lawsuit. I mean it, Kenzie. One more strike and you're out."

She jumped out of the chair. "Thank you, Keith. You're the best, you know that."

"Promise me, Kenzie." His voice was stern.

"I promise, Keith. No more waves."

Kenzie pulled over on a narrow muddy road flanked by an impenetrable wall of vegetation.

This was where he lived?

She cut the engine and climbed out of the car. After the cool air conditioning, the humidity hit her like a sauna. It was way worse than downtown Miami. She immediately broke into a sweat. It clung to her skin and made her shirt stick to her back. How did he stand it?

She inhaled the pungent swamp air and looked around. Through a gap between the foliage and the cabin, she could see the water. Flat, blue, inviting. Yet she knew it was anything but. The Everglades were riddled with dangers. Alligators, snakes, and all manner of slithery things. She shuddered. She'd been out here twice in the last four months. This was the third time. Once for every body found.

The cabin consisted of three huts joined together. A rusty sign out front said, "Legend Airboat Tours." She frowned. Did the guy who'd found the body really give airboat tours? Her police source had said he was a loner, the type of guy who kept to himself.

Reid Garrett. The name was vaguely familiar, but she couldn't place it.

She looked for a buzzer but there wasn't one, so she knocked on the door. The cell number she'd been given had remained unanswered, so she was taking a chance coming out here. Mid-afternoon with the rain coming, she thought he'd be home.

There was no answer.

She tried again, knocking harder this time.

Still no response.

Then she heard it. A thumping sound from the other side of the cabin. Someone was here. Maybe they were out back, which was why they hadn't heard the door.

She walked to the gap in the vegetation. Squeezing through, she crept around the side of the house. It was built on a wooden deck, elevating it above the soggy water line. The banging got louder.

"Hello?" she called out, not wanting to take anyone by surprise.

The banging stopped.

"Out here," called a male voice. There was an edge to it, like he was annoyed at being interrupted. Well, that couldn't be helped. She had a job to do.

The ground grew squelchy beneath her feet, so she hopped onto the deck and ducked under the railing. "I'm coming round," she said, looking for the voice.

Then she spotted him, waist deep in the water. Bronzed, shirtless, and holding a hammer above his head.

She froze. "I—I'm sorry to disturb you."

A half-naked man was not what she'd been expecting. In her head, Reid Garrett was a paunchy, middle-aged dude in a dirty tank top. A swamper.

"Can I help you?"

She eyed the hammer, still poised in the air. Thor, Viking God of

War, sprang to mind. Charging across the sky in his chariot, swinging his hammer.

"I'm a reporter from the Miami Herald. I'd like to ask you about the woman you found in the Glades yesterday."

The hammer fell. A deafening blow that made her jump.

She glared at him. "Would that be okay?"

"I'm a bit busy now."

"I can see that, and I'm sorry to interrupt. I won't take up much of your time."

He hammered in another nail. The sound reverberated around the swamp. He was wearing waders, but he'd rolled down the top to work on his tan. Sweat glistened on his body. She made a point of not looking at it.

"What do you want to know?"

"How you found her? Where you found her? What state she was in? That sort of thing."

There was a pause. Sighing, he put the hammer down and hauled himself over the railing. Water streamed off his waders, splashing the deck.

She took a step backwards.

He bent down and peeled them off. She took a sharp breath. Surely, he wasn't going to strip in front of her, but he was wearing board shorts.

"Give me a minute." He strode past her into the house.

She gazed out over the sea of grass, stretching for miles in all directions. It was a beautiful spot. Nothing but water, vegetation, and blue sky. It was peaceful too, now that Thor had stopped thundering. She could hear cicadas, beetles, and other creatures chattering about their business. A flock of birds flew low over the canal, their reflections shimmering in the still water.

"I can see why you like it out here," she said as he returned. She was relieved to see he'd put on a T-shirt. "It's idyllic."

"What did you say your name was?"

So much for small talk.

"Kenzie Gilmore. Miami Herald." She held out her hand.

He didn't shake it. His expression turned cold. "I don't have anything to say to you."

She frowned. "Why not? I thought—"

"You thought wrong. I don't talk to reporters." He shepherded her into the house. She had to move, or he'd barrel into her. "I'd like you to leave now."

"Could you just tell me where you found her?" she asked, desperate for something, anything she could print.

"The cypress swamp."

"Were you alone?" The words were coming fast now, tumbling out.

"Yes." He kept walking, driving her back toward the door.

"What condition was she in?"

He stopped. "Why? So you can publish the morbid details in tomorrow's paper?"

The hostility emanating off him was incredible. What was this guy's problem? Well, she didn't intimidate easily. "No, so our readers can understand what happened to her. Natalia was more than just a celebrity. She had a life, a husband, friends. She was a role model. Now that's all gone."

He stared at her, his expression unreadable.

She lifted her chin a notch. "Her fans deserve to know."

"She was mostly intact," he said quietly. "Her left arm had been ripped off at the elbow, and there was a bite out of her thigh, but otherwise she was in one piece. Any longer and there wouldn't have been much left to identify."

Kenzie swallowed. "How long had she been in the water?"

"It's hard to say. I'd guess three or four days, but don't quote me on that. The coroner will know more after the autopsy."

She glanced up. He sounded almost professional. That's when she saw the picture hanging on the wall behind him. A framed photograph of a younger Reid Garrett in a uniform being handed a badge. "Are you a cop?"

"Ex-cop, and I think it's time you left, Ms. Gilmore." He opened the front door.

She hovered on the doorstep. What was an ex-cop doing out here? And why wasn't he working anymore? He wasn't old enough to retire. "When did you leave the for—"

"Goodbye, Ms. Gilmore."

He shut the door in her face.

3

Reid kept his head down as he walked into the Miami PD building.

He hadn't been back since he'd quit a year and a half ago and he sure as hell didn't want to be here now, except he didn't have a choice. He'd been summoned. Lieutenant Pérez wanted to speak with him in person.

He stopped at the security desk, but instead of showing his ID card, he gave his name. He was an outsider now.

The female officer on duty called up to the squad room. A moment later, she nodded. "You can go through, Mr. Garrett. It's on the fourth floor, first door to your—"

"I know where it is."

He took the elevator, feeling the familiar jerk as it took off. He'd ridden this elevator every day for nearly 10 years. He knew every bump, every grind, every nuance. It stopped and the doors wheezed open.

"Well, I'll be. If it isn't Reid Garrett. You coming back, Detective?" asked a guy he used to work with.

"No, just visiting." He kept walking.

"Good to see you, buddy." Another officer fist-bumped him as he walked past.

"Reid, what are you doing here?" Jared, a member of his old team, came up to him.

"Lieutenant wants to see me."

His colleague slapped him on the back. "It's good to see you, man."

He kept going, ignoring the overt stares and gasps of surprise in the squad room. After the cloud he'd left under, no one expected him to come back.

He passed Jonny's desk and nodded to Detective Ryan who was leaning against it, a clipboard in her hand. She shot him a bright smile.

"Well, well, well. If it isn't the prodigal son."

Ortega.

He'd recognize that condescending son of a bitch's voice anywhere.

"'Fraid your job's been taken," he drawled.

Reid itched to punch him in the face, but he kept walking.

The door to the corner office opened and Pérez stood there, grinning. "Reid, come in"

He escaped into the Lieutenant's office, glad to see the blinds were down.

They shook hands.

"How long has it been?" Pérez asked. "A year?"

Sixteen months.

"Something like that."

"Thanks for coming in. Please, take a seat." He gestured to two chairs around a low table. "So, how've you been? You look good."

"Been keeping busy," he said.

Pérez had aged in the last year and a half. His hair, once jet black, was now greying at the temples, and worry-lines were etched into his forehead.

"Good. I heard you found Natalia Cruz." He shook his head. "That can't have been easy."

"No, but I knew it was only a matter of time. You know these psychos, Joe, they don't stop. Once they get a taste for it, it only gets worse."

This wasn't the first serial case he'd worked. Six or seven years ago, before Pérez was Lieutenant, they'd hunted down a twisted individual killing prostitutes in the Miami Bay area. An FBI profiler had been brought in to work with them, which is how he knew so much about the psychology behind it.

Pérez grunted in agreement. "Listen, Reid, I'll be straight with you. I've got my hands full with this gang war, and now the Chief is coming down hard on the department to find Natalia Cruz's killer. We're stretched thin. I'm setting up a task force and I'd like you to run it."

"Me?" Reid stared at him.

"Come back," Pérez said flatly. "You've had a year. Think of it as a sabbatical. We need you on this. There's no one else qualified to run the team, and I don't want to go outside the department."

"What about Ortega?" He gritted his teeth saying the name.

"Ortega's up to his eyeballs with the gang shootings. We're gathering intel, raiding premises, arresting everybody we can find, and yet the feud continues. He doesn't have the time to dedicate to this serial case."

Reid took a few deep breaths. "I don't know, Joe. After what happened to Bianca..."

"That wasn't your fault. You tried to pull her out, she wouldn't listen. What went down was out of your control."

"I should have followed up. I was in charge." Guilt washed over him. "She died because of me."

Pérez frowned. "She died because Alberto Torres shot her when he discovered she was a cop. That was not your doing. It's time you stopped beating yourself up about it."

"Did we ever find out who leaked the details of the op to the press?"

"It could have been anyone," Pérez said with a shrug. "Impossible to know. Besides, if Bianca had gotten out when you said, it never would have happened. She was always stubborn like that. Liked to do things her way."

Reid closed his eyes and saw her face smiling up at him. "I can do it, Reid. I can get Torres to trust me. It's the only way we're going to get the intel."

Fuck.

"I need you, Reid. The department needs you."

He sighed. "I can't, Lieutenant. I'm sorry. I'd like to help you out, but it's been too long. I'm not the same person I was back then."

Pérez got up and walked around his desk. Opening a drawer, he took out Reid's detective badge and set it down on the table. "It's yours. All you have to do is take it."

Reid stared at it for a long time, then got to his feet.

"I'm sorry, Joe."

"At least think about it," Pérez called after him as he walked out the door.

Reid got back home to find Kenzie Gilmore waiting on his doorstep. She jumped to her feet as he pulled up.

"What are you doing here?" he snapped, getting out of the car.

"We need to talk."

"I've got nothing to say to you." He walked past her and inserted his key into the lock.

"I think you'll want to hear me out."

He frowned. "What makes you think that?"

She hesitated. "I know you went to see Lieutenant Pérez today. I know he wants you back on the case."

He swung around. "How do you know that?" He'd left the department less than 40 minutes ago.

"I know a guy there, we trained together at the academy?"

"The academy?" What was she talking about? Then he got it. "*You* trained to be a cop?"

"Is that so surprising?"

He didn't reply.

"Can I come in? There are some things I need to say. About what happened...before."

He pushed open the door. "You figured it out then?"

"Yeah, I know who you are. I should have realized yesterday, but I was a bit slow off the mark. Sorry about that."

He glanced over his shoulder. Her blonde hair was pulled back in a messy bun. Perspiration glistened on her forehead and her cheeks were flushed. She must have been waiting outside for a while.

"At least give me a chance to explain."

He met her gaze. Clear, direct, and very blue.

"Okay, fine." He stood back to let her enter.

She shot him a satisfied smile as she snuck past him into the cabin. It was stifling, and he immediately opened the sliding doors to let in some air.

"You could do with AC in here," she said as he turned around and gestured for her to take a seat.

"Tell me about it."

He waited until she sat down on one of the wicker armchairs before doing the same. "Okay, Ms. Gilmore, let's hear it."

"Well, first I wanted to apologize for what happened after I wrote the article. I never in a million years thought anyone would get hurt, let alone killed."

The article needed no explanation. They both knew exactly what she was referring to.

Reid clenched his jaw. "What did you expect would happen? I had an undercover agent embedded within the cartel and you published an article telling the whole of Miami about it. It didn't take them long to figure out who the snitch was. Bianca didn't stand a chance."

"I didn't know she was still undercover," Kenzie explained. "My source told me she'd been extracted."

He scowled at her. "Who is your source?"

"I can't tell you that."

"Goddamnit! Whoever he is fed you false information. The entire op went to shit because of him. Lopez got away, and I lost a valued colleague. I'd think twice about using him again."

Valued... cherished... loved.

He should have insisted she get out. What was she thinking, taking matters into her own hands? But that was Bianca. Headstrong, stubborn, gutsy. That's what he'd loved about her. And it still hurt.

He took a steadying breath.

"He was right about you, though. Wasn't he?" Kenzie said. "Pérez did ask you to come back and lead the task force."

"What of it?"

"Are you going to do it?"

"No. I'm not a cop anymore."

There was a pause.

"You know, I wanted to be a cop more than anything. My father was a detective, back in the day. I grew up wanting to be just like him."

He watched the emotion flicker across her face. "Then I broke my leg during a training exercise and my dream went up in smoke."

"Now you're a reporter."

She scoffed. "An investigative reporter. It was the closest I could get to being a cop."

He gave her a hard look. "Why are you telling me this?"

"Because you've got the opportunity to do what I always dreamed of doing, and you're turning it down. I don't get it."

"I have my reasons."

"Because of the Lopez case? Because you lost a colleague?"

"She was more than a colleague."

"Ah, I see." Kenzie stared at him for a long moment. "And what do you think she'd say? Bianca, do you think she'd want you to quit? To just walk away?"

Reid scowled. "Why do you care so much?"

"Never mind. It doesn't matter." She looked away, towards the deck. "Anyway, I just wanted to clear the air. I would never have published anything that put someone's life in danger. I wanted you to know that."

Yeah right. "Even if it sells papers?"

"That's not fair."

"Isn't that what you do?"

"No, I search for the truth. I find out what really happened."

He contemplated this. "Is that what you were doing when Bianca was killed? Searching for the truth?"

She jutted out her chin. "I was trying to reassure the public that the police had things under control. Like I said, I didn't realize a sting operation was in progress, or that your colleague was still undercover. That's not the information I was given."

"Perhaps you better double-check your information before you go to print next time."

"I do. I double-source all the time now. Don't worry, I learned my lesson." Her eyelids fluttered. "I received massive backlash from the police department about that article. It wasn't easy for me. I felt guilty that she was dead. Responsible, even. And I got a written warning from the newspaper. I nearly lost my job over it."

He fell silent. He wanted to believe her, that she didn't know about Bianca still being in play, but he wasn't sure he could. Those big blue eyes looked innocent enough, but then he'd interrogated many suspects with the same wide-eyed stare who turned out to be guilty as sin. Just very good at hiding it.

Now he trusted no one.

"Is that what you wanted to tell me?" he asked. It was getting late, and he wanted to finish repairing the deck.

"There is the small matter of Natalia Cruz's husband, DJ Snake," she said. "I was on my way to talk to him and thought you might like to join me. He won't talk to cops. Not a fan."

He tilted his head. "What makes you think he'll talk to you?"

"I know him. We're friends." Her eyes sparkled. "Did you know Natalia walked out of her hotel room after a fight at a party last weekend and didn't come back. That was the last anybody saw of her."

Reid didn't know that. "Was she reported missing?"

"Not officially. The police went to the hotel the next day, but when they found her suitcase and clothes missing, they assumed she'd left voluntarily. No missing person's report was ever filed."

Reid scratched his head. "So, this girl was missing for a week, and nobody thought it strange? Did she do that sort of thing often?"

"According to her husband, never. He was convinced something had happened to her, but no one believed him."

"Until she turned up dead in the swamp."

Kenzie looked him in the eye. "That's right. Interested yet?"

He sighed, then picked up his car keys. The deck could wait.

4

"How do you know this guy?"

He'd followed her to DJ Snake's house in the exclusive North Links Country Club area of Hialeah. It seemed traveling together was one step too far for the suspicious ex-cop. Still, Kenzie had gotten him to come with her. That was something. His insight would be invaluable to her investigation.

"I wrote a piece on him once, citing him as one to watch. Back then he was an up-and-coming DJ making waves in the South Beach clubs. News networks picked up the article, and it caught the eye of one of Miami's top music producers." She spread out her arms and gazed up at the sprawling modern house with its landscaped gardens, "privacy" wall, and three-car garage. "Now he's got a multimillion-dollar record deal and a five-bedroom mansion."

"Impressive."

"He's expecting me. I called ahead and made an appointment."

They walked up to the front door and rang the bell. Reid gestured upwards. The beady eye of a security camera stared down at them.

A Hispanic woman in a maid's outfit opened the door. "Can I help you?"

"We're here to see DJ Snake," said Kenzie.

"One moment."

"What's his real name?" asked Reid, as the maid shuffled away.

"Eric Snider." Kenzie hid a grin. "He's from a middle-class family, grew up in Coral Gables. Had a pretty normal upbringing, although he makes out it was harder than it was. His rags to riches story is just that."

A few moments later a lanky man with boy-band good looks and expertly gelled hair sauntered down the passage to greet them. He still looked twenty, although Kenzie knew him to be in his early thirties.

"Kenzie, darling. How are you?" He embraced her warmly. His gaze darkened as it flickered over Reid. "I thought you were coming alone."

"Lovely to see you, Snake. You haven't changed a bit." She turned to Reid. "This is Reid Garrett, he's working with me on the case. I hope you don't mind?"

No way was she going to mention he was an ex-cop. That would not go down well. Snake was notoriously outspoken in his dislike of the police after an incident involving a raid at a house party a few years back. He'd spent 24 hours in police custody before they let him off with a warning, an experience he hadn't relished, although he'd used it to embellish his bad-boy image.

"I guess not." Snake eyed Reid as he shook his hand. Reid was at least a head taller than the DJ and much broader. "If he's a friend of yours."

Kenzie broke into a grin. Snake was intimidated but trying hard not to show it. Reid had that effect on people.

"Come on in. I'll get Lucinda to bring some lemonade to the terrace. Unless you'd prefer something stronger?" He glanced at Reid.

"Lemonade's fine," he said.

They walked through the marbled entrance hall, cool and minimalist. There were few ornaments or personal items. No paintings, no photographs. No sign that Natalia had ever lived there.

A paved terrace overlooked a swimming pool and a hot tub. Palm trees swayed around the edge of the garden providing dappled shade, but they sat under an awning on the terrace. Lucinda brought out a jug of lemonade and three glasses.

"This is stunning." Kenzie gazed longingly at the pool. Diamonds danced on the surface. It was bluer than the sky. The mansion felt more like a resort than a home.

"I love it." He lowered his head. "Although it's not the same without Natalia."

Kenzie gave a sympathetic nod. He'd provided the perfect opening. "I can imagine. I'm so sorry for your loss."

"Thank you." He took a deep breath. "I can't believe they found her all the way out in the Glades. It's unbelievable."

"When was the last time you saw her?" Reid asked.

Kenzie got up to pour the lemonade since it didn't look like Snake was going to do it. "Was it at the party at the Sand Club last weekend?" she inquired.

"Yeah. That's the night she disappeared." He bit his lip. "I knew something bad had happened to her. I told the cops as much, but they didn't believe me." He grimaced. "No surprises there. Useless f-ing bunch."

The muscles in Reid's jaw tightened.

"Why don't you tell us what happened?" Kenzie said quickly. "Talk us through the night of the party."

He pulled a pack of cigarettes out of his pocket and lit one. "You don't mind, do you? It calms me down."

Kenzie remembered him telling her once that he suffered from ADHD. She shook her head.

Snake took a long drag, then exhaled into the air. "We checked into the hotel that morning. Natalia went to the spa and I hit the gym."

Kenzie saw Reid's gaze roam over his slender physique.

"Was she acting normal?" Kenzie asked. "Was she herself?"

"Yes, completely. She was in a good mood. We had a leisurely day, then got ready for the party and went downstairs to check on the preparations."

"What was the reason for the party?" asked Reid.

"To celebrate the launch of my new album, *Miami Beat*."

Reid gave a blank nod, while Kenzie gushed, "Great album. Congrats on topping the charts with *Sunshine Kiss*. I love that track."

She saw Reid raise an eyebrow. Kenzie didn't particularly like dance music and certainly hadn't bought any of Snake's albums over the years, but she had done her homework.

The DJ smiled weakly. "Thanks. That song always reminds me of her. I wrote it the day we first kissed."

"That's tough," said Reid, surprising her. Perhaps the man was human, after all.

"What happened next?" Kenzie got them back on track.

"The guests started to arrive. We mingled. Things got a little raucous."

"I believe Bella Montague was there?"

Snake paused. It was a loaded question. Bella was Snake's ex, and at one point, everyone thought they'd get married. Then he met Natalia, and six months after a whirlwind romance, they were hitched.

"Yeah, Bella was there. We didn't invite her, she came with someone else."

"I heard there was an incident?"

He sighed. "There always is with Bella."

"Bella is Snake's ex," explained Kenzie when Reid shot her a quizzical look. "How long were you together?" she asked Snake.

"Nearly four years," he said.

"Wasn't it through Bella that you met Natalia?"

"Yeah, that was the problem. Bella and Natalia were friends. I'd met her a couple of times before but hadn't really gotten to know her. Then one weekend we all went on a friend's yacht. Beautiful 28-footer. Bella got seasick and spent most of the outing throwing up below, so Natalia and I started talking, and we hit it off."

"Love at first sight," breathed Kenzie. Not that she believed in such things, but she had to play the game. For him she was the wide-eyed reporter, the super-fan. Last month she'd been a guileless party girl, frolicking on the Congressman's super-yacht. She merged effortlessly from one role to another. Too effortlessly. Sometimes she forgot who she was.

"The very next week I broke it off with Bella and took Natalia out."

"That must have gone down well," murmured Reid.

Snake scoffed. "You can say that again. Bella went nuts. She yelled abuse, slandered me on social media, then got drunk and begged me to take her back. It was humiliating."

"And then came the engagement party," said Kenzie, leading him down the path.

Snake shook his head. "I had to have her forcibly removed."

"I saw the photographs." Kenzie grimaced.

"Not the kind of publicity I was hoping for," he said. "Anyway, she seemed to calm down after that. I think she finally accepted that we were getting married. We didn't invite her to the wedding, obviously, and we hadn't heard from her until the launch party last week."

Kenzie reached for her glass. "Did she embarrass herself at the launch party too?"

"Yeah, but nothing compared to her usual drama. She was drunk and traded insults with Natalia before her date took her home. He didn't realize how cut up she still was."

"It must be hard seeing your friend marry your ex-boyfriend," mused Kenzie, looking for a reaction.

Snake shrugged. "Bella and I weren't suited. We're such different people. Natalia and I clicked straight away. We're two of a kind. You know when you just know?"

Kenzie nodded. She had no idea. It had never happened to her. Not at first sight or otherwise. Reid was suspiciously quiet.

"Do you want to ask anything?" She threw him a glance.

Reid found his tongue. "The night she disappeared, what happened? Did she go back to her room? Kenzie mentioned she'd packed a suitcase?"

Snake stabbed out his cigarette and lit another. His drink went untouched. "At about eleven, she said she had a headache. It was unusual for her. Normally I have to drag her off the dance floor. I took her back to our suite, made sure she was okay, and went back to the party. When I got back around one, she was gone."

"Is that when you called the police?" Kenzie asked.

"No, first we looked for her. Some friends helped me search. We were all pretty drunk by that stage, but we scoured the hotel. She wasn't anywhere to be found."

"Did you check the camera footage?" asked Reid.

He shook his head. "I think the cops did. They came to talk to me the next day. By that stage I was frantic. I'd called her father. He got onto the Chief of Police."

Kenzie knew they were golf buddies.

"We need to view that footage," Reid said.

She nodded. "Snake, can you get us into the hotel? The security cameras might tell us when Natalia left."

He glanced at his watch. "Um, yeah, I can, but not this evening. I've got to go out. Can we do it tomorrow?"

"How's nine o'clock?" Kenzie wanted to get an early start before the hotel got busy.

Snake looked dubious. "Can we make it ten? I'm not at my best first thing in the morning."

"Sure, ten's fine." She glanced at Reid who gave a curt nod.

In a desperate move, Snake reached across the table and grabbed her arm. "You'll help me find out what happened to her, won't you Kenz?"

"Of course. You know I'll do everything in my power to see her killer brought to justice."

He squeezed her wrist. "I know you will, Kenz. If anyone can get to the truth, it's you."

5

The Sand Club was a pretentious, over-priced boutique hotel on South Beach. Reid had Googled it on his phone before meeting Kenzie and couldn't believe the eye-watering prices.

He had to admit it was stylish, though. The art deco lobby extended seamlessly onto the sand, the blinding white marble floor broken by alcoves of exotic plants.

"It's one of the hottest spots to hang out at," Kenzie told him as they waited for Snake to arrive. Security wouldn't let them past the front desk.

"What happened at the engagement party?" Reid asked to kill time. "You said Bella had a meltdown."

"God, yes. She went ballistic. Got hammered and lashed out at Snake. How could he steal her best friend? Who did he think he was? She hopes he burns in hell. That sort of thing."

"Sounds like fun."

"Yeah. I wasn't there, but I heard it was spectacular. The media went wild, and Bella had to be forcibly removed from the premises."

Reid shook his head. "Do you think she could have killed Natalia?"

Kenzie did a double take. "I thought it was the Swamp Strangler who killed her."

"We won't know that for sure until after the autopsy, and even then, it will be difficult to tell. No DNA was found on any of the victims, there's nothing linking them other than the way they died."

"Raped and strangled," she murmured.

"And dumped in the swamp."

"Are you saying someone could have killed her and made it look like the Swamp Strangler?" Her eyes were huge. He could almost see her journalist's mind working overtime.

"I'm saying anything's possible. We have to keep an open mind."

"We?" She grinned. "So, you're going to help me?"

He grunted. "That's what I'm doing, isn't it?" He wasn't thrilled by the concept, but he wanted to speak to the husband, so here he was.

They turned around as Snake hurried in.

"Sorry I'm late. Traffic was diabolical. Hello, Kenzie darling." He kissed Kenzie on both cheeks and nodded at Reid who nodded back.

"Let me have a word with Luis and then we'll take a stroll around the hotel."

He walked up to the reception desk and said something to the girl standing there. She shot him a wide smile and picked up the desk phone. A short time later Luis, a well-dressed Latino man—who Reid assumed was the hotel manager—arrived.

They shook hands, shoulder bumped, and slapped each other on the back, then Snake beckoned them over. The security guard eyed them curiously as they walked past and Reid gave him a slight shrug."

"These are my friends Kenzie and Reid," he said. "They're helping me find out what happened to Natalia."

Luis shook their hands, somber now. "It's great to meet you. I'm sorry about the circumstances. How can I be of assistance?"

"We'd like to see any footage you might have of the night Mrs. Snider was taken," Reid said. "In the corridors, the lobby, the gardens."

"Of course. We can arrange that. I'll get Roberto to set it up for you. In the meantime, do you want a drink at the pool bar?"

"Maybe later, Luis," said Snake. "Right now, we'd like to see the room."

Luis didn't blink. "I'll get you the keycard."

He spoke to the receptionist who handed him a card. "Luckily that room is not occupied. We have a booking for Friday, but it's empty now, so I can show you myself."

"That's very kind of you." Kenzie flashed him a smile, turning on the charm.

Luis smiled back. "Which newspaper did you say you were from?"

"The Miami Herald. I'm doing a piece on Natalia's disappearance."

"Terrible business," he murmured.

"Did the police interview you?" inquired Reid.

He shook his head. "Not really. They did look around the hotel after she disappeared, but haven't been back since her body was discovered."

They would, once the task force was operational. This was the first place he'd come looking. The scene of her last appearance.

Kenzie pursed her lips. "My source at the police department says they think she left on her own accord and was abducted elsewhere."

"That's bullshit," snapped Snake as they walked down a plush corridor. "Why would she leave? She was happy. *We* were happy."

"You hadn't had a fight?" asked Reid as they stopped outside a VIP suite. "A disagreement?"

"No. What are you implying?" His boyish face darkened. "I told you, she didn't leave on her own account. She wouldn't have. When I saw her back to the room, she was perfectly happy."

"Apart from the headache," said Reid.

"I'm sorry, Snake. We have to ask these awkward questions," Kenzie explained in her soothing voice. "You have no idea how many people lie to the police."

"Well, I'm not." He sulked into the room. "And you're not the police."

Not anymore, no.

Snake stood in the middle of the luxurious room and looked around. "I remember it like it was yesterday," he said. "My heart stopped when I got back and discovered she was gone."

"What did you do then?" Reid followed him into the suite. The lounge was spacious and classy with pale leather sofas, a granite-topped bar and recessed lighting. Glass doors opened onto a massive private patio surrounded by palm trees and other lush vegetation.

"I ran back to the party and rounded up a couple of dudes to help me look for her."

Reid opened one of the doors and stepped onto the vast patio. "She could have gone out this way," he said. "Are there cameras out here?"

"Only in the main pool area," Luis confirmed. "These luxury suites are secluded. The guests value their privacy."

Reid peered through the tropical vegetation. "Where does it lead to?"

"If you go straight ahead you get to the beach, but if you angle to the right, it leads to the pool area."

"She could have walked out of the hotel to the beach and no one would have known."

Luis glanced nervously at Snake. "I guess so."

"When did you notice her suitcase was gone?" Kenzie took the DJ's arm and steered him back inside.

"Early the next morning. We'd searched the whole hotel by that stage," he said, his voice coarse. "It was only when we got back to the room that I thought to check the wardrobe. Then I noticed her case was gone."

"And her clothes?" asked Kenzie.

"Yeah, some of them," he nodded.

"What was she wearing when she disappeared?" Reid studied Snake, looking for signs he was lying.

He didn't hesitate. "When I left her, she was wearing her yellow cocktail dress. She said she was going to run a bath and get into bed."

"Did she?" asked Reid.

"What?"

"Run a bath?"

"Crap." He blinked several times in rapid succession. "I didn't think to look. I don't think so, but when I came back later, I'd already had a few. I'm not sure I would have noticed if the bathtub was wet."

Reid ground his jaw. This guy was useless.

They went back downstairs and viewed the security footage. Roberto, the hotel's security expert, brought up the feed from the camera in the VIP suites' corridor. He'd located the relevant date and time period.

"That's us going downstairs," pointed out Snake. They watched the couple walk hand in hand along the corridor. Snake said something and Natalia smiled up at him. It was clear she was besotted with him. She certainly didn't look like a woman about to run out on her marriage.

"There's a camera near the Sandbar, where the event took place," said Roberto helpfully.

"Can we see it?" Reid asked.

He pulled it up. There were beautiful people everywhere. Long dresses, smart suits, leather trousers, even pink hair. Champagne bubbled as the guests smiled and mingled.

"There's Bella." Kenzie pointed to a slim figure in emerald green. Her strawberry blond hair was styled in a high bun. She appeared perfectly behaved.

"Can you fast forward a few hours?" asked Reid.

They watched as a clearly inebriated Bella lurched around the pool, often veering dangerously close to the edge.

"I'm surprised she didn't fall in," sneered Snake.

"Did you talk to her?" asked Kenzie.

"Yes, briefly. Earlier on. She congratulated me and hoped I didn't mind her coming. What could I say?" He shrugged.

"Who's that with Natalia?" asked Kenzie as a woman in a sleeveless black dress with a severe bob could be seen waving her hands in the air.

"That's Natalia's PR agent, Gabriella Vincent."

They watched as the two women argued. Eventually, Natalia swiveled on her heel and stormed off towards the bar.

"That didn't look too friendly," Kenzie murmured.

"Whoa!" Reid watched as Bella stumbled up, gripped Natalia's arm, and hissed something in her ear. They couldn't see Bella's face, but her body language screamed anger and resentment.

"I should have kicked her out as soon as I saw her," hissed Snake, his eyes glued to the screen.

Natalia jerked away as if she were stung and fled to Snake's side. He put an arm around her waist and said something to Bella's date who'd now appeared. He seemed embarrassed by the whole debacle. A short time later, he took Bella firmly by the arm and led her back into the hotel.

"That was the last we saw of them," said Snake.

The time stamp read ten forty-seven.

"Can we go back to the corridor?" asked Reid.

Roberto pulled up the camera by the VIP suites.

"Same time," said Reid.

They watched as Snake could be seen leading a weary Natalia back to the room. He had his arm around her waist, and she was leaning against him.

"Was she drunk?" asked Kenzie.

"A little woozy," he said, "but she was complaining about the headache here."

Reid frowned. He hadn't seen her drink much at the Sand Club. In fact, in nearly all the shots, she didn't have a drink in her hand. It was only after the fight with the PR agent that she went to the bar, where Bella confronted her.

Snake opened the door and led Natalia inside. The time stamp read ten fifty-eight. At ten past eleven, Snake reappeared in the corridor. He said something before he closed the door. Reid wasn't the best lip reader in the world, but it looked like, "I'll see you later." Then he closed the door and walked back to the pool bar.

Kenzie met his gaze. She was thinking the same thing he was. There was no way Snake could have been involved in his wife's disappearance. He was in the clear.

6

"It did look like she'd packed up and left," said Kenzie as they left the hotel. "If she was abducted, she wouldn't have taken a suitcase."

"Unless someone wanted to make it look like she'd walked out on her own accord." Reid stepped back to avoid a cyclist.

Kenzie gnawed on her lip. "Do you think someone would go through all that trouble? I mean, if you're going to make it look like she ran out on her husband, why dump her body in the swamp for someone to find? It doesn't make sense."

"Unless the killer didn't expect her to be found," Reid finished.

"How could he not? Two other bodies have surfaced in the last four months in the same area. He must be stupid if he thought this one would simply disappear. Even if the gators got her, there'd still be evidence."

Reid was silent. Kenzie wished she knew what he was thinking.

"I don't know," he eventually said. "I agree, it doesn't make sense. Despite what her husband claims, it does look like she left the hotel on her own. If that's the case, then her killer must have targeted her after she left."

"That's incredibly unlucky, if it's true," mused Kenzie. "But bad things happen to runaways all the time. They're vulnerable, desperate, easy prey."

"Except, Natalia was none of those things," Reid pointed out. "She had money. Tons of it. She wouldn't have ended up on the street or even in a seedy motel. She'd have stayed in five-star luxury."

"Not easy prey, then," corrected Kenzie. "But that doesn't mean the Swamp Strangler didn't intercept her."

"The only way she could have left that hotel room unseen is if she went out the patio door. She can't have gone to the pool area, or she would have been picked up by the cameras, which leaves the beach."

Kenzie frowned. "With her suitcase? At eleven o'clock at night?"

"She was obviously keeping a low profile." Reid was thinking out loud. "Why else go that way? It's difficult, she'd have had to carry her suitcase over the sand, and where did she get picked up? She'd have had to backtrack around the hotel to the road."

"She may have had someone waiting for her," suggested Kenzie. Then her face lit up. "Can we check the CCTV cameras in the street outside the hotel? Maybe one of them caught her getting into a vehicle?"

"I don't have the resources for that."

"But you could," she pressed. "If you agreed to lead the task force, you'd be able to access all the case files."

"To feed them back to you, you mean?"

Kenzie grinned. "Why not? I like to think we're a team. After all, I got you into this."

"I was involved long before you knocked on my door," he gritted out. No way was he teaming up with her. "I discovered the body, remember? Besides, if I'm back on the force, I can't work with you. My lieutenant would go nuts if he knew I was collaborating with a reporter."

She grinned cheekily. "You say that like it's a bad thing."

He had the grace to smile.

"Okay," she sighed. "What do you suggest? Without that camera footage we won't know whether someone picked her up or not."

"I'll speak to Jonny. He was on my old team. He *might* be able to get us access to the CCTV footage."

"See?" She beamed at him. "I knew having you as a partner would pay off."

"I haven't done anything yet," he grunted. "And we're not partners."

They crossed the street and walked to the next block where their cars were parked. The sun was directly overhead, and the temperature and humidity were increasing by the minute. Kenzie blew a strand of hair off her face.

"Where would she go?" Reid asked thoughtfully. "Once she left the hotel."

"You mean assuming she was trying to get away from her husband?"

"Yeah. Where would be the first place she'd go?"

"If she couldn't go home… To her father's perhaps? I heard they were close."

Reid's Ford Ranger pickup beeped as he pressed the button to unlock it. "Then let's go talk to him."

Rhys Arnold lived in a waterfront mansion in what was known as Millionaires' Row. Kenzie knew that the properties along the Fort Lauderdale Intracoastal Waterway sold for exorbitant prices, but seeing them sprawled out over leafy lawns, next to palm trees stabbing the sky, was something else. "Did you know Bugsy Siegel and Al Capone also owned properties here?" she told Reid.

"I didn't, no."

She'd gone with Reid in his pickup truck, since it was pointless for both of them to make the 45-minute drive in bumper-to-bumper traffic. He was warming to her. He still didn't trust her—and he probably never would—but he was definitely thawing.

"Properties start around the eight-million-dollar mark," she said as they drove down a palm-lined avenue towards the water. "And that's conservative."

"How did Rhys Arnold make his money?" asked Reid. "I know he's retired now, but wasn't he in waste management or something?"

"That's right," Kenzie said. She'd spent the evening reading up on him. "He founded Environ Waste Services back in the sixties. They're one of the largest waste management providers in the country. They do residential, commercial, industrial—you name it. I read they have landfill disposal sites, recycling plants, gas and power production plants. It's a massive enterprise."

"Smart guy."

"That's not all," she continued. "He also started Auto Retailer, based here in Fort Lauderdale, which sells new and used vehicles and associated services. They have more than 350 outlets nationwide."

Reid let out a low whistle.

They pulled into a short, paved driveway flanked by a showy display of red, pink, and lavender flowers. The house was designed in the Spanish Colonial style, with stuccoed walls, a red-tiled roof, and windows in the shapes of arches with wrought iron balconies.

Reid gestured to the security cameras, one above the garage and another hidden in the gables, but she'd already seen them.

"He's security conscious," muttered Reid as they climbed out of the car.

"I think everyone along here is." Kenzie gazed up at the enormous arched front door with carved detail. Alongside was a buzzer and an intercom system.

She pressed the buzzer.

A female voice with a Hispanic accent said, "Who's there?"

"It's Kenzie Gilmore. I'm an investigative reporter from the Miami Herald," she replied. "I'm here to talk to Mr. Arnold about his daughter's murder."

There was a pause.

Footsteps sounded on the tiled hallway, and then the door was flung open.

"What do you want?"

Mr. Arnold was a bald, stocky man in his early sixties. He had a hard face and suspicious eyes that roamed over both Kenzie and Reid. "I don't speak to the press." He sneered the last word.

"I'm trying to find out what happened to Natalia." Kenzie aimed for the soft, sympathetic approach. "This is Reid Garrett, formerly with the Miami PD. He's assisting me in my inquiries."

She felt Reid stiffen beside her.

"I told what I knew to the cops."

"I'm sure you did," Kenzie said with a smile. "But we're dedicating a lot of time to this investigation, time the police force doesn't have. Could we ask you a few questions about the night she disappeared?"

"I thought the police were putting a task force together to deal with this." He opened the door a little further.

"Yes, they are now, and they've asked Detective Garrett here to lead it," said Kenzie.

Reid cleared his throat.

"Hmm..." Arnold scrutinized Reid for a long moment, then nodded. "Alright then. Come in. I don't have long, but I'm willing to do whatever it takes to find out what happened to my daughter."

Kenzie shot Reid a triumphant look as they stepped inside.

Arnold led the way through the terracotta-tiled entrance hall, down a wide flight of stairs and out onto the terrace. The house was cool, although having the doors open was dissipating much of the cold air. Not that the billionaire worried about such things.

"You have a beautiful home," complimented Kenzie, gazing over the lush green lawn to the water's edge.

He grunted. A woman came out to see if they wanted anything, but Arnold waved her away. This wasn't a social call.

"When did you last see your daughter?" Reid asked, diving straight in.

The billionaire sat slightly forward, his head stiff and unyielding. Kenzie could see the pain in his eyes, the grief he hadn't fully dealt with but was trying to hide.

"Two weeks ago. She came to see me. We had lunch together."

"That would have been a week before the launch party at the Sand Club," said Kenzie.

Her father nodded. "She mentioned it, but only briefly. She was proud of her husband's achievements." There was something in his tone.

"DJ Snake has done very well for himself." Kenzie watched his face. His lips pressed together, his eyes hard. Rhys Arnold was not a fan of his daughter's husband.

"Why he calls himself that ridiculous name, I have no idea."

"It's to do with the tattoo on his chest." Arnold's dark eyes narrowed even more.

"Did you get along with your son in law?" asked Reid, who'd also picked up on Arnold's stiff demeanor.

"Not really. I don't consider hanging out in clubs and bars to be a suitable career choice, but that hardly matters now."

"Have you had any contact with Eric?" Reid wanted to know.

"Not since they discovered Natalia's body." His voice cracked as he said her name.

Reid nodded, letting the silence drag out. Partly out of respect, and partly to give the billionaire time to compose himself.

Kenzie took over. "Mr. Arnold, was Natalia her normal self when you last saw her?"

"Yes, of course. Why do you ask?"

"All the signs point to her leaving the Sand Club the night of her disappearance. Her suitcase was missing, as were some of her clothes."

He shook his head. "I may have disapproved of Eric, but Natalia was crazy about him. She didn't have a bad word to say about him. I can't see her walking out on her marriage. I just can't see it."

That's what Snake had said too.

"And she didn't come here or speak to you that night?" Kenzie asked. At the color that rose into his cheeks, she added, "I just want to make sure we're not missing anything."

"No, I would have told you if she'd come here. It wasn't like her to run away. If she was unhappy, she'd have told me."

"Were you close?"

"I thought so," he said. "Since her mother died, it'd only been us. I know I worked too hard when she was growing up and didn't dedicate enough time to her, but we'd reconnected in recent years."

The lonely little rich girl, Kenzie thought.

"Listen, I thought the task force was supposed to be looking into this." Arnold rested his hands on the table. "What's being done about it? Have you investigated her phone records, her last-known position? What about her car? CCTV footage? There must be something that can point you in the right direction."

"We're working on all that, sir," Reid muttered.

"Well, pick up the pace, won't you? It's been days since you pulled her out of that swamp. Christ, what a place to end up." He swiped at his eyes.

"We're sorry for your loss," Kenzie soothed.

He gave a terse nod.

They got to their feet. "If there's anything else you can think of, anything that was worrying her or that she might have mentioned when you last saw her, please let us know." Kenzie handed him her business card. He pocketed it without a word.

"What do you think?" Kenzie asked Reid once they got outside, and the heavy wooden door had shut behind them.

"I think that's a man in mourning," Reid said.

"I agree. I believed him when he said he hadn't heard from her."

Reid sighed. "No help there. He's as much in the dark as the rest of us."

They got into the car when both their phones beeped.

Kenzie glanced at hers. It was her source at the police department. She read the text and felt her heart skip a beat. Reid, who'd read his own text message, also appeared shocked.

"She wasn't raped," whispered Kenzie, glancing up at him. The autopsy results had just come through. "It wasn't the same MO as the others."

Reid met her gaze. "We're looking for a different killer," he said. "It wasn't the Swamp Strangler."

7

Reid had little to say on the way back to South Beach. Kenzie was also thinking things through. This new development was forcing them to look at the case from a different angle.

"It could have been any one of them." He pulled into the parking garage where Kenzie had left her car. "Bella, that PR woman, the other guests. Any one of them could have snuck outside and surprised Natalia in her suite."

"Are we saying she didn't leave on her own, now?" Kenzie squinted at him.

Reid pulled into a vacant parking spot. "Think about it. The Strangler may have intercepted her if she'd left on her own, but if we've ruled him out, it's unlikely another serial killer just happened to come across her, strangle her, and dump her body in the swamp."

"Which brings us back to Snake's theory," surmised Kenzie. "That she was kidnapped from the hotel room sometime after eleven o'clock."

Reid turned off the engine but neither of them moved.

"We're going to have to go through that camera footage again," he said. "We need to know if anyone left the party early."

"We know Bella did," she said. "Her date took her home after the drunken argument with Natalia."

"Let's speak to her and her date, if possible." Reid was conscious of how many *we*'s he was using. He didn't want a partner, but if he was going to do some preliminary investigative work on Natalia's murder, he needed Kenzie's connections. He didn't have a badge to rely on. That was still in his lieutenant's desk. "We need to check her alibi."

"I'll set it up," Kenzie said.

"I'd also like to have a word with Natalia's PR agent. She seemed pretty upset with Natalia at the party."

"I can get her details from Snake." Kenzie pulled a worn reporter's notebook out of her handbag and scribbled a few notes. "There's something else." She tapped the notepad with her pen.

"What's that?"

"Whoever kidnapped Natalia knew she was alone in her room."

Reid nodded. "Yeah, I thought of that too. It must have been one of the guests. Someone who saw her husband take her back to the room and return to the party."

"Do you think it was a spur of the moment thing?" Kenzie frowned.

"I'm not sure. Kidnapping someone like Natalia takes planning. If she'd been strangled and left in the hotel room, I'd say yes, it was more likely to be spontaneous. But with her body missing, making it look like she ran away." He shook his head. "That says premeditated."

Kenzie was watching him. "In that case, the killer must have arranged for her to go back to her room early. Snake said she was woozy. Maybe he drugged her?"

Reid, whose thoughts had been following the same lines, nodded. "Agreed. She complained of a headache. Drugging her would ensure she'd go back to her suite."

"It's even more imperative we scrutinize that footage of the party," Kenzie said. "We might see who doctored her drink."

They went back to the hotel, but the manager was far less cordial without his VIP customer around. "I'm afraid I can't give you a copy of the recording," he said. "Like I said before, our guests value their privacy."

"But we've already seen them," insisted Kenzie.

"You viewed them on the hotel premises," Luis said. "If I release a copy, it could be on YouTube by sunset." He looked her up and down. "Or in the tabloids."

"I work the crime beat," Kenzie said stiffly.

"Don't sweat it." Reid tapped her shoulder. "I've got an idea."

"It's not like we were going to post it all over social media," she fumed as they stomped away.

"He doesn't know that," pointed out Reid. "Listen, I've got to go see Lieutenant Pérez this afternoon. I think I can get a warrant for the camera footage."

"You're going back." She fixed her clear gaze on him. "I knew it."

"Not permanently." He stifled a grin. "I'm not going to be involved in the task force either, but I do have an idea that might work."

"Oh, yes?" She raised her eyebrows.

"I'll tell you tomorrow." He wasn't going to say anything now in case the lieutenant didn't go for it.

She pulled a face. "You may have noticed that patience is not one of my strong points."

He couldn't resist a chuckle. "See you tomorrow, Kenzie."

Fewer people raised their eyebrows this time as Reid walked across the squad room to Lieutenant Pérez's office. He knocked, then entered after Pérez beckoned through the glass.

"Does this mean you've agreed to come back?" Pérez took his glasses off and threw them down on his desk. His shirt was crinkled, and his hair was mussed up like he'd run his hand through it too many times.

They didn't relocate to the comfy seats this time.

"Temporarily," Reid replied.

Pérez frowned. "I don't understand."

"I assume you're not going ahead with a task force now that the autopsy revealed she wasn't sexually assaulted."

"We are," Pérez rocked back on his chair, a habit Reid remembered from before. "Sure, she wasn't raped, but that doesn't mean it wasn't our guy. Everything else is identical, down to the strangulation marks."

"Different MO, though." Reid frowned.

"There's a number of reasons why he didn't sexually assault her," Pérez rationalized. "He could have been disturbed, interrupted somehow. Perhaps she lashed out, and he killed her before he had time to do it. Hell, perhaps he couldn't get it up. Who knows?"

"It's possible." Reid would give him that much. "But it's also possible that someone else murdered her. Someone who wanted to make it look like she was a victim of the Swamp Strangler." He grimaced as he said the words.

Pérez stared at him. "You think this was someone else?"

"Yeah. I've been doing some digging and there are a couple of people with motives. Her husband's ex, Bella Montague, for one. She hated Natalia. Accused her of stealing her man."

"That doesn't mean she killed her," argued Pérez.

"I've seen security footage of a party at the hotel where Natalia disappeared. Bella Montague had an altercation with the victim before she left the party. She had plenty of time to sneak back to the suite and surprise Natalia."

"I thought Natalia left that hotel by herself." Pérez sprung up and paced the room. "Didn't she take her stuff with her?"

"Her suitcase and some of her clothes were missing," Reid confirmed.

Pérez spread his hands. "There you go. She walked out on her husband. Happens all the time, particularly amongst those celeb types."

Reid frowned. "I'm not so sure, boss. Normally, I'd agree with you, but Natalia was in love with her husband. I've spoken to several friends who confirm that. Even the victim's father agrees, and he doesn't like the guy much."

"You spoke to Rhys Arnold? Jesus, Reid. He's the one insisting we put a team on this."

"I know. Listen, what do you say to this? Let me investigate Natalia's death. It might have nothing to do with the other two murders. Your task force can concentrate on those, on finding a link between the two dead girls."

"And if it does?"

"Then I'll hand over what I've discovered," he promised. "Anything to do with the Swamp Strangler, and your boys have priority."

Pérez thought for a moment, then he opened the desk draw and took out Reid's badge. He put it down on the table.

"Welcome back, Detective."

8

"You can't work here." Kenzie stalked around the cabin. "There isn't even a decent Wi-Fi signal."

"I've got a desk at the precinct if I want it," he said.

"Do you want it?" She tilted her head to look at him. He was leaning against the deck, arms folded across his chest. He'd just told her he was officially investigating Natalia Cruz's death. He'd been reinstated.

"Not really. I'd prefer it if the rest of the department didn't know what I was doing. It may become necessary to work with them, but for now I'd like to keep it under wraps."

"Aren't they your old team?" she said. "Surely they'd be happy to work with you again. From what I hear, you were a great cop."

He snorted. "Who'd you hear that from? Your source at the department?"

"No, not him." In fact, her police contact hadn't been very complimentary towards Reid. Quite the opposite, in fact. His animosity had surprised her. "I ran into Vic Reynolds last night. He was my father's partner back in the day. He only had good things to say about you."

"Captain Reynolds was your father's partner?" Reid's eyes widened in surprise.

"Yeah, when he was still on the force. They go way back."

"And you told him we were working together?"

"Not exactly. I didn't think that would go down too well. I told him I'd interviewed you about the body in the swamp."

"Ah," Reid nodded.

"He said it was a shame you left the force, and he'd always hoped you'd go back some day."

"Did he now?"

She flashed him a grin. "And now you have."

He looked out over the water. "For now."

"Can I see it?"

"See what?"

"Your badge. I never got mine, you see." She'd come so close. Only a few months left to go, and then the blasted accident.

He took his badge off his waistband and handed it to her. It was heavier than she'd expected. The weight was reassuring in her palm. To think she'd almost had one of these. How different her life would have been. She'd been at the newspaper for nearly 10 years now. That was 10 years she could have been a cop, chasing down bad guys, putting scum behind bars. Fighting for justice for the victims of crime. Victims who'd gone missing, whose bodies had never been found. Victims like her mother. Yet all she'd done was write about it.

Sighing, she handed it back.

"You could reapply?" he offered, correctly reading her expression. She'd noticed that about him. He was good at reading people. A skill honed over a decade of service, no doubt.

"I've got metal pins holding my left knee together," she said. "I'd never pass a physical."

"Sorry to hear that."

She shrugged. "I came to terms with it a long time ago."

"What happened?" he asked.

"Car wreck. Three months before I was due to graduate."

He grimaced. "That's tough."

"Yep." Tough was an understatement. It was the day her world had fallen apart, the day her dreams had been ripped to shreds. The weirdest part was she couldn't even remember most of it. The drive home. A screech of tires. An ear-splitting crash. Colored lights flickering through her subconscious. Muted voices.

"Kenzie, can you hear me?"

"Shit, she's not responding."

"Somebody call an ambulance!"

Then waking up in the emergency ward. Visits from her colleagues at the academy. Concerned faces and well wishes, but there was nothing they could do. There was nothing anyone could do. Her left knee had taken the brunt of the smash. It was destroyed. It took three surgeries and four months of rehab to put it back together again.

"Anyway, listen. You can work at my place if you want. I have fast internet, cell phone signal, and air conditioning as a bonus."

He shifted uncomfortably. "Thanks, but I don't think that's a good idea."

"Why not? I'm usually at the office, anyway."

He hesitated.

Was he worried he'd be crossing the line? Working in her home meant he'd be in her space. Less able to do what he wanted. One thing she'd learned about Reid Garrett in the short time she'd known him was that he was fiercely independent.

"The thing is, there might be information I can't share with you. I'm officially a detective again. This isn't a team effort anymore."

Was he serious? After they'd come this far?

"I don't see why. We want the same thing. We've got the same goal. To see Natalia's killer brought to justice."

"Kenzie, that's not how it works. Cops and reporters don't pair up and solve crimes."

"Well, they should," she huffed.

"And you can't write about this investigation. Not until it's over."

"But…"

"I'm sorry, Kenzie. I did warn you this would happen."

"What about the camera footage? Can I see that at least?"

"I've requested a warrant. I'll let you know if I find anything," he said.

"That's it? After I got you into the hotel? After we interviewed Snake and Rhys Arnold together? You're going to ditch me, just like that?"

"I don't want to, but I can't discuss an ongoing investigation. You know that. This"—he waved his hand between them—"puts me in a very difficult position."

"I'd say these are exigent circumstances, wouldn't you?"

"Not really. I'm grateful for your help, but I can't be your primary source. Everything we discover is going to go straight into the Miami Herald."

"Why am I here then?" She threw her arms into the air. "I thought we were going to talk to Bella Montague today. Unless you don't want my help with that?"

He stood on the deck, legs apart, arms still folded, clearly at odds with himself.

"What if I promise not to submit anything without your approval?" She hated herself for saying that. Usually she refused to be censored by anyone, particularly law enforcement, but if it meant working the case with him… "I won't mention the investigation. I'll have to post updates, but you can sign off on those. When we bust this case open, I get the exclusive. That's the deal."

He pursed his lips. "You promise you won't publish a word without my consent?"

She gritted her teeth. "I swear."

His penetrating gaze bore into her, and she knew he was asking himself if he could trust her. She met his gaze head on, her own clear and sincere.

"Okay," he breathed, finally. "But not a word to anyone. If this gets out, I could get into deep shit."

"My lips are sealed. No one will know we're working together."

His phone buzzed. He glanced at it. "Warrant's come through."

"Great, why don't you pick up the recording and meet me at my place? I'll text you the address."

He hesitated, but only for a moment. "Okay, see you in an hour."

They must have watched the video at least five times. Kenzie's eyes were burning by the time she looked away from the screen.

"I give up. I can't see anyone leaving the party after Natalia goes to bed."

Reid scratched at his eyes. "I haven't seen anything obvious, yet someone must have. Nobody tampers with her drink, either. She gets handed it by the barman, sips it until Bella comes up to her and hisses something in her ear. They exchange a few harsh words, then Bella's date leads her away. She finishes the drink, then 20 minutes later tells her husband she's going back to the room."

"What if whatever made her groggy wasn't in the drink?" wondered Kenzie.

Reid frowned. "Where could it be from? As far as I can tell, she ate one or two canapés, the same thing everyone else was eating. Those couldn't have been touched, otherwise there'd be a bunch of people with headaches and dizziness."

"True." Kenzie thought for a moment. "What about earlier? When she first arrived at the party. She had a glass of champagne to relax."

"I saw the bartender open the bottle," Reid said. "Still, I guess it's possible someone slipped something into her glass. I can't see any evidence of it, but she's not always in the frame. There are a few instances where she's out of sight of the camera."

"Maybe the killer knew where the cameras were located," said Kenzie. "Or is that a stretch?"

"No, could have surveyed the venue beforehand. We don't know who we're dealing with yet."

"What do you say we take a break and talk to Bella Montague? I told her agent we'd be coming round today, so we shouldn't leave it too long."

"Does she know what it's about?" asked Reid.

"I told her the paper wanted to get her take on Natalia Cruz's murder." Kenzie smiled. "She thinks it's a publicity thing."

"Bella's staying at the Four Palms Hotel," Kenzie told him as she climbed into the passenger seat of his Ford pickup. He hadn't mentioned going in two separate vehicles, so she assumed he was okay with it. Reid seemed more relaxed around her now, less distant. He wasn't happy with the arrangement, but he'd accepted it. They needed each other.

"Doesn't she live in Miami?" he asked.

"Yeah, I don't know why she's at the hotel. Perhaps she's there for an event or a shoot or something."

Reid parked across the road and they walked into the lobby of the Four Palms. It wasn't as snobby as the Sand Club, and the receptionist smiled at them as they walked up. "Can I help you?"

"We're here to interview Bella Montague." Kenzie showed her press ID card.

"Yes, of course. If you'll take a seat in the lounge, I'll let her know you're here."

"Thank you." Kenzie led the way to a chic lounge area outside of the lobby. Comfy leather chairs were dotted around the room, interspersed with lush indoor plants, and lit by recessed lighting.

They didn't have to wait long.

Bella glided into the room wearing a floor-length white dress which complemented her golden tan. Her strawberry blond hair had just the right amount of blond streaks to look natural and her nails were painted a warm coral. She wasn't as beautiful as Natalia Cruz, but there was a sensuality to her that was hard to ignore.

"Bella, thank you for seeing us." Kenzie got to her feet. She smelled a warm, exotic fragrance. "Please, won't you sit down?"

Bella sat, crossing her long legs in front of her. The white dress, which was buttoned all the way down the front, slid open displaying a delicate ankle and a smooth calf. "What is it you want to know?"

So gracious and cordial, but then again, she thought this was a piece on her.

"We'd like to get your take on Natalia Cruz's murder," began Kenzie. They'd agreed on the way here that she'd take the lead in the questioning, and he'd step in only after she'd established a rapport.

"I was shocked when I found out." She lowered her voice. "It was no secret we'd fallen out, but I wouldn't wish her dead."

"You were best friends, weren't you?" Kenzie probed gently.

Bella glanced down at her hands. "We were, once. We went to school together. Things were much simpler in those days, before…" She petered off.

"Before you met Eric?"

A nod. She glanced up. "Yes. I was with Eric for four years, long before he became famous."

"It must have been a blow when he began dating your best friend?"

She stiffened. "It was. The worst part was I introduced them. I could kick myself for that." She shook her head. "But I had no idea he'd ditch me for her."

There was venom in her words. The pain still raw, even though her adversary was dead.

"What about now?" asked Kenzie. "Have you been in touch with Eric? Is there any chance of a reconciliation?"

She pursed her lips, her eyes sad. "I doubt it. I did extend my condolences, but too much has happened to go back. Too many hurtful things have been said."

"I understand," murmured Kenzie. "You were at his launch party, weren't you?"

She seemed surprised at the question. "Yes, I went to offer my congratulations. I bear Eric no ill will."

"Did you speak to Natalia?"

Her head snapped up. "Why do you ask?"

"Only because a guest saw you two arguing."

"That was my fault." She hung her head. "I find it hard to keep my animosity in check, particularly after I've had a few. I tried to be understanding, but she hurt me very badly."

Kenzie gave a sympathetic nod. "Did you leave after the exchange with Natalia?"

"Yes. Dave—my date—took me home. I'm ashamed to say I would probably have created a scene if he hadn't."

"Did you go straight home?" cut in Reid.

Her gaze turned to him. "Oh, er, yes. Dave drove me home and I went straight to bed."

"Did he stay with you?"

Another shake of the head. "No, not that night. I was too upset."

"Can anyone vouch for you?" Reid cut to the chase.

"I–I don't understand." Bella glanced from him to Kenzie and back again. "Are you asking for my alibi?"

"We just want to know if anyone can confirm you were at home after the party?" said Kenzie, more softly.

"Well, Dave, but he left after dropping me off."

"No one else? Not a housekeeper, a neighbor?"

"No. Why are you asking me this?" Her back straightened and she squared her shoulders. "Am I a suspect now?"

"Natalia was abducted from her hotel suite at some point after you left. We're looking into what happened and would very much like to rule you out." Kenzie kept her tone even.

"I thought this was an article on me?"

"Oh, I apologize if you got the wrong idea. I'm an investigative reporter looking into Natalia Cruz's death."

Bella stood up. "I think this interview is over."

"Sit down, Miss Montague." Reid's voice didn't warrant arguing with. She glanced at him, then sank back into her chair. "Who are you? I know you're not a reporter."

"Detective Reid Garrett. Miami PD." He showed her his badge. "Miss Gilmore is assisting us with our inquiries."

Her green eyes darted back to Kenzie. "You tricked me."

"No, Bella. We do want your take on what happened. I told Detective Garrett that you'd cooperate because you had nothing to hide. That is true, isn't it?"

Her shoulders slumped. "Of course I don't have anything to hide. I'm sorry, I thought you were accusing me of having something to do with Natalia's death."

"No, we're merely trying to establish the truth," said Kenzie.

Reid leaned forward. "Now, can anyone confirm you were at home?"

She shook her head. "No, I don't think so. I went inside and straight to bed. Dave didn't even come in."

"Can you think of anyone who would want to harm Natalia?" asked Kenzie.

Bella frowned. "I thought it was that serial murderer, the Swamp Strangler, who killed her."

"It's one of several lines of inquiry," said Reid.

She gave a tentative nod. "Oh, I see. Natalia and I hadn't been close for a long time, so I don't know what else was going on in her personal life. I'm sorry I can't be of more help."

"Okay, thank you Miss Montague." Reid got to his feet.

"That's it?" Bella got up too.

"For now, yes. If we have any more questions, we'll be in touch."

Once outside, Kenzie asked, "What do you think?"

"I'm not sure. I couldn't get a read on her. I think she's hiding something, but does it have anything to do with Natalia's disappearance?"

"Yeah, she did seem a little cagey, I agree."

"One thing I know for sure," said Reid, "is that she doesn't have an alibi for the time Natalia disappeared."

"So, she's still a suspect," summed up Kenzie.

"Very much so."

9

Reid couldn't get rid of the feeling that he was missing something. After dropping Kenzie back at her apartment, he drove home, grateful for the air conditioning in the car. The different aspects of the case rolled around in his mind, but nothing took hold.

Back at the cabin it was stifling. The air seemed to stand still around him.

He stood on the deck and stared over the water to where it had all begun. Where was the Swamp Strangler now? Was he, at this very moment, stalking his next victim? Somehow, Reid had veered off the path of the serial killer and onto finding out who murdered Natalia Cruz.

After the autopsy report, he was convinced the two cases were separate, unlike Pérez who'd sourced a detective from Miami-Dade to lead the task force. Jonny had texted him an update earlier today. Other than the lieutenant, only his old teammate and the rookie, Detective Ryan, knew he was involved. He was hoping it would stay that way.

In the background, the television showed scenes of the most recent spate of gang shootings in Miami. A gang banger had been murdered in his car by a group of four men, armed with fully automatic weapons. Reid looked over his shoulder. The car resembled Swiss cheese. He dreaded to think what the occupant looked like.

Ortega had his hands full with that. If anything, the violence was escalating. They needed to take drastic measures to get it under control. The police were dealing with a full-out gang war.

There was brief mention of the ongoing investigation into the Swamp Strangler, with Natalia Cruz suspected as his third victim. A police task force had been formed to hunt down the killer, and Captain Reynolds from the Miami Police Department was confident they'd have the man in cuffs before long.

Reid snorted. Good luck with that. With absolutely nothing to go on, things weren't looking very good for the hastily assembled task force.

It was too hot to sit indoors, so Reid took his beaten-up laptop outside where there was a slight breeze and replayed the video of the launch party. Heavy clouds dotted the horizon. It would rain soon. They needed it to break the humidity.

He went through the video frame by frame, looking for anything to explain Natalia's spiked drink. After finding nothing, he went through it a second time, looking for anyone leaving the party shortly after Natalia.

He rubbed his eyes. Other than Bella's boyfriend escorting her out, nothing jumped out at him. During the third run-through, he spotted it. The PR woman, what was her name again?

After her altercation with Natalia by the swimming pool, she retreated to the other end of the bar, where she ordered a drink and knocked it back. Clearly agitated, she took a few deep breaths and was then joined by another couple. They talked for a few minutes and then moved to the far end of the swimming pool.

The camera above the bar covered the length of the pool, so Reid could see her in her emerald-green dress, talking and laughing, the argument with Natalia seemingly forgotten.

Reid forwarded the video slowly, keeping his eyes pinned on the green dress.

There.

At eleven twenty-two, she was gone. No green dress.

He rewound it and watched for the moment the PR woman walked out of the frame. Eleven twenty-one she moved off to the side and out of the camera's line of sight. It was a subtle movement. Nothing sudden, nothing to catch the eye. She simply melted into the shadows and disappeared.

Heart pounding, Reid flicked to the footage of the hotel lobby. It was as he'd thought, she didn't pass reception. Not at eleven twenty-two or anytime afterwards. Back at the party, the green dress was gone.

He forwarded the video to the end of the night just to be sure, but she didn't come back. She'd disappeared in the direction of the beach.

Kenzie curled up on the couch with her laptop. Her mission was to delve into Natalia Cruz's background and find out all she could about the woman who had stolen DJ Snake's heart.

Natalia was born into money. By the time she came along, her father was already a multi-millionaire. He'd married a local stunner called Silvana who he'd met at the country club. Her father had been one of Cuba's richest businessmen before he'd fled the country of his birth to come to America.

But Silvana was too beautiful and, in the end, had been enticed away by a wealthy Texan oil baron. She died a few years later in a gas explosion at the family ranch. According to the photographs Kenzie could find, Natalia was the spitting image of her mother.

Heart-shaped face, long glossy brown hair, expressive eyes, and full, luscious lips. She was sexy too, with an hourglass figure, a slim waistline, and impressive cleavage. No wonder Snake fell so hard for her.

But what was she like?

Kenzie looked up some blog posts and articles written by reporters she knew and spent the evening calling them. She asked the same question every time. What did you think of Natalia Cruz?

"Vacant."

"Not to speak ill of the dead, but she was a complete airhead."

"Sweet, but not the brightest candle on the cake."

"Beautiful, but not much there."

"Spoiled and entitled. Not much going on upstairs."

Kenzie poured herself a glass of sparkling water and went back to her laptop to write up her notes. The consensus was the same. Natalia was spoiled, beautiful, but lacking in the intelligence department.

That was interesting. A person like that would need someone to handle their financial affairs, and someone as wealthy as Natalia would need it more than most. Did she have a trust fund? Did her father control her finances? It wasn't a question they'd thought to ask him.

Her husband would inherit her fortune since she hadn't made a will, so he had the most to gain by her death. Except he was the one person they'd cleared. It couldn't have been him.

It was after ten when her cell phone buzzed. She didn't recognize the number.

"Hello?"

"Miss Gilmore, it's Rhys Arnold here. You asked me if I knew of anyone who'd want to hurt Natalia."

"Yes," she breathed.

"Well, I've thought of someone."

"Who is it, Mr. Arnold?"

"When Natalia was last here, she mentioned she was going to fire her PR agent."

"Fire? Are you sure?" A visual of a woman with a short, dark bob in a sleeveless black dress sprung to mind.

"Yes, I'm certain. I remembered this afternoon. Natalia said she thought her PR agent was stealing from her."

"Really? Did she say how?"

"No, I'm sorry. I suspect she was overcharging for her services, they all do. And possibly skimming off the top. I suggested she get an auditor in, but Natalia wasn't like that. She didn't enjoy confrontation. She said it would be easier for all concerned if she just got rid of her. No drama."

Except there had been drama at the launch party. Gabriella had been livid with Natalia and confronted her. Natalia had gone running to her husband's side, only to be ambushed by Bella, who'd had too much to drink. So she'd taken refuge in her room.

Kenzie thanked Natalia's father, then hung up. She stared at her notes, thinking. Gabriella had a motive. If she was scamming Natalia, she wouldn't want that coming out. It would affect her reputation, her business. It might even land her with a court case.

She sent Reid a text message.

I think we need to talk to Gabriella Vincent.

Her phone buzzed almost immediately.

Agreed. Can you set it up?

Sure, I'll text you the details in the morning.

He sent her a thumbs up in response.

Kenzie smiled. Reid didn't strike her as the sort of man who used emojis, but at least they were on the same page. Gabriella Vincent had just become their number one suspect.

10

Gabriella Vincent was a striking woman in her early forties. Her severe bangs hung just below her eyebrows, brushing her eyelashes. How it didn't annoy her, Reid had no idea. It was annoying him just looking at it.

"What can I do for you?" she asked once they were seated around a glass table in her office. The air conditioning hummed and there was a jug of coffee on the table in front of her. She didn't offer them any.

"We'd like to ask you some questions about your late client, Natalia Cruz," Reid said. He'd filled Kenzie in on what he'd seen on the video footage, and she'd told him what Rhys Arnold had said.

Her face fell. "Sad business, that. Tragic."

"How long had she been a client?" asked Kenzie, setting the stage. She was good at putting people at ease and lowering their defenses before Reid swooped in for the kill. It was an unconscious strategy they'd adopted, but it worked. He had to admit, they made a good team.

"About five years."

"And what exactly did you do for her?" Kenzie tilted her head to the side. Polite, inquiring, non-threatening.

Gabriella pursed her lips. "My company managed her publicity. We made sure she was portrayed in a certain light, maximized press opportunities, booked interviews and television appearances, that sort of thing."

"I believe she was trying to make a name for herself as a singer?"

Reid glanced at her in surprise. That was news to him.

"Yes, that's right, although to be honest, she wasn't very good at it. Her husband's influence helped. He wanted to use her in his latest album, although that never happened."

"What was your relationship like with Natalia?" Kenzie kept her tone casual.

"I like to think we were friends. We'd grown close over the years."

Kenzie smiled. "Did she ever confide in you?"

"Sometimes." Her eyes shifted off Kenzie and onto the table.

"Did she ever mention problems in her marriage or with anyone else?"

"With her husband, no. They were blissfully happy. With her husband's ex, yes. That woman was a menace. Couldn't get over the fact Natalia had stolen her man. It was getting a bit old, to be honest. I mean come on, we've all been there. Time to move on." She looked at Kenzie like she ought to know what she meant.

Kenzie gave a tiny nod. Reid wondered if she had been there.

"We heard a rumor that Natalia was going to fire you," cut in Reid.

Shock and then denial spread across her face.

"I don't know where you heard that, Detective, but it isn't true. We had a good working relationship."

"She told her father she suspected you were stealing from her."

Gabriella sputtered. "That's ridiculous. He must be mistaken. My company is above reproach."

"Then you won't mind if we have a look at your accounts?" Reid said.

Her face reddened. "Of course I mind. You can't come in here and accuse me of fraudulent practices and demand to see my books."

"I think you'll find I can." Reid handed her the warrant he'd rushed through that morning. Pérez had been skeptical but accommodating. "This is on you," he'd told Reid. "The department doesn't have time to sift through this woman's accounts."

Kenzie arched an eyebrow but didn't comment. She hadn't known about the warrant.

Gabriella stared at him.

Reid slid a card over the table. "Please email a copy of your current financials to that address. Failure to comply will mean obstruction and I'll have no choice but to arrest you."

The shocked expression turned hard. "Why are you so interested in my finances?"

He folded his arms across his chest. "You can see how it looks. If you were stealing from Natalia and she was about to report you, that would give you a motive to silence her."

She gasped. "I didn't have anything to do with her death. I was at a party when she disappeared."

"Actually, you weren't," Reid said. "You left the party at twenty past eleven. Maybe you'd like to explain why you walked down to the beach and didn't leave via the hotel exit?"

She looked confused for a moment.

"We saw video footage of the party," Kenzie explained more gently. "When you left, you headed down the path to the beach. A bit dangerous that time of night, wasn't it?"

"I needed to clear my head," she said.

"Is that because you had an altercation with Natalia before you left?"

She sighed. "Okay, fine. You're right. Natalia was going to terminate my services. But it wasn't because of the reason you think. She wasn't happy with the way we were representing her. She felt we could do more for her singing career." Gabriella spread her hands. "I tried. I really did, but nobody wanted to take her on. Like I said, she wasn't good enough. Talented Latina singers are a dime a dozen in this city."

Kenzie frowned. "Then why did she tell her father you were stealing from her?"

"I have no idea. Perhaps she was trying to justify it. Who knows?"

"What did you do after you walked along the beach?" he asked.

"I went back to my car and drove home."

"Can anyone vouch for you?"

"I don't think so." She clicked her fingers. "Actually, yes. I stopped at a gas station on the way."

Kenzie met his gaze.

"Which one?"

"Bay Point Shell, on Biscayne."

"Okay, we'll check it out. Thank you, Ms. Vincent."

Her guarded expression told him it wasn't a pleasure.

She got to her feet.

"I still need to see your finance records," he said.

Her lips pressed together. "I have nothing to hide."

"Great, I'll expect them this afternoon."

They walked into the morning sunshine. "She's hiding something," Kenzie said as they walked back to Reid's car.

He tended to agree. "It might just be her finances. We need to check out her alibi. The gas station is bound to have a security camera."

"We could go there now," Kenzie said. "It's not far away."

The Bay Point Shell was a 24-hour gas station with a convenience store. Reid spotted two security cameras attached to the outside wall, pointing at the pumps. Sitting behind the checkout was a portly man in a straining shirt and faded denim jeans. He had a hangdog expression and dark rings under his eyes.

"You the owner?" asked Reid.

The man nodded. "Bill Preston. What can I do for you?"

Reid showed his badge. "I need to see your security footage from the night of July sixteenth."

He scowled. "Don't you need a warrant for that?"

Reid gritted his teeth. Everybody was an expert these days. He was about to say he could get one when Kenzie lowered her voice and leaned in. "We're following a lead on the Swamp Strangler."

His eyes lit up. "Seriously? You think he came here?"

"That's what we need to check."

He turned to the computer behind the checkout. "Give me a moment. July sixteenth, you say?"

"Yeah," grunted Reid. He shot Kenzie a look.

"It worked, didn't it?" she whispered back.

Preston tapped away and then said, "Here you go. Saturday night."

"Do you mind if we come round?" Reid asked. The counter was piled high with racks of candy and other last-minute items.

"Sure."

They crowded into the narrow space behind the counter and stared at his screen. The quality wasn't great, and the video was in black and white, but they could still make out the vehicles coming in for gas.

"Can you forward it until eleven twenty p.m.?" asked Reid.

Preston did so, then stood back as the footage played in real time. Nothing happened. Nobody came in or out of the gas station.

"Speed it up again," ordered Reid.

Preston did so and the images flashed past, blurry and jumpy.

"There!" Kenzie grabbed Reid's arm. "That's her, I'm sure of it."

Preston slowed it down to real time and they watched as Gabriella Vincent climbed out of a smart Mercedes Benz and filled up the tank. She used her credit card to pay at the machine, without coming into the store.

"It's definitely her." Reid's heart sank. "She was telling the truth."

"Eleven forty-seven." Kenzie read the timestamp. "I suppose she could have gone back to the beach. We don't know what time Natalia was taken."

"The Swamp Strangler's a chick?" gaped Preston.

"An accomplice," whispered Kenzie.

Preston gave an uncertain nod.

"Snake got back to the room at about one in the morning and she was gone," Reid said. "That's a window of at least an hour."

Gabriella got back into her car and drove out of the frame.

"She was heading in the opposite direction," murmured Reid.

"Yes, but she could have turned around up ahead and we'd never know. This could be her alibi. Maybe she planned this, just like she planned everything else."

Reid bit his lip. It was possible, he'd give her that much, but something in his gut was telling him it wasn't her.

They thanked Preston and got back into Reid's pickup truck.

"I'm going to get forensics to sweep the hotel room." He started the engine.

"I thought they'd already done that?"

"Nah. Natalia was never reported missing, so the hotel suite was never a crime scene. The police paid Snake a visit the next day, but they didn't check for blood or DNA in the hotel room."

Kenzie paused, then said, "You're thinking the killer must have subdued Natalia somehow."

"Yeah. If she didn't leave voluntarily, he or she must have carried her out."

"What if she was drugged?" Kenzie pointed out. "There'd be no trace evidence left in the suite."

"I still think it's worth a shot."

She nodded. "Yeah, I agree. It's a pity they didn't send in CSI the day after she vanished. There might have been signs of struggle, or like you said, some DNA lying around. Now, the room would have been cleaned several times over."

"Blood is hard to remove," Reid said. "You can still pick it up months, if not years, after the event."

"Let's do it, then," said Kenzie. "Let's send them in."

He couldn't resist a grin at the "let's." "I'll call them now."

11

Kenzie was fascinated by the crime scene investigation process. She always had been. As a girl, she'd watched the forensic team sweep her own house, serious men dressed in white from head to toe painstakingly searching room by room. They found nothing, of course. No trace of her mother.

She'd disappeared while at the Christmas market, not from their home. At the time, Kenzie had been confused by the sudden invasion of police officers and forensic specialists, but later, she understood they'd been investigating her father.

The spouse or partner was always top of the suspect list. On the day her mother vanished, Kenzie had been with her father and Uncle Larry at the market. Kenzie's friend, Bethany, had also been there, and Bethany's parents. Kenzie had gone to Santa's Grotto with them, while her father and Larry went to sample the mulled wine. Her mother had wandered off, never to be seen again.

The police had scoured the area, but there was no trace of her. Nobody had seen a thing. The woman in the red coat had simply vanished.

"You okay?" asked Reid.

She turned to him. "Oh, yeah. Sorry, I was miles away."

He gestured to the room. "They haven't found anything. No blood on the carpet or the walls. They already changed the bed sheets, so there's no chance of finding anything there, but I had hoped." He trailed off.

"Me too," she said. Finding Natalia's blood in the room would have backed up their theory that she'd been abducted.

"There are other ways of subduing a person," said Kenzie. "The kidnapper could have strangled her in the hotel room before carrying her off."

"That's a possibility." Reid glanced around. "If the patio doors were unlocked or open, he could have snuck in and surprised her."

"I suppose it's pointless checking for prints?" Kenzie said.

"Yeah, with all the guests that have opened that door, it'll be impossible to isolate any suspects."

She sighed. "Now what?"

"Let's walk down to the beach and trace Gabriella's steps. I have to get back to work. I've got Natalia's bank statements to go through, and Gabriella's finance records."

"I can help," Kenzie said. "Let me do the bank statements. You take the finances."

He hesitated. "Thanks. Do you have a printer?"

She grinned. "Sure. I told you, I have everything."

Kenzie lived in an updated one-story villa on East Bay Harbor Drive. It had a paved pathway leading to the front door and a small porch where she could sit and watch the sunset.

"Nice place." Reid followed her up the path to the front door.

"Thanks. I bought it with the money my father left me, almost a decade ago." She blew a strand of hair out of her face. "It feels like yesterday."

"How'd he die?" Reid asked.

"Heart attack. He retired from the force the year before, and I always said it was the inactivity that killed him."

"I know the feeling."

She let them into the house. "Are you saying you're glad to be back on the job?"

"In a way. This is only temporary for me. I doubt I'll go back full time."

"Why not?"

He didn't reply.

"Because of what happened before?"

"Yeah." He shifted his weight onto the other foot. "I can't get past that. It was my investigation. My team."

Kenzie turned to face him. "But not your fault. You didn't pull the trigger. You couldn't have known what her target was going to do." She swallowed. "Just like I couldn't have known he was going to read my article. Or that your girlfriend was still undercover."

Reid moved a pile of books out of the way and put his laptop bag on the table.

"It's terrible that happened," she said. "But you can't beat yourself up about it."

"So everybody says."

She picked up the pile of books and moved them onto the floor. "Sorry about the clutter. I need to get more bookshelves."

Reid eyed the rows of bookshelves on the wall behind her. "I'm not sure where you're going to put them."

She laughed, easing the tension. "I'll find somewhere."

Kenzie put on a pot of coffee and took two ice-cold waters out of the fridge. She handed one to Reid. "Did you say you wanted to print those bank statements?"

"Yeah, if you don't mind."

"No problem. It's a wireless printer. I'll get you the code."

When she got back, he was looking at a framed photograph on a side table. "This you?" He pointed to the blonde child.

"Yeah, with my mom. That was taken a couple days before she disappeared."

Reid's eyes widened. "Your mother disappeared? What happened to her?"

She shrugged, trying to appear nonchalant, yet knowing he'd see right through her. "No one knows. There was a police investigation, of course, but nothing ever came of it."

"I'm sorry," he said. "I had no idea."

"It was a long time ago."

"Is that why you became a cop?" he asked.

The way he was looking at her, like he could see into her soul. "You mean did I become a cop because I couldn't save her?"

He nodded.

"No. I'm not that cliched." Maybe she was. "My dad was on the force. I think I just wanted to be like him. He raised me after she disappeared."

"He sounds like a great guy."

"Yeah, he was." Most of the time.

She changed the subject. "Why don't you print those documents and we can get started."

He logged onto his laptop and set up the printer. Within five minutes they heard it spitting out pages in her study. Kenzie didn't want to be rude, and the study wasn't big enough for two, so she brought the copies and her laptop to the living room and set up on the other side of the round table.

"These are Gabriella's finance records." She passed him a pile. "I'll take the statements."

They got to work. Kenzie started with the most recent and worked backwards, going through each entry line by line. She looked for anything unusual or strange. Natalia spent a lot of time and money on spa treatments and lunches at the country club. Almost every day there was an expensive, frivolous purchase.

"The lives of the rich and famous," she muttered.

"Find anything?" Reid asked.

"Not yet. You?"

"All looks legit, but if she was stealing money from Natalia, the cards would have been charged for things that didn't exist or services Natalia hadn't requested. I don't know what those are."

"I'll take a look later, if you like," Kenzie offered. "A second set of eyes is never a bad thing."

She'd been at it for 45 minutes when she whistled under her breath.

Reid glanced up. "What?"

"I've found an anomaly." She stabbed the page with her highlighter. "Natalia made a substantial payment to a company called AF Investments."

"How much is substantial?" he asked.

"Two hundred and fifty thousand dollars."

"Okay, that is substantial. What is AF Investments?"

"I'm not sure. I'll look it up."

Kenzie typed the name into a search engine. "According to their website, they're an investment consulting firm catering to a small number of exclusive clients."

"Are they based in Miami?" he asked.

"Yep. Downtown area." She glanced at the time on her phone. "They're still open."

"Great. Let's pay them a visit."

Reid pulled up in front of the high rise housing AF Investments and gazed at the concrete and chrome monstrosity. "Do we know what floor they're on?"

"Sixteenth." She strained her neck. "How do we get in?"

"Over there." The entrance was hidden under a promenade station platform with steps and walkways overhead. There was no parking on the street, so they drove into a nearby parking garage.

"How do you want to play this?" Kenzie asked.

"What do you mean?"

"Well, there might be a better way than flashing your badge and demanding to know what Natalia was paying him for."

"There is?"

She grinned. "We could pretend to be prospective investors. Natalia recommended the firm and we've come to find out more about it."

"You think that'll work?"

She shrugged. "It'll get us an appointment. If he's dodgy, as soon as he sees your badge he'll clam up and we'll be lucky to get anything out of him."

Reid considered this. She had a point. His usual forthright approach might not be the best way forward in this instance.

"Okay, we'll do it your way, but just until we're in there. If he doesn't give us the information, we're going to have to revert to Plan B."

"Fair enough."

Her eyes gleamed, and he realized she was enjoying this. "You like playing a part, don't you?" he said as they got out of the car. "You like being somebody else."

"If it gets me what I want." She shot him a sideways look.

"You're very good at it. Manipulating people into talking to you."

"Thank you. I think. Anyway, let's not jinx it. AF Investments might not be so open to manipulation as others, especially if they're manipulators themselves."

They entered through a set of automatic glass doors that hissed shut behind them. They found themselves in a vast, brightly lit lobby. There was nothing in it other than two elevators.

"The only way is up," remarked Kenzie, pressing the button to open the doors.

They flew up to the sixteenth floor, where the elevator announced their arrival with a loud *ping*. Reid rested his hand on his weapon, beneath his shirt. He wasn't a fan of sudden entrances, particularly when he didn't know what was on the other side of the door.

He didn't have to worry. They emerged into a small, welcoming foyer composed of plush carpeting and a leather sofa under a permanently sealed window. There was no receptionist, just a pad on the reinforced glass door with a button on it.

Reid inspected it. The sticker read "AF Investments."

He pressed it, then waited. Kenzie came to stand beside him.

A female voice said, "Yes? Can I help you?"

He glanced up and saw the omnipotent eye of a security camera bulging down at them. He forced a smile. "Hello. We don't have an appointment, but we'd like to speak to someone about investment opportunities."

A pause.

"Take a seat. Someone will be with you shortly."

Reid shrugged at Kenzie and they sat down.

A short time later, two men approached the door. Both were wearing expensive Italian suits, but while one was middle-aged and balding, the other was in his late thirties, broad-shouldered, and definitely packing.

Reid stared at the younger man and froze. He'd recognize that face anywhere. Every line, every curve ingrained in his memory.

"You okay?" whispered Kenzie.

He didn't answer. He couldn't. He never thought he'd see that face again.

Kenzie followed his gaze. "Who is he?"

Reid gritted his teeth and tried to remain calm. "That's the man who killed Bianca."

12

There was no time to ask Reid for an explanation before the two men shook hands and the soundproof glass door opened.

"I'll be in touch," the younger man said, before pressing the button to summon the elevator. It opened immediately, again with a loud *ping*.

The older man turned to them, a practiced smile on his lips. "I'm sorry to keep you waiting. I'm Antonio Fernández. I believe you wanted to talk to me about investment opportunities?"

"Yes, that's right." Kenzie stood. "I'm Kenzie and this is my husband, Reid."

Reid had gone white and seemed to have lost the ability to speak. His eyes were still on the closed elevator the younger man had disappeared into.

"Do you have time to see us? I'm afraid we don't have an appointment." She flashed her dimples at him and he melted.

"I think I can squeeze you in. Follow me."

She elbowed Reid in the ribs and shot him a look that said, Get a grip! She couldn't have him falling apart on her now.

Whoever that man was, it would have to wait. They had a job to do.

Fernández led them down a corridor to an office at the end. It was sparsely furnished but had big windows overlooking the city.

"Lovely view," Kenzie complemented, playing for time. She needed Reid to pull himself together.

"Thank you. One of the bonuses of being this high up. Please, take a seat."

They sat. Reid seemed to have regained some of his color.

"Now, what can I do for you?"

"Well, a friend mentioned she invested with you, and we've just come into some money, so we thought we'd explore our options. Would you mind telling us more about what you do?"

His chest puffed out. "Of course. We're a brokerage firm with a contemporary approach to wealth management. We always put our customers first." His smile didn't reach his eyes. "We offer a wide range of services, including personalized financial advising and retirement planning, as well as expert investment research. We'll invest on your behalf and develop a portfolio that suits your needs and focuses on your financial goals."

"Sounds excellent," said Reid, getting into the role.

"What do you need from us?" asked Kenzie.

"It depends entirely on your budget," Fernández said. "You'll meet with a financial advisor who'd take you through the process. We'll develop a strategy for you, build a portfolio, and take it from there. Do you mind if I ask who referred you to us?"

"Natalia Cruz," said Kenzie. "Before she..." Her face clouded. "Well, you know."

She could have sworn Fernández paled, but he recovered well. He cleared his throat. "We were all shocked to hear what had happened to her."

We? So far, he was the only person Kenzie had seen on the whole floor. The female voice who had greeted them via the intercom seemed to be just that, a voice, and there were no employees walking around, no office banter, nothing.

"Yes, it was a terrible shock," she replied. "It makes you realize how vulnerable you are, as a woman." Kenzie clutched Reid's hand.

"That's why you've got me." He smiled and squeezed back. She almost believed him.

"What exactly did Ms. Cruz say about us?" Fernández asked.

"Oh, she didn't go into detail." Kenzie tossed her hair over her shoulder. "She mentioned a couple of firms and you were one of them."

"Do you mind telling us what you did for Natalia?" Reid asked.

"That's confidential," he said.

"She paid you two hundred and fifty thousand dollars." Reid watched as the man's eyes widened behind his glasses. "That's a lot of money. Must have been a good investment."

"H–How do you know that?" he stammered.

Reid took his badge out of his pocket and placed it on the desk. "I looked at her bank statements."

The man stared at it. "You're a cop?"

"Got it in one." Reid leaned forward. "Now, you can tell us what Natalia paid you for, or we'll get a warrant, confiscate all your computers, rifle through your files, make an unholy mess, and probably uncover a whole bunch of other things you don't want us to know."

Kenzie had to admit, he was intimidating. She was grateful she was sitting next to him and not on the other side of the desk.

"We managed her portfolio." He wiped a bead of sweat from his forehead.

"Could we see it?" asked Kenzie.

"I can't give it to you. It's confidential."

"I guess I'll have to get that warrant after all." Reid pulled out his phone.

Unfortunately, Fernández called his bluff. "I'm afraid I can't hand over the files without one."

Shit.

Kenzie clenched her fists.

At that moment, a barrel-chested man with tough eyes and an ill-fitting suit marched into the office. Kenzie didn't have time to wonder where he'd come from before he grabbed Reid's arm and hauled him out of the chair. Kenzie leaped to her feet.

Reid shrugged off his hand. The two men glared at each other.

Kenzie's heart skipped a beat. Please let them not get into a fight now. Both men were clearly armed, and she didn't want to be caught in the crossfire.

"It's okay," Fernández said. "They were just leaving."

She exhaled.

"We'll be back," Reid promised. "You can count on it."

"You do what you have to." The financial advisor gave a slimy grin before his henchman ushered them out of the office.

"Well, that wasn't suspicious at all," Kenzie said as they got into the elevator. "I thought that guy was going to physically throw us out. Fernández is definitely hiding something."

"Without a doubt. I'll get a warrant and come back tomorrow. We'll tear that place to shreds."

Reid was angry. His body was stiff and the veins in his neck stood out. But she wasn't entirely sure it was because of Fernández.

"Who was that man in the lobby?" she asked, as they descended to the ground floor.

His voice hardened. "Alberto Torres. He works for the Morales cartel."

Kenzie gasped. "You're kidding! The Mexican drug cartel?"

"Yeah. He was the one Bianca seduced to infiltrate the network. He's the one who shot her."

Kenzie stared at him. He was almost pulsing with angry energy.

"What was he doing here?" she whispered.

"That's what I'd like to know."

They walked to the car and got in. Kenzie's investigative mind was working overtime. "Do you think he's investing with Fernández's company?"

Reid scoffed. "No, that's not an investment company. It's some sort of Ponzi scheme. I'll bet my house on it. He's not investing for the Morales Cartel, he's laundering money for them."

"Oh, my God." She fastened her seat belt as Reid drove out of the parking garage. "This is huge. Local Miami Firm Launders Money for Mexican Cartel." She could see the headline.

Reid turned to her. "You can't write anything about this. Not yet. We don't know what the connection is. I'm just guessing, but it'll be something along those lines. You can count on it."

"I can't write about anything I haven't proven, or at least double-sourced. What are you going to do?" She wasn't sure she wanted to know the answer. She had a horrible feeling Reid was about to go rogue on her.

"I need to talk to my lieutenant. If Torres is in town, then the Morales cartel is still active in Miami. They may even be mixed up in this gang war."

"You're going after him?" It was more of a statement than a question.

"I have to. He killed one of our own. I can't let that go."

Kenzie turned away. "What about Fernández? Are you still going to get a warrant to search the premises?"

"Of course. I'll arrange it this afternoon, and we'll raid the place in the morning."

"Won't that give them ample warning?" she said.

"Yeah, but it can't be helped. They won't have time to doctor their books, and if they do, we'll pick up on any discrepancies."

"I hope you're right."

He dropped her off at home and picked up his laptop. "I'll work on Gabriella's finances this evening," he said. "I'll let you know if I find anything."

Feeling restless, Kenzie went into the office. She wanted to write up what had happened today and file a preliminary report on both Natalia Cruz and AF Investments. There were two big stories there, and she wanted to be ready when they broke.

"It's about time," her Editor-in-Chief called as she walked in. "I was wondering if you still worked here."

"Sorry." She approached him. The open office was emptying now that it was the end of the working day, with only a few die-hards chasing deadlines. "I'm on to something, and it's big."

"Come, let's talk."

She took a seat in his office, and he poured them both a cup of coffee. "What's happening? How's that cop you're working with?"

"He's fine. We're making progress." At least, she thought they were. She told Keith what they knew. "We don't think Natalia Cruz was killed by the Swamp Strangler."

"You're shitting me?" His eyebrows shot up.

"Different MO, but nobody knows yet."

"This could be big, Kenz." He rubbed his temple. "I want to make sure we're the first to break it."

"We will be. We're also chasing some leads. There are several suspects, including an investment firm who was scamming her. And get this, we also think they're laundering money for the Morales cartel."

Keith spluttered out his coffee. "Seriously?"

"Garrett recognized one of Federico Lopez's men. He was coming out as we were going in. They looked like friends, or at least business associates."

"Holy shit. Can you get proof?"

"We're going back with a warrant tomorrow to confiscate their computers and records. Garrett has a team at the department who will scrutinize them for fraudulent activity. If they're laundering funds, they'll pick it up. Then I'll have my proof."

"And Garrett is prepared to share this information with you?" Keith frowned.

She didn't blame him for being skeptical. Cops and reporters weren't usually a good mix. "Kind of. As long as nothing I write jeopardizes the investigation. I'll have to clarify that with him before we go to press."

Keith's frown deepened.

"I know," she said with a wave of her hand. "I don't like it either, but it's the only way. I'd have nothing without him."

"Well, we can't wait forever," Keith said. "Make sure you have something for me soon."

"I will," she promised.

13

Alberto Torres.

Reid increased the speed and felt the airboat accelerate beneath him. He was hoping the wind would clear his head and drive away the memories. Seeing him standing there had been a shock to the system. In that instant, he'd been catapulted back 16 months to when Bianca had died. That last frantic text message.

They know!

Then nothing.

He'd known then she was dead. That's when he'd ordered his team to descend on the bar. Sure enough, there she was, lying in a pool of her own blood in the back office.

The place had been cleaned out, the safe left open. The only evidence they'd found was the dead body of his agent.

His agent.

Until now, everyone had assumed Lopez and Torres skipped town.

Yet here he was, as calm and cocky as ever, shaking hands with an investment fraudster. Business as usual. What else was he doing there if not laundering the cartel's ill-gotten gains?

Reid swung the wheel hard to the right and felt the boat slide across the water. He executed the turn and then sped out towards the cypress swamp where he'd found Natalia's body.

A flock of birds flew low beside him, keeping up with the roaring jet engine. They veered off as he approached the swamp, as if they sensed something bad had happened there.

He stared at where he'd spotted the yellow dress. Nothing was there now. Just grass and reeds and a tangle of roots. She hadn't even changed after the party. That meant she hadn't had time to have a bath before her attacker had grabbed her. Chances were, he or she had come in right after Snake had left the room, or perhaps they'd been lying in wait the whole time.

Could it have been Fernández who'd ordered the hit? Had Natalia realized he was conning her and threatened to go to the authorities? But then why dump her body in the swamp? Why not just ditch her on a roadside, or leave her in the hotel room?

Unless they wanted to make it look like she was another one of the Strangler's victims. Perhaps they wanted to allay suspicion, send the cops on a diversion. Except they hadn't known about the sexual assault. The police had deliberately withheld that information from the public.

At first, it was thought it would create too much of an outcry. A dead girl was bad enough, but raped, too? Then, when the second victim had been found, Pérez had purposely held back the details. "That's something only the killer knows," he'd said, and he'd been right. Withholding that information had been a smart move to rule out any copycats.

There was a problem with that theory, though. Fernández couldn't have known Natalia would leave the party early. Not unless he'd had a spy, someone who'd spiked her drink.

The other possibility was that he hadn't known. He or his hit man had broken into the room, planning to hide until Natalia and Snake got back, then he was going to take them both out. Perhaps he'd make it look like a murder-suicide. When Snake had returned to the party, he'd had to change his plan.

Reid's pulse quickened. That could be it. He'd run it past Kenzie tomorrow and get her opinion.

He bit his lip. Listen to him. Since when had *he* started running things by *her*. A reporter. He crinkled his nose. Until recently, he'd considered them the scum of the earth. Bottom feeders, scavenging on the victim's pain.

But Kenzie was different. She cared. She wanted to find the truth. That was her sole aim. In that respect, she was just like him. He hoped he wasn't making a huge mistake by trusting her. If the Lieutenant found out, or if she broke their agreement and let something slip. Christ, he couldn't even bear to think about it.

Another wild turn and he was heading back the way he came. She was a good investigator, though. Better than he was in some ways, not that he'd ever admit it. He enjoyed working with her. That was a first. Usually, he flew solo. Even at the precinct, he'd been more of a leader than a team player, which was why he'd risen so quickly through the ranks to Sergeant.

He slowed down and cruised for a while, raising a hand in greeting to another tour operator as he passed. If he got fired for sharing information with Kenzie, he could always take tourists around the swamp. It wasn't the worst job in the world.

An hour later, he sat on the deck with his laptop, sipping a cold beer and going through Gabriella's financial statements. He highlighted a few discrepancies worth further investigation. A large sum of money had been paid to a magazine for an exclusive of the wedding, but several large amounts had been paid to other publications. A thousand dollars here, fifteen hundred there. Why was she paying them if there was an exclusive deal?

He googled those other publications and found they didn't exist. Gabriella had fabricated them to extort money from Natalia, and she'd been too naive to realize. He recalled Kenzie telling him she was considered vacant and an airhead. Perhaps that's why she'd been so easily taken advantage of.

Her PR agent had been ripping her off. Fernández had conned her into that fake investment scam. He sighed. Where was her husband in all this? Or her father? She had two strong men by her side, but neither had guided her.

He made a mental note to ask them about it in the morning.

His phone buzzed.

Pérez.

"Hey, LT. What's up?"

"Meet me for a drink at Smiley's?"

"Sure, now?"

"I'll be there in five."

Smiley's was the kind of bar you didn't go to unless you were desperate, or a local. It was filled with gatormen, prostitutes, and swampers. Most nights, folks fought, bled, and drank themselves silly. Still, it was early enough to be reasonably safe—for a police officer.

Nobody in the area knew Reid was a cop. He'd gone there a few times over the last year and a half, mostly when he'd first moved into the cabin and thought drowning his sorrows was a good idea. He didn't want them to find out now.

Pérez walked in wearing jeans and a T-shirt. He got a few stares, but was crumpled enough to not arouse suspicion.

"You look like you need a drink."

Pérez grunted. "Rough day."

Reid ordered two beers. "To what do I owe the honor?"

"I thought I'd swing by and see how you're doing? God knows, I could use a drink." He glanced around. "I haven't been to this dive since I was a teenager. Even then, I was too scared to come here at night. The day was bad enough. It was the first time I saw a man passed out cold. At noon."

Reid laughed. "It hasn't changed."

"How's the investigation going?" Pérez asked.

Reid filled him in. "Three suspects, none with a steadfast alibi. Bella Montague, the disgruntled ex, was home alone. Gabriella Vincent drove home via a gas station—security footage confirmed she was there—but she could have driven back to the hotel. And then there's Fernández. We're raiding his office tomorrow morning as soon as they open." He took a long pull of his beer.

"Motives?" asked Pérez.

"Bella Montague hated Natalia for stealing her man, Gabriella Vincent was ripping her off, and Fernández was scamming her. Out of the three of them, he's the top suspect. I think he may have taken a hit out on Natalia. She was naïve, people took advantage of her, but I think she saw through this one. She was going to report him to the authorities, so he took her out."

"Can you prove any of that?"

Reid shook his head. "Nope. Not yet."

"You're absolutely convinced this has nothing to do with the Swamp Strangler?" He glanced around as if he expected to see the serial killer sitting at the bar. It wasn't the most unlikely prospect, given the place's reputation.

"Pretty much. Until we can prove otherwise, I think we need to treat Natalia's death as an isolated incident. How's the task force coming along?"

Pérez grimaced. "I put Jonny in charge."

"What about that guy from Miami-Dade?"

"His wife went into labor early. There wasn't anyone else. I hope Jonny can handle it."

"He'll be fine," said Reid. "It'll be good for him."

"I've put Jared and Chris on it, too. I can't spare any more men."

Reid nodded. They were both decent detectives. They'd get the job done.

"So far, they haven't found a link between the girls," Pérez told him. "The first two were out of towners, and Natalia was local. None of them knew each other. None of them stayed in the same hotel. It's a mystery."

"Yet somehow the Strangler targeted them. Concentrate on the first two. Maybe they went to the same bar or hung out at the same beach. There must be a pattern somewhere."

Pérez glanced at him over his beer. "You sure you don't want to come back and take over?"

"Nah, I'm good flying under the radar for now."

Pérez gave a sad nod and took a long swig of his beer. "What time is the raid?"

"I've arranged to have a uniformed team there at nine when they open for business."

Pérez nodded. "Keep me posted. You do realize that even if you find evidence of fraud, it still doesn't prove the bastard killed her."

"No, but it gives us enough to bring him in for questioning."

"That it does," Pérez muttered. "That it does."

14

Kenzie stood outside AF Investments' high rise and watched as the team of police officers suited up. There were eight officers in total, all wearing their Miami PD uniforms complete with utility belts, tactical vests, and weapons.

Watching them made her suck in her breath with longing. Three months. That's all that had stood between her and that uniform. Three lousy months and she would have graduated from the police academy.

She glanced down at her leg. It looked perfectly normal in her jeans, but she never wore shorts. Her knee was crisscrossed with ugly scars and part of it was still numb. Nerve damage, her doctor had said. She'd never get the feeling back.

Reid came up to her. He wore a Kevlar vest over his T-shirt and was checking his handgun. A Glock 22. Standard issue for the Miami PD.

She swallowed her envy. "You going in?"

"Yeah. Stay here until you hear from me, okay?"

"Roger that. Good luck."

He gave a terse nod and strode back across the road toward the building. She saw him address the team, and they went inside.

What wouldn't she give to be with them?

Unable to stand still, she paced up and down the sidewalk, staring at the tower block, trying to count to the sixteenth floor. She lost it after nine and had to start again. What was happening in there? Was Fernández compliant? Or had he kicked up a fuss?

She paced up and down until her phone rang.

Reid.

"Yeah?"

"It's empty," growled Reid's voice. "They left."

"What?"

But he'd hung up.

Heart sinking, she raced across the road and pressed the button on the elevator. In another minute, she was on the sixteenth floor staring at the thick glass doors that had been jimmied open. The lock lay in pieces on the carpet.

She ran down the corridor to Fernández's office and burst in. It was empty. Even the desk was gone. Reid stood there, staring out of the window. "You shouldn't be in here."

She ignored him. "They must have packed up and left overnight. Have you checked the other offices?"

"Yep, all empty, if there were any people there to begin with."

A uniformed officer poked his head around the door. "See you back at the station," he told Reid.

"Yeah, thanks Matthews." He raked a hand through his hair. "What a waste of time. You were right. We gave them too much warning."

"Clearly they had a lot to hide," she surmised, looking at the indents in the carpet where the desk had stood. "They didn't want you getting your hands on their records."

"We're going to request the CCTV footage from the building and the nearby parking garage. We might be able to pick them up on that."

"You might spot Torres that way too," she pointed out.

Reid managed a weak smile. "I'm one step ahead of you. I figured he must have left his car there, since it's the only available parking on the street. As soon as I get the footage, I'm going to find that bastard. If I can get a license number, I can trace him through that."

"Then what?" Kenzie asked. "What are you going to do when you find him?"

He gave her a long, hard look. "Arrest him, of course."

Reid headed back to the station. At a loose end, Kenzie decided to drive up to Fort Lauderdale to see Rhys Arnold. She needed more information on Natalia's background, like why she was investing with Fernández's company. Had her father not advised her on those investments?

"I wasn't expecting you." Arnold opened the door in sweatpants and a T-shirt. It looked like he'd been working out.

"I know. I'm sorry to bother you. I had a few more questions about Natalia, I hope you don't mind."

"Where's your detective friend?" He glanced behind her.

"He's tied up at work," she said. "I'll pass everything we discuss to him."

Arnold gave a curt nod. "I had two other officers from the task force here earlier asking about her. They wanted to know when I last saw her and whether she'd been in touch at all in that week before her body was discovered. I told them the same thing I told you. I hadn't heard from her since we had lunch together." He sighed. "I hope they know what they're doing."

"We're following a different line of inquiry." Kenzie wanted to put the man at ease. The task force was playing catchup, having been formed after she and Reid had already begun their investigation. To Arnold, it must look like the left hand didn't know what the right was doing.

"You think she was murdered by someone she knew," he surmised. He was an astute old guy.

"It's a theory we're working on, yes." She hesitated. "Mr. Arnold, your daughter was investing through a company called AF Investments run by an advisor called Antonio Fernández. Do you know him?"

His eyes narrowed. "That thieving scumbag. Yeah, I know him. He tried to get me to invest in his fraudulent little scheme, but I saw right through him." He scratched his bearded chin. "I had no idea Natalia was involved with him."

"Two hundred and fifty thousand dollars," she said.

"Christ." He swept a hand over his thinning hair.

"Then a further hundred thousand two months later."

Heat swept into Rhys Arnold's cheeks. "The bastard was robbing her blind," he hissed. "You know how he works, don't you? He uses the money from new investors to pay the old ones. They think their money is sitting in a trading account being used solely for trades, and when they check via an app, they see a healthy interest, encouraging them to invest more. Meanwhile, it's completely fabricated. I got a trader pal to look into it for me. I always do due diligence before I hand over large sums of money."

A practice his daughter should have also adhered to.

"Excuse me for asking this, Mr. Arnold," she said. "But why was Natalia handling her own investments? Don't you have someone to do that for her?"

"You'd think so, wouldn't you?" He snorted. "Natalia—bless her soul—was a simple girl. Naive, trusting. She received a monthly allowance from a trust I set up of which she was a beneficiary. This is what she lived off. I couldn't allow her to manage her own finances for exactly this reason. The money she handed over to Fernández came from her mother. It was a substantial inheritance left on her mother's death. I had no say over what she did with it. I had hoped her husband would advise her, but it seems he's as useless with money as she was."

He gritted his teeth. "I'll get AF Investments shut down."

"I'm afraid they've vanished," Kenzie said. She didn't think Reid would mind her passing on that information. There wasn't much anyone could do about it now. "The police raided the premises this morning. Fernández and all his staff have gone."

"All his staff." Another snort. "My pal said the entire operation was run by Fernández, some tech whiz he had working for him, and a big bastard who made sure no irate customers came clamoring for their money back."

"That pretty much sums it up," said Kenzie. "Any idea where they've gone?"

"No, but I hope you catch his sorry ass."

"We'll definitely try," she said. "And if you think of anything else, you have my card. Feel free to call me any time."

15

Reid watched Gabriella Vincent squirm on the small screen outside the interrogation room. She crossed her legs, then uncrossed them. She leaned back, folded her arms, then unfolded them and put her hands in her lap. The woman was nervous, no doubt about it.

He'd left her to stew for a good half hour, telling her nothing about why she was here.

Eventually, he barged in, folder under his arm, tossed it onto the table and sat down opposite her.

"Detective, what is all this about? Why am I here?"

"We'll get to that. This interview is being recorded, and as I understand it, you've waived your right to an attorney."

"If I don't know what I'm here for, how can I know whether I need a lawyer?"

"You're here because we have some questions regarding your financial reports that you sent us."

"I told you, I have nothing to hide."

Reid opened the folder and took out a piece of paper. He slid it across the table. "That is an extract of your payment ledger. Do you see the highlighted entries?"

She paled, but nodded.

"Those publications do not exist. I checked them out myself. You've been invoicing Natalia for bogus payments to fake publications. How do you explain that?"

Her lip quivered, but she didn't respond. She stared at the entries, a defeated look on her face.

"Ms. Vincent?"

"Yes, I heard you. I was going to pay the money back. The company ran into some financial difficulty, and I needed cash. I took the money from Natalia because I knew she wouldn't notice. It's the only time I've done that, I swear. I was going to issue a credit note next month."

Reid studied her. She was worried, but still indignant. Didn't she realize what she'd done? "You've committed fraud. I'm going to have to charge you."

"Oh, God." She sunk her head into her hands. "Please, no. You'll destroy everything. My reputation, my business."

"I can't help that."

"What if I pay it back?"

"You should ask your legal representative about that. I'm afraid I can't advise you."

She shot him a scornful look. "You don't care, do you? You don't know how hard it is running a business in this economic climate."

"I'm sorry for your troubles, Ms. Vincent, but like I said, you'll have to discuss your options with your attorney."

"Then I want her here now," she sulked.

He nodded and pushed himself away from the table. That's what he'd thought she'd say. "Give his details to my colleague and we'll call him for you."

"Lawyering up, is she?" asked Jonny, as Reid exited the interrogation room.

"Yeah, no surprises there. She admitted to the fraud, though, so that's something. I'll have to wait for her attorney to arrive before I question her about Natalia's murder."

"You think she did it?"

Reid squinted at the screen. Gabriella looked devastated as the consequences of what she'd done weighed down on her.

"I don't think so. She's guilty of swindling Natalia Cruz out of several thousands of dollars, but I don't think she's a killer."

Jonny nodded.

"How are things on the task force?" Reid asked. "Congratulations, by the way. I heard you'd been put in charge."

"It was a surprise," he admitted, the strain showing. "Hope I can live up to the lieutenant's expectations."

"You will. You got this."

He grimaced. "We're still trying to find a connection between the victims. So far, all we've got is that they were in the Miami Beach area on the nights they disappeared. We think that's his hunting ground." There was a pause. "What do you think?"

"It's possible," Reid agreed. "He may have cruised the beach bars looking for his next target. Have you checked CCTV in the area?"

"Yeah, we've just requested the footage, but there's also private security cameras in bars and clubs, literally hundreds of hours of it. Impossible to know where to start."

"Start with what you know," said Reid. "You know where the victims were, so concentrate on those bars or clubs first and work your way outward. Look for faces that appear in more than one location. Pay special attention to anyone who approaches the girls, even if it's just a bump or a nudge."

Jonny gave a purposeful nod. "Okay, thanks boss."

"Well, well. Look who's back."

Reid didn't have to turn around to recognize Ortega's mocking tone.

"I'd heard rumors, but I didn't think you'd have the balls."

"The balls for what?" Ortega was pissing him off.

"Reid," cautioned Jonny.

"To show your face around here."

Reid took a step closer to him. "I'd advise you to stay out of my way, Ortega."

"Or what?" he sneered.

Reid was at least a head taller than him and he made full use of his height now, towering over his adversary. "Or you'll get what's coming to you."

Ortega snorted, but he took a step back. He was rattled. He'd seen something in Reid's eyes that scared him.

Good, Reid thought, letting the tension ease.

"I never understood what she saw in you," Ortega murmured, before walking away.

Reid made to go after him, but Jonny put a restraining hand on his arm. "It's not worth it, buddy. You've just got back. Let it go."

His colleague was right. He exhaled and forced his shoulders to relax. Now wasn't the time to make waves. One day he'd have it out with Ortega, but not today.

Gabriella's attorney arrived in a fire engine red power-suit and a cloud of expensive perfume. "Celine Palmer." She thrust her hand in front of Reid's face.

He shook it, noting her nails matched her clothing.

"I'll take you to your client." He showed her to the interrogation room where Gabriella was beginning to wilt. It was warm inside, even with the air conditioning, and she hadn't had anything to eat or drink since she'd arrived. "You're welcome to take her some water," he added.

"Thank you, Detective."

Palmer bought a bottle of water from the vending machine and went to confer with Gabriella. Reid gave them 20 minutes, then walked in. Same folder, same no-nonsense expression on his face.

"My client tells me she's already admitted to the fraud charges." Palmer fixed her gaze on him.

"That's correct."

"She's prepared to cooperate fully," she continued. "She feels awful about what she's done and wants to put things right."

It was a bit late for that.

"That's good to know." He opened the folder. "Did Natalia Cruz know you were stealing from her?"

Gabriella gave a hesitant nod. "She suspected, but she didn't ask me about it directly."

"How do you know she suspected, then?"

"By the way she was acting. I could tell she was uncomfortable with me. Our relationship had changed. She cancelled meetings, would only speak to me on the phone, and even then, kept it short and abrupt."

"How did she find out?" inquired Reid.

"I don't know. I gave her a breakdown of everything we were doing every month, and I think she must have suspected she was overpaying for services. I can't be sure."

"Why didn't she confront you about it?"

"That wasn't her way. Natalia avoided confrontation of any kind. She'd rather walk away than confront me directly. Her husband told me she was going to let me go. She couldn't even do that."

Natalia appeared to be a sensitive, retiring, gullible woman with a below average intellect, who others had taken advantage of. Perhaps she'd always been taken care of and didn't know how to look after herself. Her beauty made her sought after, but her naivety made her vulnerable. Reid felt sorry for her. Right then, in the interrogation room, he decided that everyone who'd taken advantage of Natalia was going to pay. Gabriella, Fernández, the person who'd strangled her and dumped her body in the Glades. No one had a right to treat another human being like that.

"Had her husband fired you already?" Reid asked.

"He'd given me notice," she explained. "I had until the end of the month to tie up any contracts and end any ongoing deals with magazines and publications."

"Given your tense relationship with Natalia, I'm surprised you attended her husband's launch party."

"I couldn't afford not to be there," she said. "It was a great networking opportunity. Without Natalia's contract, I needed to source new clients. Everybody in the industry was there."

"And did you source new clients?" he asked.

"I handed out a few business cards, yes." She straightened her back.

"Before you left at twenty-two minutes past eleven."

The attorney's eyes narrowed.

"That's right," Gabriella said.

"We checked the footage at the gas station," he said. "You did stop there on your way home."

"I told you so. I wasn't lying about that."

"You left the gas station at eleven forty-seven, which means you still had time to drive back to the hotel and surprise Natalia."

"What are you getting at, Detective?" snapped her attorney. "What has this got to do with the fraudulent accounts?"

"I'm trying to ascertain whether Ms. Vincent had anything to do with Natalia Cruz's disappearance later that night."

"I told you, I didn't," she cried.

"I know what you told me," he said, "but now you've confessed to defrauding her, which gives you a motive."

She hung her head. "I was desperate. I was going to pay her back. I'm not a thief, and I'm definitely not a murderer." A sob escaped her.

Reid wanted to believe her, but he had to be sure. "What did you do when you got home?"

"I had a shower and went to bed." Her kohled eyes pleaded with him.

He'd asked the forensic tech team to look up her phone location on the night in question. If that supported her story, she was in the clear.

"Gabriella Vincent, I'm charging you with intentionally misleading Natalia Cruz with the intention of defrauding her."

"No!" She clawed at the table. "You can't do this. Please. It was a mistake. I'm sorry."

Her attorney put a steady hand on her arm.

"What about Natalia's disappearance?" Gabriella asked Reid.

"We're still looking into that," he replied. "If we have any more questions, we'll let you know."

Gabriella's haunted eyes followed him as he left the room.

16

Amalfi was a beachfront bar that pumped out music from eight in the evening to two in the morning. It was in full swing when Kenzie arrived shortly after ten. She'd met a friend, who used to work for the *Herald* before he'd been poached by one of their rivals, for a catch up and a cocktail—it always helped to know what other people were working on—and thought she'd have a quick word with DJ Snake on her way home.

This was his Thursday night gig. One of few regular appearances he still made since hitting the big time. He liked to keep his fans happy, and this was where he'd first been talent spotted, so it had a special meaning for him.

Kenzie showed her press ID card at the door and told the bouncer Snake was expecting her. He wasn't, but they wouldn't know that. They let her in, despite the groans of the impatient revelers waiting in the queue. Just in time too, as it started to rain.

The pulsing beat assaulted her senses. Snake was in full swing. She glanced up at the podium on which he stood and marveled at the ease with which he whipped the crowd into a frenzy. She remembered watching him almost eight years ago at this exact place, thinking he was going to go places. He'd been younger then, his music rawer and less sophisticated, but his talent undeniable. She'd given him a glowing review in her entertainment column.

A major music blog had picked up the article and run with it, and the crowds had flooded to Amalfi to hear the young prodigy play. More reviews followed, and the year after that, Snake had his first record deal.

He spotted her standing to the side of the dance floor by the bar and lifted a hand in greeting. She beckoned to him, indicating that she wanted to talk. He held up a hand. Five minutes left of his set. Kenzie ordered a drink and sat down to wait.

"Sorry to keep you." He finally came over, drenched in sweat but glowing, the adrenalin still pumping. "It's insane tonight."

"I'm glad to see you're doing so well." She eyed the gyrating crowd. A new DJ had stepped up to the decks, but he was nowhere near as good as Snake.

"I love this gig." He grinned. "I never want to give it up. Keeps it real, you know?"

"I do." In his industry, it was so easy to get swept along on the wave of fame and forget who your real fans were. She admired him for that.

"What can I do for you?"

"I wanted to ask about Natalia's investments," she said. "Her father seemed to think she wasn't capable of handling her own finances, and I wondered what you thought about that."

"Nats was very trusting," he said. "It was one of the things I loved about her, but it did mean she was a soft target. I tried to advise her, but I think she wanted to prove to her old man that she could look after herself. It was important to her."

Kenzie could understand that. Hadn't she been guilty of the same thing? She'd acted tough, done what she could, even joined the police academy to make him proud.

"Did you know about AF Investments?" she asked.

He frowned. "I don't think I've heard that name before?"

"Natalia invested two hundred and fifty thousand dollars with them."

"Holy shit, really?" He looked horrified.

"You didn't know?"

"Of course not. I wouldn't have let her do it if I'd have known. Not without checking them out first. Were they legit?"

"Unfortunately not." Kenzie grimaced. "They're scammers operating some sort of Ponzi scheme. I don't know the details, but I doubt you'll ever see a cent of that investment."

He slammed his fist down on the bar.

At her surprised look, he said, "I hated it when people took advantage of her."

"Did it happen often?" she asked.

"More than it should have," he confirmed. "Like I said, she was too trusting."

Kenzie patted his arm. "Thanks, Snake. I have to go, but I appreciate you talking to me."

"Are the police going after the scammer?" he asked.

"I'm sure they will," she replied. If they could find them.

"Stay and have another drink." He gestured to the barman. "I'm not on for another hour."

She was about to decline, but he waved a hand, dismissing her refusal. "Come on, babe. When did we last do shots together?"

Oh, boy.

It was very late by the time she got home.

Kenzie woke with a start as her body vibrated.

What the—?

She turned over, but it didn't stop. Then she realized she'd fallen asleep with her phone in her back pocket. She reached for it, groaning as a stab of pain shot through her temples. Tequila. Her worst enemy.

They'd been joined by a bunch of Snake's friends, and she'd

stayed with them while he'd gone back up to play. How he knew what he was doing after three tequila shots, she had no idea.

Then they'd hit the dance floor.

"Hello?"

What time was it? She glanced at the window, but the blackout blinds were down. At least she'd had the foresight to do that. The sun was blinding first thing in the morning.

"Kenzie, it's Reid. Did I wake you?"

"No, um, yeah. What time is it?"

"Six-thirty."

"Oh." She struggled into a sitting position, scowling at the throbbing in her head. It must be important if he was calling so early. "What's up?"

Water. There must be some here somewhere? She leaned over the side of the bed, looking for the bottle she kept on the floor. Water and a couple of Tylenol would sort her out.

"It's not good, Kenzie," he said. He sounded tired, like he'd been up all night. "There's been another murder."

17

The report had come in from a swamper who'd found the body along a canal on a deserted loop road leading deep into the Everglades.

It was quicker and easier to get there by boat, so Reid had gotten dressed, leaped off the deck onto his airboat, and headed into the darkened waterways. The nearest police department, Sweetwater, had dispatched a team of officers to contain the scene and coordinate with the crime scene investigators, but Reid wanted to see her before they pulled her from the water.

He drove slowly, using a powerful handheld torch to illuminate the inky black water ahead. The swamp was a different place at night. The darkness seemed to close in, the air dense with the smell of mud and wet foliage. Visibility was limited. He could only see a few meters in front of him, and the tall sawgrass on either side seemed to curl inwards toward the boat.

Reid glanced upwards at the night sky, strewn with stars. It would have been beautiful had he not been thinking about the dead girl entangled in the reeds at the side of the canal.

The engine drowned out most of the night sounds, but he wouldn't have heard them anyway. He was concentrating too hard. Twenty minutes later, he steered the boat into the canal where she was reported to have been found. Dispatch had given him the coordinates, which he'd entered into an app on his phone. Half a mile ahead.

He saw lights waving in an arch and cut the engine. The airboat drifted to the side where a man was waiting. "She's up ahead," he said.

"You alone?" Reid asked.

The swamper nodded. "Nobody got here yet."

"They're on their way."

The dirt road alongside the canal was narrow and filled with potholes. It would take the cavalcade of police cars and CSI vans at least 40 minutes to get here from Sweetwater.

"I been waiting close to an hour," he complained.

"Thank you." Reid tied his boat to a pole. "It's good to know she's not alone."

He gave a terse nod, slightly mollified. "This way."

Reid followed him down the road to where his car was parked. It was a hardy pickup truck, the kind that could easily transport a dead gator in the back.

"What you doing out here this early?" Reid asked.

"Snake hunting," he replied, not meeting Reid's gaze. "I like to get an early start."

Croc hunting, more like, but Reid let it slide. He wasn't here to arrest the good Samaritan who'd called it in. They came to a stop and the swamper pointed toward the murky water.

Reid aimed his flashlight and saw her. His heart skipped a beat. Her pale skin caught the light. Iridescent underneath the yellow-tinged swamp water. She was face-down, like the others, but her body was intact. He shone the flashlight over her arms and legs, all in one piece. The gators hadn't had a chance to get to her yet.

She was wearing a black dress. Tight and fitting, designed to entice. Her feet were bare, and her hair billowed out around her in a dark cloud.

He took a few photographs with his phone, then he called dispatch to get an ETA for the CSI team and police officers. Fifteen minutes, he was told. He took the good Samaritan's details and told him he could go home. "You might get a visit from us later today."

"No problem." The guy got into his pickup and took off down the road, kicking up loose stones and dust behind him.

In the east, the sun was poking its head above the tree line, sending orange lasers darting across the water's mirror-like surface. The sky was lightening, giving way to the day.

Reid stood by the side of the road, staring down at the girl. There was a splash downstream and a swishing sound. The predators were circling.

Putting on a pair of forensic gloves, he bent down and pulled her out of the water. Turning her over, he lay her on the roadside. He couldn't risk a gator taking a bite out of her and compromising any potential evidence. She hadn't been in the water very long. Hours maybe, as opposed to days.

This girl had been taken tonight.

The shiver that ran down his spine had nothing to do with the fresh breeze coming off the water. It would warm up later, but for now it was pleasantly cool, like last night's rain had washed the air clean.

She was young. Early twenties. Pretty, with dark hair and long eyelashes. He could see the blush staining her cheeks. Pink smudges against her ashen complexion. Her eyes were closed, the terror of the last few hours blocked out. When she'd finally succumbed, it would have been a relief. Her dress had been pulled up around her thighs and he could see that her underwear was missing.

Shit. She'd been sexually assaulted. This looked like the Strangler's work. He pulled her dress down to preserve her dignity. Nobody needed to see her like that.

Using his flashlight, he bent forward to inspect her neck. Thin, purple ligature marks were etched into her skin. A wire of some sort. He wondered if it was the same with the first two victims. Natalia had bruising too, but it wasn't as narrow as this.

Reid sat beside her and watched the sunrise. It had climbed above the trees, burning through the morning haze when he heard sirens. They were here.

"What can you tell me?" Reid asked the medical examiner as the body was loaded into the waiting ambulance. The doc, who hadn't had his morning cup of coffee, wasn't in a sociable mood.

"Not much." He snapped off his gloves and stuffed them into his pocket. "She was killed maybe eight or nine hours ago. The water makes it hard to tell."

"Cause of death?"

"Strangulation. There's petechial hemorrhaging caused by asphyxia, and she's been sexually assaulted. There's evidence of bruising and penetration, although I'm going to wait until I get her back to the lab before I explore that in more detail."

Reid nodded. "Anything else?"

He pursed his lips. "There are bruises around her wrists, which tells me she was constrained. There are also defensive marks on her forearms and some residue underneath her fingernails. I can't tell for sure whether it's human, but I've bagged her hands and we'll let you know once we've analyzed it."

A surge of adrenaline shot through him. "But it could be, right?" With a bit of luck, this victim had scratched her attacker and given them the DNA of their killer.

"I wouldn't put much stake in it yet," the doctor warned. "It could just be mud from the swamp." Reid desperately wanted to know whether this latest victim had managed to give the task force a lead. God knows they needed one.

As the ambulance and police cars prepared for the drive back to civilization, Reid cast off and headed home. He'd have a quick shower and drive to the station. There were things he needed to do, resources he couldn't access at the cabin. Eyebrows would be raised when he walked in and commandeered a desk. Rumors would circulate, but it couldn't be helped. He had a killer to catch.

18

Kenzie raced out to the Glades, driving as fast as she dared in the early morning traffic. She gritted her teeth at the stop-start tempo and heaved a sigh of relief when she finally hit the dirt road to Garrett's cabin.

She wanted to be there when he got back. There wasn't much time. Before long, news of the body would be all over the radio stations. The news networks would pick up the story and it would be in the afternoon editions. It was too late for the morning run.

His car was there, parked beside the cabin. She pulled in beside him and jumped out of her car. "Reid?" she called.

She thumped on the front door, but there was no answer. She tried the handle. It was locked. Where was he?

Walking back to the car, she put her hand on the hood. It was stone cold. Puzzled, she looked around. Then she got it. He'd gone by boat. The body was in the swamp. His airboat would have been the quickest way of getting there.

Slipping through the foliage, she made her way around the side of the cabin, like she had the first time she'd come here. Except, unlike that time when she'd found the half-naked Garrett hammering the deck, it was empty. He wasn't back yet.

Not a problem. She could wait.

She took out her phone and frowned at the single bar. How did he live like this? No signal, no internet, no AC. Just the basics.

Perhaps that was the idea. To be cut off from the rest of the world. His way of opting out. It made sense when she thought about it. He blamed himself for his colleague's death. More than a colleague, he'd said. Had he been in love with her?

She thought back to the article she'd written, oblivious to the impending consequences. How had her source gotten it so wrong? There'd been a miscommunication somewhere. A change of plan, but not everyone had been briefed. An administrative error with deadly consequences.

She'd been the messenger, and she'd got it so wrong.

Never again.

She glanced up when she heard the distant drone of the airboat's jet engine. The sun had risen now and warmed her skin. It was perfect, this time of day. Not too hot, but warm enough to make her feel cozy and relaxed. Except the reason she was here was anything but cozy.

Straining her eyes, she stared over the river of grass. The white hull of Garrett's airboat came into view. First a speck, getting bigger as he got nearer. The drone got louder until it was a hum and then a roar. He sat on the elevated seat, a stoic figure silhouetted against the fiery orange ball behind him.

Kenzie stepped back as he slid alongside the deck. He tossed a rope to her. "Tie that around the mooring for me?"

"Sure." She picked it up, wet and heavy in her hands, and tied it as best she could around the wooden railing. What she knew about knots was dangerous.

Reid climbed out, hopping over the railing and landing in front of her. His shirt was wet and there were muddy marks around his trouser legs.

"Did you pull her out?" she asked.

He looked down. "Yeah, didn't want the gators to get her."

Kenzie shivered. "Is it another one of the Strangler's victims?"

"Looks like it." He pulled out his phone, scrolled to the photographs he'd taken of her lying in the water, and passed it to her. "Here, take a look. I'm going to wash up. I'll be right back."

Kenzie sat on one of the deck chairs and thumbed through the photographs. He'd taken several, from different angles.

Face down. Dress hitched up to her thighs. Dark hair floating around her.

She was barefoot, no noticeable jewelry. Kenzie couldn't see her neck. The dress was telling, though. This girl had been dressed for a night on the town. Hitting the South Beach clubs? The Strangler's suspected hunting ground.

"She was in one piece," Reid said, returning. He'd changed and was now wearing jeans and a black button-down shirt. It looked good on him. "Doc didn't think she'd been in long."

"Was she reported missing?" Kenzie asked.

"Don't know. I'm sure the task force will look into it. Too early to say at this stage. The doc thinks it happened last night."

Kenzie shuddered. She'd been in the same vicinity last night. Drinking, dancing, all while the serial killer had been stalking this girl, waiting for an opportunity to pounce.

"I was there," she whispered.

"Where?" he raised an eyebrow. "South Beach?"

"Yeah. I went to speak to Snake. I wanted to ask him about Natalia's investments and why he hadn't been helping her."

Reid frowned. "What did he say?"

"Well, she had a trust fund that gave her a monthly allowance. Her father monitored that. But she also had an inheritance from her mother that had gone directly to her. Snake didn't interfere. He said she wanted to prove she could look after herself."

Reid shook his head.

"I know. Anyway, I hung out with him and his crew for a while. Got home late."

He studied her, his gaze lingering on the shadows beneath her eyes. "Be careful, Kenzie," he said. "There's a killer out there."

"That's what I was just thinking. While I was out having fun, he was targeting his next victim." She glanced down at the phone. "Her."

There was a pause.

"Do you have a name yet?" Kenzie asked.

"No."

"Will you let me know when you do?"

"I'll try." He wasn't very convincing.

"Please, Reid. I need this story. It'll be out soon. You can't keep something like this under wraps. May as well be me who breaks it."

He sighed and repocketed his phone. "Okay, fine. I'll call you as soon as I know something."

Kenzie grinned. "Thank you."

He didn't smile back. There was a melancholy around him. It clung to him like the muddy smell of the swamp. "Was it bad?" she asked quietly. "Seeing another one."

"Yeah. She'd been strangled like the others. Thin ligature marks, not finger indents like Natalia."

"Another reason to think this is the Strangler's work," she surmised.

He gave a terse nod.

"Was she raped?"

Reid hesitated, as if unsure of what to say.

"She was, wasn't she?" Kenzie felt the color drain from her face.

"You can't print that," Reid barked. "It's something only the killer would know. We have to hold that from the public."

She bit her lip. "It would really help if I could link this murder to the others by saying all the girls were sexually assaulted, except Natalia. That would be an edge the others don't have."

"Not yet," he warned her. "It will jeopardize the investigation."

"Okay, but you'll tell me when?"

"Yes, and you don't have to flash your dimples at me. As soon as we can make that information public, I'll let you know."

Kenzie gave up and chuckled. "All right, then. I won't mention the sexual assault. I'll give a rough description and outline how she was found. Do you want me to appeal for witnesses?"

Reid thought for a moment. "Yeah, might as well. Jonny and the task force need all the help they can get."

"I don't suppose I can use that picture?" She nodded to the phone in his pocket.

"No way. The Chief would know it was me giving information to the press. Other than the swamper who found her body, nobody else saw her like that."

"The Chief might think it was him," Kenzie argued. "Even if he denied it, no one could prove otherwise."

But Reid wasn't budging. "Sorry Kenzie. No can do."

She sighed. "Okay, then I'll have to go out there and get a photograph of where they found her. I need something to print."

"It's a forty-minute drive into the swamp," he told her. "I don't want you going out there alone."

"Then let me use the picture," she reasoned. "And I won't have to."

"Can't do that either."

She huffed in frustration. "Right, then you leave me no choice. I'll hunt down the guy who found her," she said. "He may have taken a photograph, something to show his swamping buddies."

"How will you find him?" Reid asked, the muscles in his jaw tensing. "I haven't told you who he is."

"I have ways and means," she said. At his look, she sighed. "If he's been back on the water, it'll be all over the swamp by now. Besides, I have another source, don't forget."

"Ah yes, the officer who always gets it wrong." His forehead creased into a frown. "Unless he's on the task force, he's not going to know shit."

Kenzie didn't reply. She got to her feet and made her way to the door. Keith would insist on a photograph of the crime scene, at the very least. She was heading out to the swamp, whether Reid liked it or not.

"Kenzie, stay out of the Glades," he warned. "It's not safe."

"For a woman, you mean?"

His mouth hardened.

"Thanks for the info." She opened the door. "If I find out anything else, I'll let you know. I'm not stingy with my intel."

All she got was a grunt in reply.

19

Damn, Kenzie.

He knew she would head out to the crime scene, despite what he'd said. Part of him wanted to go with her, but he couldn't. He was due at the office. He'd already texted Pérez and told him he was coming in.

She was on her own this time.

His desk would be waiting. It was time to face the music.

Reid parked in the police department parking lot, in the same spot he used to park when he'd worked here. Old habits.

He scanned his ID at the reception desk, then made his way up to the homicide department on the fourth floor. The lift stopped with a jerk. He took a deep breath and stepped out.

The office was buzzing with activity. He spotted Ortega's team on the left-hand side, their desks arranged to face each other. Officers darted about, on the phone, collecting printouts, talking in hushed voices. They were planning something big, a crackdown. Reid could tell. He knew the signs.

Ortega glanced up, his brow raised in surprise. Then he glanced away again, as a team member said something. It must be important if it was enough to distract him from Reid's entrance.

"Hey, Reid. Good to see you," called an ex-colleague, as he walked to the Lieutenant's office.

"Garrett," said another, raising his head in greeting.

Pérez saw him coming through the office's wide windows and opened the door. "Garrett, good to see you. Come with me, I'll show you to your desk. You're all set up and ready to go."

Thankfully, he was positioned on the right, across the walkway from Ortega's team. The corner desk, they used to call it. The one nobody wanted because it was out of the way. Now it was perfect for his solitary mission.

He got a coffee from the kitchen and screwed up his face. It was as bad as he remembered. Back at his desk, he logged on to the computer and pulled up the security footage he'd requested of the night of Natalia's disappearance.

The Sand Club had reluctantly handed it over when issued with a warrant. He stared at the parking lot. Valet. Guests only.

There was Bella's date's car, a silver Nissan Altima. They'd arrived just after eight, Bella in a striking rose-patterned gown and her partner in a suit. The event hadn't stretched to rate a tux, but it was glamorous.

Reid fast-forwarded to when Bella was led out, stumbling and flushed. Her date said very little as they waited for the valet to bring the car around. He opened the door for her, and they got in and drove off.

Before switching to the CCTV footage of the street outside the club, Reid trawled the footage for Gabriella's vehicle. He knew she'd slunk away via the beach path, so he wasn't surprised to find she hadn't parked on the property.

He scanned the street for Gabriella's vehicle. After an hour of searching, he found it parked on Fifteenth. Had she always intended on leaving early, or did she just not want the hassle of waiting on a valet?

He scanned the footage for either vehicle returning before two a.m.

Nothing.

He didn't see Bella's or Gabriella's car come back. It wasn't an exact science. There were side streets he couldn't access and garages further down the beach, but on the surface, it looked like they'd both been telling the truth.

There was an adrenaline-fueled moment when Ortega's team left on a raid. Mid-morning. Strange time, but perhaps they had to wait until a bar opened or the major players were in situ. He watched them depart, sensing their excitement, remembering what it felt like to be on a bust.

"I damn well hope they get them," growled Pérez, coming over. "We need to get the situation under control."

Reid didn't ask who Ortega's team was after, not that Pérez would tell him anyway. Not his case.

"How are you doing?"

"Been going through the security footage at the club. So far nothing."

"That's dog work," Pérez muttered. "Shout if you need any help. Detective Ryan can give you a hand."

"Happy to be of assistance, sir," she replied from across the office.

He turned around. "Thanks. I'll let you know."

The next task he wanted to do himself.

Reid loaded the footage from the street camera opposite the building occupied by AF Investments. It was aimed at the Metrorail station but caught the front of the building in its line of sight. He increased the speed, letting it run until midnight. Nothing out of the ordinary. He suspected Fernández would wait until things quieted down before he moved in.

He was right.

At ten past one in the morning, a large moving van pulled up outside the street entrance. The usually bustling downtown street was deserted. Green-tinged street lamps cast an eerie glow, like a scene from an alien movie, or maybe that was just the camera. He watched as the back of the van opened and six men jumped out, all wearing balaclavas and gloves. Slick bastards.

They hurried inside, a fast walk, not a run. Reid played the recording in double time until they came back out carrying an assortment of office furniture and equipment. The big items came out first: desks, tables, chairs. Next, printers, computers, and boxes of files.

He checked the timestamp. They'd emptied the office in under 20 minutes.

The men jumped back into the van and drove off. The driver hadn't left the vehicle, and the engine had been running the whole time. A perfect getaway.

He never saw Antonio Fernández.

Reid sighed and kicked back his chair. He should have listened to Kenzie. He'd underestimated the scam artist. They should have gone in armed with the warrant and left him no wriggle room. Still, there was one other thing left to check.

He pulled up the CCTV for the parking lot next to the building. This was a warrant he'd snuck in under the pretense of looking for Antonio Fernández's vehicle. The Ferrari wasn't hard to find. Fernández parked on the same level every day. Reid made a note of the license plate. He'd get Ryan to run it through the DVLA database.

Now for the real reason he wanted the parking garage footage.

Torres.

It had been late afternoon when he and Kenzie visited AF Investments. He was guessing four-thirty. Torres had been leaving as they arrived.

Reid studied the video recordings of the elevator entrance to every floor of the parking garage from four o'clock to five o'clock on that afternoon until he found it.

Torres emerged from the elevator and strode across the lot to an Audi TT convertible. Sweet ride. Clearly, he wasn't trying to remain incognito. Perhaps they figured with the current chaos between the street gangs, the pressure was off.

Except, Reid never forgot.

Reid watched as Torres put the top down and reversed out of the parking bay. Even through the grainy camera lens, he looked suave and handsome, his shoulders relaxed, his chin tilted back, cheekbones cutting shadows into his face. The arrogance of the man. Going about his daily business with blood on his hands. So much blood.

Reid shut his eyes. He could see the carnage in the bar with crystal clarity. The shouting as they barged their way in, the shots fired, hitting the deck. Arresting the gangsters who were still there. The feeling of dread as he proceeded through the bar shouting Bianca's name.

The silence that greeted him.

The *knowing*.

Then the proof. Her body lying in the back office. A bullet through her head.

The medical examiner had said she'd died instantly. Massive cerebral trauma. The bullet had literally blown her brains out.

Then the pain. The gut-wrenching realization that she was dead. That he'd never see her again. Never laugh with her or kiss her against the wall behind the precinct.

He exhaled.

"You ok?" asked Ryan, coming over. "You sure there's nothing I can do?"

He glanced up, mentally dragging himself back to the present. "Actually, yeah. You can run these plates for me."

He scribbled Torres and Fernández's plates on a Post-it Note from a pad he'd stolen from Ortega's desk and handed it to her.

"Sure."

He liked she didn't ask questions. Just headed back to her desk to do what he'd asked.

Reid turned his gaze back to the video and pressed play. He

watched the convertible ease out of the parking lot and into the Miami traffic.

I'm going to get you, you bastard, he promised. *No matter what it takes.*

20

"The moving van belongs to a company called New Horizons," Ryan told Reid a short while later. "They hire out vehicles for business and industrial shipping, moving, that sort of thing."

Reid wrote the name down on his pad.

"Do we know who hired it?"

"Yeah," she grinned. "The van was rented to a guy called Phoenix Bender. He works as a security guard at a building downtown."

"Downtown? Which street?"

"Southwest 1st Avenue."

Reid drew in his breath. "That's where AF Investments is located."

"So he's part of it?" she asked. He'd briefed her about the failed raid.

"I'm not sure. Do you have an address for him?"

She handed him back the Post-it he'd given her. She'd written his home address and phone number on it.

"Thanks. Any luck on those other two plates?"

"Yeah, the Ferrari, is registered to AF Investments at the address you raided."

He grimaced.

"The Audi convertible is also registered to a company, Regal Holdings, and the address looks to be a warehouse at the port."

He arched his eyebrows. "Thanks, that's great."

Regal Holdings. The cartel always had illusions of grandeur.

"Want me to dig deeper? I've got the time."

"Aren't you working on the task force?" Reid inquired.

"No, not unless they need reports or filing." She rolled her eyes. "Jonny's waiting for the lab results on the fourth victim, Mimi Silverton."

"Is he at the morgue?"

"Yeah, and Jared and Chris are talking to her family and friends, trying to trace her last known whereabouts."

They were following standard operating procedures in a homicide.

"You could do some digging into Mimi's background," he suggested. "Unless you've already done that."

"No, I haven't." She hesitated. "Use my initiative, you mean?"

"Yes, you're obviously a competent officer. Instead of sitting around waiting, you could put together a profile on the victim, where she went to school, where she went to college, who her friends were, her social media profiles. Flag anything suspicious. Look for links with the other victims."

She broke into a wide grin. "You know what? I will. Thanks for pointing me in the right direction, Detective Garrett."

"Please, call me Reid."

"Okay, Reid." She flushed and went back to her desk.

Her potential was wasted writing up reports and filing them. He'd have to have a word with Jonny. As short staffed as they were, they could use her on the task force.

Without telling anyone where he was going, Reid packed up and left the office. He drove out to Biscayne and investigated the industrial area where the container operators were located, searching for the address of the warehouse Ryan had given him.

Eventually, he found it hidden behind a huge container yard. It was wide, half a football field, with corrugated iron roller doors and tiny smudged windows. There didn't appear to be anyone around.

Reid parked a few streets away and approached the building on foot. He looked for signs of activity, of loading or unloading, of workers going in and out, but there was nothing.

The place was deserted.

A security camera was mounted to the front of the building above the main entrance. He circled the property but didn't spot any more. Was the warehouse alarmed? He assumed so. He pasted his face against a smudged side window but couldn't see anything. Inside was dark.

No, wait a minute. There was a flicker of light coming from a doorway toward the back. An office, perhaps?

He went around the back, but all the windows on this side were boarded up or too filthy to see through. Then a door opened and he heard voices.

He froze, hunkering down at the back of the building, praying whoever it was wouldn't come his way. He was in luck, the voices faded. He snuck around the side in pursuit. Two men, casually dressed, definitely packing judging by the bulges at the back of their shirts. Security guards doing a checkup.

When they'd walked off toward the docks, he glanced at his watch. If they were going to the port, they wouldn't be back for a good 10 minutes. Time to poke around.

Reid approached the door out of which the two men had come. It was locked. Taking out the lock-picking kit he'd brought with him, he went to work. Within a minute, he was inside.

He was in a small, dark corridor. The only window, the one he'd looked through before, was small and grimy.

There were two doors. One right in front of him and another at the end of the corridor. He chose door number one and cracked it open. This was the warehouse. It was large and mostly unused. There were a few machines for lifting and storing containers, but not much else.

Ducking back into the corridor, he approached door number two and turned the handle. It wouldn't budge. Once again, he went to work on the lock. This one was trickier. Finally, he felt it give and pushed open the door.

The office was dark on account of the blinds being down, so he switched on the light. At first glance, it looked neat and organized. Everything had a place. A desk stood under the window, clear of clutter. No paperwork or used coffee cups. One wall was lined with shelves filled with rows of files. There was a filing cabinet on the other side, and above it a picture of an old-fashioned ship riding the high seas.

A typical warehouse operator's office.

He inspected the files. Regal Holdings. Orders, delivery notes, invoices. Everything looked legit.

He approached the desk. Was this Torres's office? Was he running the company, using it as a front to manage the cartel's illegal imports? After the bust that had gone south a year and a half ago, Lopez and Torres had vanished, presumed to have gone back to Mexico to regroup.

Now they were back and operational again.

There was no laptop or computer, so Reid began opening drawers. There were lists of invoices, shipping inventories, container numbers, and schedules. He took pictures of them all on his phone. He'd study them later when he had time.

It was the same as the back office in the bar they'd raided, where Bianca had died. Tidy, orderly, methodical. All the hallmarks of Torres.

The Cuban had run the cartel's Miami interests with an iron fist. He seldom made mistakes. Even when they'd raided the bar that fateful day, they hadn't had enough to hold him. It was one of the reason's Bianca had stayed under.

"We need more, Reid. We need actual proof of a shipment."

Is that why she'd been killed in his office? She'd found something?

A shiver ran down his spine. Bianca had done well to break through Torres's defenses, but she was a beautiful woman. Sexy. Provocative. She'd worked her way up through Vice and was no stranger to going undercover in a short skirt and tight top.

He grimaced, thinking of her at his mercy.

"He doesn't scare me," she'd told Reid once. "He's all bark and no bite."

Well, it was his bite that had gotten her in the end.

In the bottom right-hand drawer, he found a black notebook. He flicked through it, but it was just scribbles. Docking times, order numbers, ship names. He took a couple more pictures just in case, then put it back where he'd found it.

Time was ticking by. He'd been inside for over five minutes.

He pulled open the filing cabinet. Again, everything was ordered alphabetically. He had no doubt these were legit company records. Torres wouldn't be so stupid as to leave incriminating evidence lying around for anyone with a warrant to find.

That would be stashed in a safe somewhere or hidden in a place that wasn't easy to find.

His gaze fell on the picture of the old ship.

Moving quietly across the office, he took the painting down.

Bingo.

It was a heavy-duty safe. Old school. Without a block of C_4, he had no way of opening it. He put the painting back.

Reid took one last look around and was about to exit the room when he heard the side door open.

Shit, they were back.

He flipped the light off and hid behind the door. Had they seen it? There was quite a big gap under the door.

Footsteps approaching.

Hurriedly, he reached out and turned the latch. The lock clicked into place. There was a knock.

"Boss, are you in there?"

Reid didn't reply. Pulse racing, he glanced around for a way to escape. He sure as hell couldn't go out the way he'd come in.

He pulled up the blinds, inspecting the windows. They were old and rusted, but he might be able to open them.

"Hello? Boss is that you?" came the voice again.

He grunted as he swiveled the tarnished metal lever. It hadn't been used in years. Finally, it gave, and the lock loosened. He pushed the window outwards. It was stiff and groaned in protest, but opened enough for him to climb out.

Just.

He grabbed Torres's desk chair and positioned it underneath, then jumped up and swung a leg over. It wouldn't be long before the guards figured out he was opening a window and came around the back.

He heard a quick, deep interchange as they discussed what to do, then there was a thud as a shoulder pummeled into the door. They were going to break it down. Another thrust and the door gave a little more. One more burst would do it.

Reid swung his other leg over and jumped down onto the ground outside, scraping his arm as he went.

Shit.

He couldn't leave his DNA there. They might call the police to report the break in. A place like this, though, he seriously doubted it, but he couldn't take any chances.

He used his sleeve to wipe down the frame. A forensic team would still get his skin cells off it if they knew where to look, but to the naked eye, it appeared spotless.

There was a combined shout as the door came splintering off its hinges and landed on the office floor.

Reid took off along the wall at a sprint. He didn't look back. By the time the men got to the window, he'd rounded the corner and was headed for the container yard. They'd never find him there.

He zigzagged through the jungle of containers, trying to put as much distance between himself and the warehouse as possible. There was shouting as the two men came after him, but it faded out after a while, and he figured they'd given up. This was one of the biggest container yards in the state. Finding him would be impossible.

They'd go back and look at the security footage, except he wasn't on that either. Then they'd report the break-in to their boss. Torres wouldn't be happy, but with no laptop and an unbreakable safe, he didn't have anything to worry about.

One thing was for sure, though. The Morales cartel was back in business, and they were operating out of The Port of Miami.

21

Kenzie swung in the hammock on Reid's deck and waited for him to get home. The patio doors were locked, but she was content to lie here thinking, listening to the soundtrack of the swamp.

She must have dozed off, because she woke with a start as a deep voice said, "Kenzie, what are you doing here?"

"Oh, God. Sorry, I fell asleep. I was up late writing my article."

He frowned. "On Mimi Silverton?"

"Yeah, have you seen it? It's in today's paper."

"I haven't had a chance."

She got off the hammock. "My editor, Keith, is happy with it. We're the first to report on it in so much detail." At his suspicious glance, she raised a hand. "Don't worry, I didn't say anything that would compromise the case."

"I hope not," he muttered. "Want a beer?"

"Yeah, sure."

She followed him inside. "So, what's been happening? Have you found out Fernández's whereabouts?"

"No, he's in the wind. His car was registered to the company at the same address. I did see them load the furniture and equipment into a van in the middle of the night, though. Stealthy job. In and out in under 20 minutes."

"Professionals," she said.

He nodded. "Fernández wasn't there."

"Any idea who they were?" she asked.

"The van was hired from a company called New Horizons. The owner said he rented the van to a guy called Phoenix Benson. When I spoke to Benson, he had no knowledge of it."

"Was he lying?"

"I don't think so. He said he'd lost his wallet a couple of days ago. Couldn't understand why anyone would hire a moving van with his ID. Funny thing is, he works at the AF Investments' building."

"It's very suspicious," Kenzie mused. "Are you sure he wasn't involved?"

"Ryan's checking him out now." At her quizzical look, he elaborated. "Ryan's a rookie detective at the precinct. She's helping me out."

"She?" Kenzie didn't mean to sound surprised. It was just that Ryan was a boy's name.

"Yeah, I don't know her first name. Everyone just calls her Ryan."

"Ah."

There was a pause.

"If this security guard's wallet was stolen to hire the van, then we have no way of tracking them."

"Dead end." Reid sank into a wicker chair. It creaked under his weight. "They'll lie low for a few months, then pop up somewhere else under a new name."

"And start scamming people again?" Kenzie finished.

He gave a terse nod.

She scowled. "I wish there was a way of stopping them. It's not right. Why don't the authorities do something?"

"Do what? Nobody's complained. There's no evidence of fraudulent activity. All the victims think their money is safe and sound and earning interest."

"Until it doesn't," Kenzie said.

"Exactly, and that's when they pack up, move out, and start again. We just spurred them on with our inquiry."

"I could write an article on them," she said. "I'll warn people to watch out for them. Maybe I'll make it a general piece on wire fraud."

"You do realize they're probably laundering money for the cartel. If that's the case, we're messing with some very dangerous people. You don't want to draw any attention. You'll be putting yourself in their sights. Also, if you go to print with an article like that, it could scare them off."

"The cartel, you mean?"

"Yeah, they'll go elsewhere to get their money cleaned. Then we'll have lost our only link to them."

"So, you want me to keep quiet until we have, what? The cartel in custody? You know that's never going to happen."

"No, just until I figure out what Torres was doing there, and what role AF Investments plays in the drug trafficking."

"This is about Torres, isn't it?" Kenzie watched him from over the rim of her beer bottle. "It's not about Natalia anymore. You want to find him and make him pay for what he did to your undercover agent."

"Of course it's about Natalia. That's why I'm back on the force, to find her killer." He stared at his beer bottle. "But you're right, I do want to find Torres. He's not going to get away with what he's done."

She believed him.

It was then she noticed the scratch on his arm. "What happened?"

"Huh?"

"To your arm. You're bleeding."

"Oh, that. I must have scratched myself somewhere."

Hmm. Why did she get the feeling he wasn't being completely honest with her? Still, she didn't push.

"What's next on Natalia's investigation?"

He seemed relieved at the change in subject. "CCTV backed up both Gabriella Vincent and Bella Montague's statements. From what I saw, neither went back to the club that night."

"Okay, if we rule them out, it's looking more and more like Fernández or his henchman were responsible."

"The thing that bothers me about that," said Reid, "is how did they know about the party?"

"More importantly, how did they know Natalia would leave and go back to her room?" added Kenzie.

"They must have had a mole." Reid shook his head. "It's the only solution."

"Who?" Kenzie spread her hands. "We've been through that footage a dozen times. No one spiked her drink, no one went near her other than her husband, Bella, and Gabriella."

Reid frowned. "We must have missed something."

"I'll ask Snake to take another look, see if there's anyone he doesn't recognize."

"That's a great idea." Reid perked up. "Good thinking."

She shrugged. "It's better than doing nothing. In the meantime, tell me more about this guard that had his ID stolen."

The next morning, Kenzie put on her gym outfit and drove to South Beach. Phoenix Benson thought his wallet had been stolen at a gym called Progressive Overload.

She walked inside and froze.

Oh crap.

This was not the sort of establishment that offered Pilates and hot yoga. In fact, the only equipment she could see were rows and rows of free weights and she was surrounded by giants with unreal bodies in vests that looked like they'd been spray-painted on.

Gulping, she ignored the pointed stares and made for the reception desk.

"Hi there." She gave the woman her friendliest smile, although she, too, looked like she could crush watermelons under her armpits. "I'm looking for this man. Have you seen him?"

She held up her phone. Reid had sent her a picture of Fernández's henchman, an Eastern European ex-military operator called Ivan Petrovitch.

"Who wants to know?"

She flashed her press card. "I'm investigating an incident that took place near his place of work last week, and I wanted to ask him a few questions."

The woman's gaze wavered. She knew him.

"He said I'd be able to find him here," she lied. The words fell seamlessly from her lips.

The woman hesitated, then said, "Ivan isn't here yet."

"But he'll be in later?" Kenzie asked.

"He usually comes in around seven."

Kenzie grinned. "Thank you. You've been very helpful."

Yes!

She was getting somewhere. Her hunch had been right. Ivan had stolen Phoenix Benson's wallet at the gym, then used his ID to hire the van. Any ID would do, but by targeting someone who worked at the same building, they were casting suspicion on him.

Now she had a link to Fernández.

She left the gym and walked up the road to a nearby café. She ordered a coffee and thought for a moment. Should she update Reid? Except she hadn't actually seen Ivan yet. He might not even make an appearance, in which case there was no point in bothering Reid with it.

As she watched the beachgoers sunning themselves on the blinding white sand, Kenzie made a decision. She'd come back tonight and wait for Ivan. Once she had eyes on him, she'd contact Reid. He'd be home by then. When Ivan finished his workout, they could tail him to wherever he was staying. He might lead them to Fernández.

22

Reid glanced up as Ortega's team strutted into the precinct holding a man in cuffs. They laughed and joked, showing off their catch. Ortega caught his eye and smirked.

"They got him," murmured Ryan, standing beside his desk. "Yesterday's bust was called off at the last minute, so they went in today. Apparently, this guy works for The Kings."

Reid studied the perp. A stocky, dark-haired Latino in ripped jeans, a designer T-shirt, new sneakers, and an expensive watch. Vicious gang tattoos covered his forearms. He couldn't have looked more like a gang banger if he'd tried. He had the arrogant swagger of a man who knows he holds all the cards.

"He's going to cut a deal," Reid mumbled.

Ryan shot him a surprised glance. "How'd you know?"

"Look at him. The cocky son of a bitch knows he has information that we want. He knows we'll strike a deal to get to García."

Matt Garcia. Leader of The Kings and an all-round badass with an itchy trigger finger.

Ryan stared at the gangster. He even had the audacity to shoot her a lecherous grin as he walked past. She turned away.

"I hope they're not too lenient on him."

"Witness protection, I'd guess." Reid crinkled his nose like he'd smelled something bad. "Which is more than he deserves."

Ryan shook her head, then went back to her desk.

Reid watched the interrogation on the television screen in the viewing room. Ortega was probing the gangster, whose name was David Navarro, but he wasn't cooperating. His lawyer eventually leaned forward. "My client is willing to tell you what you want to know, if you'll protect him."

"Here it comes," mumbled Reid.

Ortega laughed, trying to call his bluff. "If he doesn't talk, he'll be going to jail for a long time."

"On what charge? Possession? Intent to supply? Please, detective. We all know he'll be out in five years."

Ortega shuffled uncomfortably in his chair. The lawyer was right. They didn't have a lot to go on. If they wanted to bring down the entire gang and end the street war that had broken out, they needed to know what he knew.

"What did you have in mind?" Ortega asked.

The lawyer smiled.

Bastard.

Reid turned away. The deal would take some time to negotiate. I would need signatures from the Chief of Police and various other law enforcement organizations. Only then would Navarro be willing to talk.

As he'd thought, no burglary had been reported at the warehouse. That meant he was safe. No fingerprints or DNA to link back to him. No camera footage, either. Nothing that would send any unwelcome visitors his way.

He breathed out. Because he wasn't finished with Torres yet.

Back at his desk, Reid went through all the photographs he'd taken of the documents in Torres's study, zooming in on his phone and studying each individually.

The company was a legitimate dock loading enterprise. It

provided equipment to commercial customers in the Miami area. He saw orders for dock levelers, safety systems, industrial doors, and loading tables. It was a clever front. A way for the cartel to offload their shipments of drugs when they arrived at the Port of Miami.

Nothing in the documentation was out of place. All the orders seemed legit, but as he'd suspected, they wouldn't make it obvious. The Morales Cartel had been around a long time. They were smart, efficient, and careful.

Bianca had been their one weakness. A honey trap. She'd caught Torres's eye at a club and he'd chatted her up. A flick of her hair, a brush of her hand against his.

"Oh, I'm sorry. I wasn't looking where I was going."

He'd bought her another drink. She'd made him think it was his idea.

"Only if you're sure?" That flirtatious smile he knew so well. A sparkle in her hazel eyes.

Reid hadn't liked it. He'd never liked it, but she'd been adamant. "It's the only way we'll get in there, Reid. You know it is. He likes me. Let's run with it and see what I can find out."

So they had, against his better judgment.

It had worked better than anyone had expected. Torres had been smitten. Reid could tell, by the way he watched her. The possessive drape of the arm, the way he locked her to his side. Bianca had filtered information back to them. Times and dates of meetings, major players in the organization. Valuable intel. Some of it they'd acted on. Some they hadn't. It wouldn't do to give the game away too soon. They were waiting for the big one. The shake down that would nail the entire organization.

They didn't talk about what happened after hours. When Torres took Bianca back to his place. Reid hadn't wanted to know. They weren't an item, not anymore. Not his choice. But there were still feelings involved. He cared about her more than anyone else in the world.

Had cared.

He blinked. And Torres had gunned her down like she was nothing.

"Er, Reid, I think I have something." Detective Ryan came over, her face flushed.

"What is it?"

"I was looking into the fourth victim, Mimi Silverton, like you suggested, and I found something interesting. A potential link with one of the other victims, Natalia Cruz."

He stared at her. "You found a connection between Mimi and Natalia?"

She nodded, eyes gleaming.

He shook his head. How was that possible? Natalia hadn't been murdered by the Strangler. The MO was different. Thicker ligature marks. No sexual assault.

A connection with Natalia didn't make sense. Had he been wrong all this time? Had the Strangler been interrupted before he could rape her like the task force believed? Had he rushed Natalia? Dumped her body before he had time to finish the job?

"What was the link?"

Ryan grinned. "They were at school together."

23

It was almost seven o'clock, and Kenzie was back at the cafe next to the gym. She was working on an article on her iPad while sipping her fourth coffee. She'd switched to decaf two lattes ago, else she'd never sleep.

Working helped take the edge off her impatience. She didn't have high hopes that Ivan would turn up. After the dismal raid and Fernández's disappearing act, she didn't think the burly henchman would be so stupid as to frequent his usual gym.

Seemed she'd overestimated him.

At precisely seven o'clock, the bulky bodyguard strode up the road. Gone was the ill-fitting suit, replaced with sweatpants and a T-shirt that said RAISE THE BAR. He held a small gym bag over his shoulder.

Gotcha.

Oblivious to Kenzie buried in her tablet, he walked straight past her through the front door of the gym.

Her pulse quickened. Now to contact Reid.

She was hoping he'd come and meet her, and they could tail Ivan together. There was a strong possibility he'd lead back to Fernández.

If not tonight, then tomorrow or the next day. Reid could assign someone to watch his apartment and follow him when he left for work in the morning. They'd soon have Fernández in custody and could question him about Natalia's murder.

Kenzie felt a spark of excitement as she called Reid's number, but the phone just rang. Damnit, where was he?

Ivan would probably be at the gym for an hour, two hours max. Reid needed to get his ass down here ASAP if they wanted to follow him.

She tried again, but it was the same story. No answer. The call diverted to Reid's voicemail.

Kenzie left a message. "Hi, it's me. Where are you? I'm outside the Progressive Overload gym in South Beach and I just saw Ivan Petrovitch walk in. I'm going to follow him when he comes out, in the hopes that he'll lead me to Fernández. I was hoping you'd join me. Call me when you get this message."

There wasn't much more she could do.

She settled down to wait, but it wasn't long before Ivan burst out again. He glanced up and down the road, clearly agitated.

What happened? Then she knew. The receptionist had told him Kenzie had come looking for him. He'd realized his gym was compromised and was now getting out of there.

Shit.

She ducked behind a family who'd just arrived and were choosing a table outside. It was a lovely evening, not too humid. It had rained earlier in the day and now the sky was clear, the sun curling over the horizon, drenching the skyline in a rusty glow.

The beachfront was crowded with tourists and locals. Music was already seeping out of bars and clubs, while diners spilled out onto the sidewalk. There was a jovial atmosphere, but she had no time to enjoy it.

Poking her head out from behind a rotund woman in a caftan, she saw Ivan stalk down the street in the opposite direction from which he'd come. Was he going to warn Fernández?

She'd paid already, so she stuffed her tablet and phone into her bag and took off after him. Just then, her phone vibrated.

Reid.

Keeping her eyes glued to Ivan, she scrounged in her bag.

"Hello?"

"Where are you?" hissed her unofficial partner.

"I'm tailing Ivan. Where are you?"

"Stop it. Now. It's too dangerous." There was genuine concern in his voice.

"I can't stop. He's on the move. He left the gym in a hurry. I think he knows I was there asking about him. He's going to tell Fernández. I can feel it. If I stop now, I'll lose him."

"Kenzie, please. It's not worth it. If they spot you—" He didn't finish before Kenzie interrupted.

"They won't, I promise. How far away are you?"

"I'm on my way, but traffic's bad. It'll be a good 15-20 minutes before I get to South Beach."

"Call me when you get here. I'm heading south along Ocean Drive."

"Kenzie—" But she'd cut the call.

He didn't need to tell her how to do her job. She'd been at it for over 10 years. She'd even done a surveillance course several years back. It was coming in useful now since Ivan kept glancing over his shoulder.

"You have a right to be paranoid," she muttered at the retreating figure. "We're coming after you. You and your little fraudulent organization."

Ivan turned a corner up ahead. He was walking fast, and she had to lengthen her stride to keep up. She approached the side street cautiously, like she'd been taught. There he was, still marching along, his bag swinging over his broad shoulder.

Kenzie kept to the shadows. There were fewer people on this street, although the traffic was back-to-back. Typical Miami jam.

Horns hooted, radios were turned up, and arms rested on open windows.

The street lamps flickered on all at once. Ivan kept walking, head down. He rounded another corner and headed back the way he'd come.

She frowned, making sure to keep well back. He was employing classic counter-surveillance techniques, making sure he wasn't being followed.

He glanced behind him, but she'd already turned around, anticipating it. He didn't see her. She glanced down the street in time to see him cross the road. As she watched, he darted up another side street.

Cursing, she zigzagged through the stop-start traffic and followed him. It was dark up here. The lights were further apart and dimmer than on the main thoroughfare. There was less foot traffic, too. A man in a work suit clutching a briefcase and a woman in stilettos grappling with a For Sale sign hurried past, but apart from them, the street was empty.

Heart throbbing, Kenzie followed Fernández's henchman as he weaved his way through the backstreets. It got darker and darker and more deserted. She began to get nervous. Damnit, Reid.

She called him again, keeping well back. With few people about, Ivan would notice her if he spotted her more than once.

"Kenzie?"

"Where are you?" she whispered.

"I'm close. Are you okay?"

"Yes, I'm still following Ivan."

"Where exactly? Give me the road name." His voice was terse.

"Um." She hesitated to glance at the nearest street sign. "Corner of 14th and Euclid Avenue."

"Okay, wait there. Don't move."

"I'll lose him if I stop."

"Kenzie, I swear." She heard his frustration. "Just wait there, okay. I'm a few blocks away."

She sighed. It was dark and there was nothing but apartment blocks and some sort of church with an empty parking lot nearby. It was creepy. The hairs on her arms were standing up, a sure sign she should proceed with caution.

"Okay, just hurry. He's getting away."

She watched the hulking figure walk along the street. He wasn't hurrying, just a steady gait, gym bag over his shoulder. The urgency had disappeared. He felt safe now.

She moved forward tentatively, keeping him in her sights.

And then, he was gone.

She blinked, straining her eyes. What? Where'd he gone?

She ran forward, scanning the sidewalk. Had he gone into one of the apartments? Is this where Fernández was hiding out?

Shit, how could she lose him? He'd been right here.

She looked around. There was a dark alleyway between two blocks of apartments. He could have ducked down there. A shortcut to the street behind, perhaps?

She hesitated. There were no streetlights and lots of places to hide. She stomped her foot in frustration. If Reid were here, they could have gone in pursuit. Now she'd lost him, and they might never know where Fernández was hiding out.

She heard a soft rustling to her left, in the direction of the alleyway. She spun around, heart racing. What was that? Was there someone there?

Kenzie peered into the darkness, searching for shadows.

24

Reid saw Kenzie standing underneath a streetlight, her blond hair illuminated like a beacon, and hit the brake. The Ford pickup screeched to a halt. She turned and he saw the relief flash across her face before she ran for the truck.

"Thank God." She pulled open the passenger door. "I had an awful feeling someone was about to jump me."

"Who?" He glanced behind her down the alley. "Ivan?"

"Maybe, I don't know." She got in and shivered. "He disappeared. I thought he might have ducked down the alley, but I was worried it might be a trap. I didn't want to risk it."

"You did the right thing," he breathed, his heart rate returning to normal. "Next time, give me some notice before you go chasing after a suspect. I was worried sick."

"You were?" She smiled, her eyes teasing.

"Of course I was. Ivan's ex-Serbian military. He can snap your neck with one hand. Don't ever do that again."

Her smile vanished. "I'm not a complete novice. I know how to keep someone under surveillance, and I can look after myself. I didn't go down the alley, did I?"

No, but she probably would have if he hadn't arrived when he did. He clenched the steering wheel. "I'm sorry, but I don't need another dead girl on my watch."

She fell silent.

Reid pulled away from the curb and they drove down the street. Away from the bustle of the beach, the streets were quiet. Only one or two cars passed them as they made their way back to the main road.

Eventually, Kenzie said, "I'm sorry too. To be fair, I did call you earlier, but you didn't pick up."

"I was busy."

"And then Ivan came out of the gym so fast, I had to make a snap decision. I expected him to be there for at least an hour. That would have given you plenty of time."

He grunted. He'd seen her missed call once he'd finished discussing the connection between Natalia Cruz and Mimi Silverton with Ryan.

"You want me to take you back to your car?"

"Yeah, I'm parked on Collins."

He gave a stiff nod.

"At least we know it was Ivan who stole that security guard's wallet. They go to the same gym."

"It doesn't matter whose ID they used to hire the van," Reid said. "In fact, I'm not entirely sure Fernández was involved in Natalia's death."

"What?" She glanced across at him. "Have you got a new lead?"

He stopped at a traffic light. Now that they'd left the back streets behind, it was busy again, mostly with revelers heading down to Ocean Drive for a night out.

"Of sorts." He turned to her. "We've just discovered Natalia Cruz went to school with the fourth victim, Mimi Silverton."

A myriad of emotions flew across Kenzie's face. Surprise, suspicion, denial, and then acceptance. He knew how she felt. He'd felt the same way.

"Seriously? There's no mistake?"

"Nope."

"Jesus." She ran a hand through her disheveled hair. "What does it mean?"

"I don't know." He sighed. "I've been trying to make sense of it."

"They knew each other?" she murmured, thinking out loud.

He nodded. "Same year. Even if they weren't in the same class, they would have known each other."

"Could it be a coincidence? They're both from Miami. It's not too implausible that they would have gone to the same school."

When he didn't immediately reply, she said, "Is it?"

"I don't believe in coincidences."

"No, me neither. But if it isn't a coincidence, then what?" She faded off, a horrified look on her face.

"It means they were both murdered by the same person," finished Reid.

There was a long pause. The lights changed. Reid drove forward, then turned onto Collins Avenue.

"Did we get it wrong?" she whispered. "All this time the Strangler took Natalia?"

He inhaled through his nose, then pursed his lips. The same thought had been ricocheting around his brain for the last few hours. "I think it's something we have to consider."

"Shitballs."

He sniffed. "You can say that again."

Reid pulled up behind her car. The air was heavy with confusion and uncertainty. He could almost hear her brain ticking over.

"If that is true, we're saying the killer targeted them because they were at school together." She frowned. "That was so long ago. Why would he target them now? And what about the other two victims? They didn't go to the same school. They're from out of town. It doesn't make sense."

"No, it doesn't."

"The first two victims aren't linked, are they? They didn't go to the same school too?"

"No." He watched her logically work through what they knew.

"This guy might be targeting women who'd spurned him in the past, or something like that, but if there's a connection, I can't see it. Unless," she petered off.

"Unless what?"

"Unless he jumped around as a kid. Maybe he went to all their schools, met all four girls, and now he's paying them back for rejecting him."

"Over a decade later?"

She slumped in her chair. "I know, right? Why now? None of this makes any sense."

Reid cut the engine. The AC fell silent and heat filled the interior. Even at this time of night, it was oppressive.

"I'll mention it to the task force. They should look into it, anyway. Just in case."

"Not only students, look at teachers too."

Reid studied her. Her cheeks were flushed from her dash across town and her eyes glinted in the dim light of the car. "You know, you would have made a good detective."

Her face lit up. It was the first genuine expression of happiness he'd seen. The times she'd put it on for their witnesses and suspects didn't count. "Really? You think so?"

"You've got the mind for it."

She met his gaze. "Thanks. That means a lot."

"It's true." He glanced away.

She put her hand on the door handle. "I'd better go. Let me know if you find anything else."

"Kenzie."

She turned back.

"You can't breathe a word of this to anyone. We could be way off base here."

"I know. The world thinks Natalia was the Strangler's third victim, so there's nothing new to report."

He gave a curt nod. "Okay, see you soon."

She got out, closed the door, and gave him a little wave. He waited until she was safely in her car and saw the lights go on before he eased back into the traffic.

Kenzie had taken a risk tonight. When Reid had gotten that last phone call, his heart had started racing and his mouth had gone dry. He'd driven like a crazy man to get to her. The only thought in his head had been, *please no, not again.*

That confused him. Why was he so concerned about Kenzie? He hardly knew her. Yet he'd felt such a gut-wrenching sense of panic when he'd thought she was in danger.

It was because of Bianca. It had to be. Even though his feelings for Kenzie were nothing like what he'd felt for Bianca, she was still his responsibility.

He rationalized it as he drove home. It was because of her he was back on the force, that he was working this case. It was her lead that had started this investigation. He owed her for that. It was the whole reason he'd agreed to this informal partnership, or whatever you'd call it. Highly irregular, but he couldn't cut her out, not after everything she'd done for him.

Now she was his problem. And given her curious nature and her stubborn determination to get the truth, he had his hands full. Strangely enough, that didn't bother him. If he were honest, he enjoyed working with her, a freakin' reporter.

Now *that* was something he never in a million years thought would happen.

25

Kenzie woke early the next day. Her head was pounding with unanswered questions. If there was a connection between two of the victims, there must be a connection between all of them.

She grabbed a mug of coffee and took it into her study.

It was time to take a closer look at all four victims. She knew the task force would look into it too, but she trusted her own research. She was thorough, and she thought they might miss something.

"Always double-source," Keith had drilled into her, and after the screw-up with Miami PD's undercover op last year, she'd learned that lesson the hard way.

The first victim, Sarah Randall, had been the youngest of all four girls at eighteen. She'd been in Miami for Spring Break, a time usually filled with making fun, if raucous memories. Kenzie remembered hers. Even though all she'd wanted to do was become a cop, her father had made her go to college before she applied to the police academy at twenty-one.

She'd gotten her diploma in journalism, because she'd always been good at writing and it meant staying up to date with cutting-edge stories and world events. She'd also figured that one day, when she had kids of her own and could no longer work in the field, she could write about it and work from home. Little did she know that day would come before she'd even graduated from the academy.

Sarah's friends had reported her missing after she failed to return to the hotel the next morning. Initially, they thought she was with a guy, but when she didn't materialize, they began to worry. By then, it was already too late.

She'd gone to a public high school in Tallahassee called Markham High. Kenzie couldn't get a list of teachers' names. The task force would have to do that. The last place Sarah was seen was The Ocean Club, a hotel beach bar popular with spring breakers.

The second victim, Miranda Hodge, was from Orlando. She came from a normal, middle-class family and had moved to Miami five years ago to work at a real estate agency. Her social media profile said she went to Lakeland High School, which appeared to be one of the best public high schools in the state, according to the reviews she'd found on the internet. An ambitious young woman with a good education, enjoying a night out with friends in one of the beachfront bars. Kenzie looked up the name. Go Social! Miranda had left to walk back to her car and was never seen again.

Kenzie tapped her finger on her mouse. Both Sarah and Miranda had been taken in the South Beach area after a night out. Then there was Natalia, who also disappeared in the same part of town. She'd been abducted from her hotel room at The Sand Club, or had she left on her own accord and been targeted while making her getaway?

Mimi Silverton. Radcliffe High School, Miami. The same as Natalia and Bella Montague. Were they friends? Reid had told her she'd disappeared after going dancing at a club called Maxine's near the beach. Again, same area. *That* was obviously the Strangler's hunting ground.

Kenzie wrote down the names of the various establishments. It was time to scout them out. Walking in the victims' footsteps would give her a better sense of how the killer had stalked his prey. Perhaps he'd chatted them up, then followed them out. Somehow, he'd lured them back to his place.

Kenzie parked in the nearest parking garage to all four bars. It was situated at the north end of Ocean Drive where it met 15th Street. She exited via the main entrance and emerged onto the busy street. Hotels towered on all sides, dwarfing even the palm trees. It was a scorching hot day and sweating tourists in shorts and T-shirts mingled with locals on their way to the beach or out for lunch.

She started walking and stopped when she came to one of the bars or restaurants on her list. The first thing that struck her was that they were all at the top end of the street, close to where she'd parked. The killer had limited his target area to a few blocks.

She visited all four places. The Ocean Club was spacious, with a large outdoor pool bar, although it would have been packed and rowdy during spring break. Go Social! was a much smaller, nonetheless classy joint with a late-night DJ and an array of mind-boggling cocktails. Not so easy to spy on someone without being noticed.

The Sand Club she knew, so she didn't go inside, although she stood at the main entrance and studied it. The killer could have targeted Natalia during her husband's launch party, but how would he have known she'd go back to her room alone? If they were sticking to the Strangler theory, he'd have nabbed her when she left her room later that night.

Kenzie walked around the hotel. Apart from the valet parking outside the main entrance, there was a parking lot around the back, as well as the path from the ground floor suites to the beach. Reid had checked the CCTV footage both at the front entrance and the rear parking lot and found nothing.

She stood on the beach and stared up at the hotel. Where had Natalia gone after she'd walked down the path? She'd need a vehicle or an accomplice to pick her up. She had that heavy suitcase with her, and she was still wearing her party dress. A hurried escape then. No time to waste. But why? Why leave her husband when she was so happily married?

She blew a strand of hair out of her face and located the path leading up to the suite. She didn't go up it, merely stood looking at it, then turned around and surveyed the beach.

Ocean Drive was pedestrian only, which meant the closest parking garage was the one on 15th where she'd parked. She wondered if Reid had checked there to see whether either suspect had come back to the hotel later that night.

She was about to go into the final bar on her list when she spotted Snake walking along the beach. He was hard to miss with his tattoos, skinny legs, and mop of ruffled, dark hair.

Was that—? Kenzie did a double take. He was walking with Bella.

Now *that* was interesting.

She walked over to them, bright smile firmly in place. "Hi, how are you guys?"

They froze.

"Oh, Kenzie. Lovely to see you." Snake recovered first, leaning in for a kiss. Bella took a few steps back.

"I'd better be off," she said. "It was nice bumping into you, Eric. I'm glad you're doing better. Let's talk again soon, yeah?"

He nodded, unsure what to say.

Bella shot Kenzie a furtive smile and strode off the beach.

"I hope she didn't leave on my account." Kenzie studied Snake, looking for signs that he was back with his ex-girlfriend.

"No," he said hurriedly. "We just bumped into each other. She was asking how I was getting on."

"And how are you getting on?" Kenzie asked.

"I'm okay. I go through phases where I really miss her, you know? Then others when I think I'm okay."

She gave a sympathetic nod. "It's hard, but you'll get there."

Her eyes followed Bella off the beach. She turned right and disappeared behind the palm trees.

"Hey, listen." Snake perked up. "I'm having a beach party on Saturday. You wanna come?"

"Sure, that sounds great. Text me the details."

He nudged her. "You can bring a partner, if you like."

"Thanks, but I'll probably just come alone. You know me." She gave a self-deprecating laugh.

He shook his head. "Time to get settled already, Kenz. I'd like to see you happy."

"Thanks, but I am happy." She squeezed his arm.

"Suit yourself. Saturday, 9:00 pm. I'll text you the address."

She waved as he set off back the way he'd come.

Kenzie sat down on the hot sand and gazed at the waves rolling in. The sea looked cool and refreshing, and she was hit by a sudden urge to go swimming. Unfortunately, she didn't have her bikini on, or she would have.

She supposed Bella and Snake could have just bumped into each other like he'd said, although the way they were walking, shoulder to shoulder, heads down, deep in conversation, it looked like they'd been talking a while.

Still, Snake had no reason to lie, unless there was something going on between them. She thought about this possibility for a while, then pulled out her phone to call Reid.

26

"How do you feel about going to a beach party with me tomorrow night?"

Reid hesitated. Was Kenzie asking him out on a date?

"Um, sure."

Even more bizarrely, he accepted. There was even a twinge of excitement as he said the words. He hadn't been on a date since Bianca, and they hadn't really dated. They'd had sex a couple of times after work, then she'd called it off. It wasn't worth their jobs.

"Snake is having a party, and I thought it would be a good opportunity to snoop around."

Ah.

"Yeah, sounds good. Maybe we can talk to some of his friends who were at his launch party. Get their take on it?" He hoped his recovery was believable. Of course, she wasn't asking him out on a date. Why would she? They were working the case together, that was it.

He couldn't believe his thoughts had even gone there. What was wrong with him?

"That's what I thought. And guess what? You'll never believe who I just ran into?"

"Snake?" he guessed.

"With Bella Montague, and they looked pretty close, if you know what I mean."

"Really? Are they an item again?"

"I'm not sure. They were walking along the beach together, oblivious to the rest of the world. I interrupted them and she took off. He pretended they'd just bumped into each other, but I think it was more than that."

"That *is* interesting," he mused.

"We can check out their status at the party," she said.

"You'd better send me the details."

"Better yet, why don't you pick me up at seven-thirty?"

"Um, yep. I can do that."

"Cool. See you tomorrow." She hung up.

"Wow." She looked incredible. She'd styled her hair so that it twirled around her face in blond tendrils, and for the first time since he'd met her, she was wearing makeup. Her blue eyes looked positively luminous. He realized he was staring and cleared his throat. "I mean, you look great."

She laughed through glossed lips. "Likewise."

Her coral-colored dress encased her figure like a seashell, then flowed softly to mid-thigh. It was sexy without being too provocative. Perfect for a celebrity beach party. She wore flat gold sandals and her toenails were painted the same color as her dress.

He suddenly felt self-conscious. He'd worn his best pair of jeans and a navy-blue shirt shot through with silver and open at the neck. It was his most stylish shirt, even though it was still Miami-casual. That was about as formal as he got.

"Shall we?" She stepped out and closed the door behind her.

For a work event, this sure felt like a date.

"So, Bella and Snake, eh?" he said once they'd set off.

"I know. She could be biding her time since Natalia died," Kenzie pointed out. "I wouldn't put it past her."

"She was hung up on him," Reid agreed. Kenzie's perfume was drifting across to him. Warm, feminine, intriguing—a lot like her. Then the air conditioning kicked in and the fragrance dissipated.

"I've just had a crazy idea." She turned to him. "What if Bella and Snake were having an affair? That would give Natalia a reason to leave him."

"But they hated each other. Bella had a meltdown every time she was in the same room as Natalia."

"What better way of disguising their affair?"

He glanced at her. "Do you really think they'd be that sly? The negative publicity almost ruined Bella's reputation."

"What reputation?" Kenzie said, not unkindly. "She's a nobody. Her only claim to fame is being Snake's ex."

"I don't know." Reid drove towards the South Beach hotel where Snake was hosting his party. "Everyone said how happy they were. Even on the hotel security they looked like a couple in love."

"Appearances can be deceiving." Kenzie shrugged. "I do it all the time."

"You pretend to be someone you're not?"

"Yeah, when I'm investigating a story. It's easier than you think."

He didn't reply.

It was a beautiful evening for a beach party. There was little to no wind, the air was warm, and the sun lingered over the horizon, painting the sky in shades of gold.

DJ Snake was working his magic on the decks. There were about a hundred guests.

"Who's who in the music industry," Kenzie told him. "That guy's from *Radio Times*, and that's the editor of *Tuned*, the up-and-coming music magazine for the digital age."

They each got a drink and began circulating. "There's Bella." Reid gestured to the strawberry blond in a tantalizing black dress.

She was barefoot and had strings of pearls around her neck that jangled as she danced. She was with a group of friends, her back to DJ.

"She's not even looking at Snake." He watched as she threw back her head and laughed.

Kenzie drew them into conversation with a young woman who had bright pink hair and a diamond nose-ring. "Checking out the opposition?"

The woman laughed and embraced Kenzie. "Just enjoying the party, hon. He's on fire tonight."

Snake mixed a new track seamlessly, grabbing the audience's attention. There were several whoops of approval.

"Reid, meet DJ Fleur. Fleur, this is my friend, Reid."

He admired the way she'd teased the celebrity while still coming across as warm and friendly. He bet Kenzie was one of the cool kids at school. Always in the in-crowd. She certainly looked the part, flitting around with the glamorous guests. Or was she acting? Turning on the charm to integrate herself into the trendy music set. He realized he didn't know. She was that good. "Hi, great to meet you, Fleur."

He, on the other hand, felt like a fish out of water. He wasn't the most social at the best of times, and he'd certainly never been cool or trendy.

The DJ threw him a seductive smile. "My pleasure."

"You were good friends with Natalia, weren't you?" Kenzie said.

"Yeah, I was devastated when they found her body in the swamp." She shook her head. "We all thought she'd left him."

"Why'd you think that?" asked Reid.

Fleur looked uneasy. "There was talk that Snake wanted to put her in his next album, but his producers refused. They said she wasn't good enough, that she'd ruin the album." She grimaced. "Bitter pill to swallow, but let's face it Natalia wasn't a singer. Sweet girl, but not musically gifted." And this coming from her professed friend.

Reid pursed his lips. "Did that cause a rift between them?"

"Yeah, she thought he should have stuck up for her, but he sided with his producer. I mean, you're not going to jeopardize your career, are you? Not when a contract's in the balance."

"What?" cut in Kenzie.

"Shit, man. Forget I mentioned it." She glanced at the stage as if Snake could overhear what she'd said.

"They were going to drop him?" Kenzie persisted.

She lowered her voice. "I heard a rumor that he wanted to renegotiate his contract. He felt he wasn't getting paid enough. Even accused the management company of withholding commission."

"He kept that very quiet." Kenzie glanced at Reid.

"I only know because I'm with the same management company," she said. "They were talking about him being overvalued."

"What do you think?" asked Reid. "Is he overvalued?"

She shrugged. "He's not pulling the same kinda sales as he used to, but the fans still love him. And you know what this industry's like." She looked at Kenzie. "All it takes is one slick remix and you're smiling again."

"True." Kenzie nodded in agreement.

Reid had to take their word for it. What he knew about the music industry was dangerous.

A couple of Fleur's friends came up, and Kenzie and Reid stepped away.

"He can start his own management company now." Reid watched Snake as he jumped up and down, one hand on the massive set of earphones, the other on the turntable. "He's inherited a fortune from Natalia."

Kenzie followed his gaze. "Very convenient."

27

"I'm going to talk to Snake's friends." Kenzie motioned to a group of guys about Snake's age, also sporting tattoos and designer jeans. "I want to question them about the night Natalia disappeared."

"You know them?" Reid frowned at the way they were tossing back shots from a bottle of tequila.

She grinned. "Yeah. I party with them sometimes."

"I see."

She laughed. "Don't be such a party pooper. Go talk to Dave."

"Who?"

"You know, the guy who was at the launch party with Bella. The one who took her home that night."

"Gotcha."

He strode off, beer in hand. Kenzie watched him go. She could tell he felt awkward, but was hiding it well. His height and imposing physique gave him an air of confidence he didn't feel, not with this crowd. He was more at home with cops and ex-cons, like her dad. She got it.

Kenzie'd had to grow up fast when her mother disappeared. She'd learned to mask her feelings, to hide her emotions and put on a brave face. To smile when she didn't feel like it and to feign interest when all she wanted to do was curl into a ball and cry.

She'd done it so often it had become natural. Now she flitted from group to group, role to role with ease. A definite skill in her job.

"Hey." She joined Snake's friends. "Got one for me?"

Paul, a good looking and self-proclaimed bachelor, grinned. "Sure thing, Kenz." He poured her a shot. "Cheers."

They knocked it back. The spirits stung her throat but brought a welcome warmth. They chatted a bit and then she asked about the night Natalia went missing. "You guys helped look for her, didn't you?"

Paul nodded soberly, though his eyes were beginning to glaze. "Yeah. We turned that hotel upside down. She was nowhere, man."

"I know this is a stupid question, but did you actually go into their suite? Was there any sign of a struggle?"

"I don't think so. I mean, it didn't look any different than usual," he said. "Nothing on the floor or broken or anything. Is that what you mean?"

"Are you working now?" joked a guy called Nathaniel. He'd come on to her once or twice, but she preferred to keep it friendly. He'd known Snake for years, since before he was famous.

"I am doing a follow-up piece on Natalia," she admitted. It wasn't a lie. "I'm trying to figure out if she left on her own accord or if she was taken. What do you guys think?"

May as well put it out there. It never hurt to get some general feedback.

"Her things were gone," said Nathaniel. "Not that we noticed at the time. But that's what Snake said the next morning."

"You didn't notice her things missing when you checked the room that night?" Kenzie clarified.

"No. We were looking for her. We checked the room, then the rest of the hotel."

"She definitely left on her own, although nobody could figure out why," said Paul. "Least of all, Snake. He was devastated."

"I'm sure. They looked so happy to me," said Kenzie.

"They were," agreed Paul. "I sure as hell didn't see it coming."

"Me neither. And then when they found her body." Paul shook his head. "That was just awful."

"You going to have another shot or what?" Nathaniel said, unwilling to let the party mood drop.

She laughed and held out her glass. "Damn straight. Fill me up."

The tequila had kicked in by the time she found Reid. He was still in conversation with Dave, who, it turned out, had been a firefighter for 12 years before he'd become a property developer. "Hey, there you are."

He turned and smiled, his eyes crinkling. He appeared much more relaxed now. In fact, he almost looked like he was enjoying himself. "Kenzie, you know Dave, right?"

"Yep. Hi, Dave." She flashed him a smile.

"Dave was just telling me how he met Bella," Reid said.

"Oh?"

"Yes, he rescued me from a burning building," sang a feminine voice. They all turned as Bella sauntered up.

"Seriously?" gasped Kenzie.

"Yeah." Dave chuckled, embarrassed. "Although Bella tends to exaggerate."

She slipped an arm around his waist. "He's being modest. My apartment block caught on fire and we couldn't get out, so I went out onto my balcony. Dave climbed up a ladder to rescue me."

"That is so romantic," said Kenzie, a tad wistfully.

She didn't miss the look Reid gave her. Ignoring it, she said, "Is that when you started dating?"

"Not exactly," Bella said. "I was still getting over Snake, so it took a while, but eventually, I caved." She glanced up at Dave. "He was, or rather he has been, very patient with me."

He shrugged. "Some things are worth waiting for."

Kenzie envied his certainty. She snuck a furtive glance at Reid. He had a strange, faraway look in his eyes.

"It certainly doesn't seem like she's pining for Snake," she said to him later when they'd moved on.

"No, I didn't see any indication that she and Snake were an item, even undercover," he added.

Kenzie bit her lip. "I must have been mistaken on the beach. I thought I saw something that wasn't there."

Reid nudged her. "I never took you for a romantic."

"I'm not."

"Could have fooled me. I saw your expression when Bella described how Dave had rescued her. You went all gooey."

"I did not." She swatted him on the arm, but she couldn't help flushing. There was a side to her that wanted the happily ever after, but there was another, more realistic side that knew there was no such thing. "That was the tequila."

He laughed. "Okay, if you say so."

"Did you ask Dave about the launch party?" Kenzie changed the subject.

"Yes, I did. He insists he took her straight home. She was more than a little drunk. He said she always got like that when Natalia was around. She was really hurt when her best friend ran off with her boyfriend."

"I suppose it was a double blow," Kenzie mused.

"Yeah, but she seemed okay tonight. Cheerful, but sober."

"I agree. She was in a good mood, but not drunk. Perhaps now that Natalia is gone, she'll be able to move on with her life."

"It must have been hard seeing them together all the time, particularly when they had the same group of friends." His gaze rested on Bella's dancing figure. Her strawberry blond hair whipped around her face, turning bronze in the laser beams that were now flashing over the crowd.

Kenzie felt the music vibrate through her. Snake was getting to the end of his set, and the music was getting more frenzied. Reid scrunched up his forehead like she did when she felt the beginning of a headache coming on.

"Should we go?" he asked.

Kenzie glanced up at Snake, whipping the crowd into a frenzy. He had a look of euphoria on his face, even though he was drenched in sweat. "I think I'd better stay for a while and talk to Snake. It would be rude to leave now."

Reid nodded. "You don't mind if I—"

"No, not at all." This wasn't his scene. It wasn't hers either to be honest, but Snake had invited her personally and she ought to stay long enough to say hi. He wouldn't be long now, she could tell by the climactic beats that the song was in its final throes. "I'll call you tomorrow."

"Thanks." He hesitated, and she thought he was about to say something when Nathaniel came prancing over.

"You owe me a dance, young lady." He drew her into the crowd. She waved at Reid and saw him frown before he turned and stalked off into the night.

They danced for another five minutes, their bodies gyrating under the lasers. Snake kept the crowd going, piling on the tension until they were screaming with anticipation. Then the beat dropped and everybody went mad, jumping up and down, raising their hands like worshippers.

She played along, swishing her hair and shouting with all the others. To anyone watching, she was having the time of her life.

Finally, the song ended and the music faded out. There was laughing and clapping, and the sweaty dancers made their way to the bar or the pool for a dip.

Kenzie went up to Snake. "Wow, that was incredible."

"Thanks." He was grinning from ear to ear. "You have a good time?"

"Great time," she smiled back. "But I've got to work tomorrow, so I just came to say goodbye."

"You're leaving already? Fleur is getting on the decks next. You should stay for a set."

"I'd love to, but I can't. I've got an early start."

Other people came up to congratulate him. Kenzie was getting shouldered out.

"I'll call you in a couple of days," she promised, then backed away.

She walked through the hotel and out the front, looking for a cab. When none appeared, she decided to call an Uber. There was no parking in front of the hotel, so she walked down the road, eyes on her phone to pull up the app.

She ordered the Uber and ran a hand through her hair, lifting it off her hot and sticky neck. She hadn't danced like that in years. Her ears were still ringing from the music. It had been very loud. Snake must have paid the hotel a large amount of money to use their private beach and create such a racket.

She glanced at the app. Two minutes away.

A rush of hot air made her turn around, but not before she felt a thud and stars exploded in her head. The sidewalk rushed up to meet her. She tried to see who'd attacked her, but all she could make out was a shadowy shape before her world went black.

28

Kenzie woke up to see Reid's face staring down at her. "Kenzie, thank God."

"Reid?"

Where was she? She scrunched her eyes against the bright light. Her head throbbed. She felt the back of it and found a large lump. "What happened?"

"You were attacked." Reid released her hand, and Kenzie realized he'd been holding it. He looked pale, like he hadn't slept.

"Attacked?"

"A passerby found you on the sidewalk with your phone in your hand. Do you remember anything?"

She screwed up her forehead, trying to think, but everything was murky. "I felt a rush, like someone running up behind me—then pain. They must have hit me on the head. I don't remember anything after that."

"Was it a man or a woman?" He leaned forward.

"I don't know. I can't—" She closed her eyes as the throbbing became too much. "I don't think I saw them."

"Don't tire her out." A nurse smiled at her. "Welcome back. I'm just going to check your vitals."

Kenzie noticed an IV in her arm. She was connected to a machine that beeped lazily beside her. The nurse checked the various numbers, then nodded. "All looks good, but you need to rest. You've got a nasty bump on your head."

No kidding. She felt like a herd of elephants were stomping through her brain.

"How did you know I was here?" she asked Reid once the nurse had gone.

"The person who found you called me," he said, his voice even. "I was the last dialed number on your phone."

"Ah." That's right. She'd called him to invite him to the party. That was the last phone call she'd made.

"How long have you been here?"

"A while. I'm just glad you're okay."

Her eyes flitted to the window. Slices of sunlight filtered through the open blinds. "What time is it?"

"Mid-morning, you've been out a while. They did a CT scan, but luckily there was no internal bleeding. You've got a concussion, though. You'll have to take it easy for a while."

"I was waiting for an Uber," she said.

He grimaced. "I should never have left you there by yourself." Guilt and anger flickered across his face.

"It's not your fault," she said. "You didn't know this would happen."

"Still, I should have driven you home."

"I'm fine, Reid. Really, you don't have to worry, and please don't feel guilty about it. At least we know we're on the right track."

"We do?" He scowled.

"Yeah, we've ruffled someone's feathers, haven't we? So much so that they felt compelled to issue a warning." She pointed to her head and gave him a bleak smile.

"I don't see how you can think this is a good thing. You could have been killed."

"But I wasn't. Either he didn't want to kill me, or he didn't have time. I was on a busy street, after all. He couldn't just pick me up and carry me over his shoulder. Someone would have noticed."

"I'll appeal for witnesses," he said.

"I think it was a warning," she continued, as if he hadn't spoken. "Maybe even for you."

"Message received," he said grimly. "From now on, you're going to be extra careful. Until this guy is caught, you're not to go anywhere alone. Do you hear me? Particularly at night. In fact, I'll come and stay at your place for a night or two after you get out of the hospital. Just to be safe."

"Honestly, Reid. I'm fine. You don't have to babysit me." She was touched by his concern, even if it did border paranoia.

"If it's the same person who killed those four women, he's dangerous. I'm not taking any chances."

"We're back to that theory, are we?" she asked.

He raked a hand through his hair. It stood up in all directions, giving him an impish look. He hadn't shaved. Two-day stubble covered his jaw. The dark shadows beneath his brown eyes made them appear almost yellow in the fluorescent ward light.

"Right now, I've no idea. I've got to go to work, so I'll see what the task force has discovered, if anything. The lab results should be back from Mimi Silverton, which may give us a few more leads." He shook his head. "I still can't get my head around the fact that Natalia, Bella, and Mimi were at school together. That must be relevant."

"Don't forget to ask the task force for a list of teachers at that school. Then cross check them with the other two victims' schools."

His face softened. "Yes, ma'am."

She grinned. "Sorry, I'm getting ahead of myself."

"No, it's okay. I'll follow up on that."

She gave a little nod and leaned back against the pillow. The pounding was so loud it was drowning out his voice. "I think I'd better rest now."

Reid stood up. "I'm glad you're okay."

"Yeah, me too."

"I'll call you later. I meant it about not being alone. If you don't want me coming over, ask someone else to stay. A girlfriend or something."

"I'd rather have you," she said without thinking.

At his surprised look, she gave an embarrassed chuckle. "I mean, I'd rather have a law enforcement officer guarding me than a beautician."

At his confused look, she explained. "Mandy's the only other person I'd ask to stay with me, and she's a married mother of three from Fort Lauderdale. She's also a beautician."

"Ah. In that case, I'll see you later."

"Navarro's about to make a deal," whispered Ryan, as Reid walked into the precinct. Pérez stood in front of the viewing screen with Captain Reynolds. It wasn't often he graced them with his presence. On it, Reid could see Ortega sitting opposite their arrestee from the raid and his lawyer.

He walked over. Both men nodded to him, then went back to watching the screen.

"It's a turf war," Navarro was saying, his voice tinny through the speakers. "There's fresh product on the streets and both gangs want a piece of the action."

"Where are they getting it from?" asked Ortega.

Navarro hesitated.

Ortega leaned forward. "You want this deal or not?"

"The Morales cartel."

"What?" spluttered Pérez.

The captain looked furious. "I knew those bastards would be back."

Reid said nothing, but inside he was seething. Now they knew Torres was back, too.

Ortega was asking who was in charge. "Is it 'The Wolf'?"

Lopez's street name.

Navarro nodded. "Yeah, he's their main man, although Alberto Torres is running the show. He's the one distributing the product."

"Do you know where we can find him?"

Reid held his breath.

"Nah," said Navarro. "We communicate via burner phones. They give us the time and place, and we do as instructed. You don't mess with the cartel, not if you want their business."

And everybody wanted their business. Their drugs were pure, cheap, and plentiful. If you didn't, someone else would. Hence the turf war between the Kings and the Warriors.

"I want that number," Ortega said.

Navarro nodded.

"I knew this would happen," said Reynolds. "Cartel's destroying this city. I'm not going down this road again. This time we're handing it over to the DEA. They wanted it, they can have it." He stalked off back to his office.

The DEA had given them a hard time last year, but since it had been Miami PD's operative undercover, they'd backed off. Then when it had all gone to shit, they'd said, "Should've let us handle it." Maybe they'd been right. At least that way Bianca would still be alive.

Pérez looked at him. "You okay, Garrett?"

"Yeah, why wouldn't I be?"

"Navarro bringing all this up again."

He shrugged. "Not my case. I agree with the captain. Let the DEA handle it." That would put Ortega's nose out of joint. A small consolation.

Pérez grunted. "Yeah, I'll give them a call now. Fill them in."

"Let's talk about Matt Garcia," Ortega was saying.

An hour later, four officers from the Drug Enforcement Agency arrived. They escorted Navarro out, much to Ortega's dismay.

"They're taking him to a safe house until the trial," Pérez told them. "It's not our problem anymore."

Ortega was fuming. "It was our case. We could have handled it."

"Concentrate on the turf war," the lieutenant told him. "He gave you names and addresses. Pick up those bastards and let's put an end to this chaos. Leave the Morales cartel to the DEA."

Ortega glanced at Reid.

"If you hadn't screwed up, we'd have gotten them the first time."

Reid debated smacking him in the face, then decided against it and went back to his desk.

At lunchtime, Reid slipped away unnoticed.

He drove back to the warehouse. This time, the roller doors were up and two flat-bed trucks with cargo handling equipment were parked outside. A foreman was managing the offload. The morning rush was over and they were storing the equipment back in the warehouse. It looked like any other legitimate business.

He scanned the yard for Torres's Audi. There it was, parked at the end behind the trucks. He was here. It was business as usual. The arrest of David Navarro hadn't spooked them.

Good.

Reid delved into his backpack and pulled out a home security camera. He'd bought it online a few years back but hadn't used it since he'd moved to the Glades. It connected to his phone, so he could log in and monitor the activity whenever he wished.

He got out of the car and looked around. Opposite the warehouse was the massive container yard. Giant Lego bricks extended into the distance as far as the eye could see. It would be difficult to mount the camera there.

Diagonally across the road was a prefab style building with a sign that said Calvin Exports on the front. It didn't look like it was in use. The windows were filthy and there was an unkempt feel about the place. That would do.

He walked around the back and looked for a place to climb onto the roof. A pipe ran up the wall next to the window. Grunting, he put his foot on the ledge and hoisted himself up, holding onto the pipe for support.

Using the top frame of the window as a foothold, he pulled himself up so that his head was level with the roof. Gripping the pipe, he swung his legs up and rolled over. He was up.

He leopard-crawled across the flat surface until he had a bird's-eye view of the warehouse yard. The camera had fresh batteries and would last a couple of days before he'd have to come back and change them.

He set it up, angling it towards the warehouse. Then he checked the image on his phone. The front of the building was visible, as was the side door where he'd broken in. He couldn't see the far side where Torres had parked his car, but he figured the entrance was more important. Besides, he'd see the car when it drove in.

He pocketed his phone and slid back down the pipe.

Ortega had been desperate for Torres's whereabouts. Reid could have put him out of his misery and told him about the warehouse, but then they'd descend on this place, guns blazing, and Torres would disappear again.

Reid wanted the Morales foreman right where he could see him. A drug charge was too good for that bastard. He was going to pay for what he'd done to Bianca. Reid would make sure of it.

29

When Reid got back to the station, it was buzzing with activity. Jonny, Jared, and Chris were all talking at the same time, phones glued to their ears.

"What's happened?" he asked Ryan, whose fingers were flying over her keyboard.

"We got a break in the case." She stopped typing and glanced up. "It's a big one."

"What is it?"

Pérez came striding over. "Garrett, it looks like you might have been right all along."

He frowned. "About?"

"The Montague girl," he said. "She's involved, no doubt about it."

"Bella?" Now he was really confused. "Will someone tell me what the hell is going on?"

"Bella Montague's car was picked up on a traffic camera going south towards the Glades the night of Natalia's murder," supplied Ryan.

He stared at her. "Bella's car?"

"Yeah."

He remembered Dave saying how drunk she was. That he'd dropped her off at her apartment and she'd gone straight to bed.

"Are you sure?"

"Clear as day," said Pérez.

Ryan handed him a photograph. It was black and white, and the quality wasn't great, but he could clearly see Bella driving her Honda Civic. She had both hands on the steering wheel, her eyes focused straight ahead. She didn't look drunk. Not even slightly inebriated.

"That's her alright," he muttered. Then his gaze flickered to the person sitting beside her. "Who's that?"

"*That* is what we need to find out," growled Pérez.

"His face is dark."

Ryan looked up. "We've sent it to the tech team to see if they can enhance it, but at the moment, all we have is that shadowy figure."

"It's a man." Reid studied it. Height-wise, he was taller than Bella, his head nearly touching the roof of the car. He had an angular chin, but not much else was recognizable. It was impossible to tell whether he was broad or skinny, blond or dark, or what color his skin tone was.

Dave? He strained his eyes. No, he didn't think so, although if he was turning to the side, maybe.

Snake? Again, impossible to tell. It could be someone else entirely.

"She could be connected to the Swamp Strangler." Ryan's eyes gleamed.

"Given the link with the fourth victim, that's a distinct possibility," agreed Pérez.

Jonny rushed over. "We're bringing her in," he said. "I've sent a squad car to pick her up. We're going to question her in connection with Natalia Cruz's murder, and maybe she'll let something slip about the others."

Reid went back to his desk. There was a heaviness in his chest, the kind that comes when you know you've been duped. Bella had lied to him. She hadn't been drunk at the launch party. It had all been a farce. Her spat with Natalia, was that for show too? Is that how she'd slipped whatever it was into Natalia's drink?

And if that was all an elaborate performance, then was her relationship with Dave real?

Reid got the distinct feeling that Dave was being played for a fool. Unless he was her accomplice, but he couldn't see it somehow. Dave was a standup guy. He rescued damsels in distress off burning balconies. He didn't dump their bodies in the Glades.

No, the guy in the photograph must be someone else.

The timestamp on the photograph had said 2:11am. The timing fit. He thought through the possible sequence of events.

Natalia had retired to her room at eleven. Bella, or her accomplice, must have broken into the hotel suite, attacked Natalia, and carried her out via the patio entrance. They stuck her in Bella's car and drove her out to the Glades to dump her body.

The question was, did they do it to make it look like the Swamp Strangler's victim, or was Bella in cahoots with the Swamp Strangler himself?

He was betting on the former. Serial killers didn't team up with bitter ex-girlfriends. It just didn't happen. Still, the task force was convinced they were all related, thanks to the school connection. That reminded him, he needed to check on the list of teachers and students.

But he didn't have time, because at that moment, Bella walked in, escorted by two policemen.

"This is outrageous!" She flung her head back in a fiery display of pique. "I want my lawyer."

"You'll get a lawyer," said Jonny, who'd read Bella her rights. He turned to Jared. "Put her in interrogation room one."

Pérez came out of his office and watched Jared lead the suspect away. "Hard to believe that beautiful creature is a cold-blooded killer."

"We don't know she is yet," cautioned Reid.

Pérez raised an eyebrow. "The camera doesn't lie."

"It's circumstantial," reminded Reid. "Sure, it doesn't look good, but it doesn't mean she murdered anyone."

"That road only leads to one place," Pérez said. "The swamp."

That was true. It was the road he took to get home every day. It curved past his cabin, past the Gator Inn and Smiley's Bar and to the dirt loop road that wound deep into the swamp. One way in, one way out. Unless you had a boat.

"All I'm saying is a jury will argue that's not concrete evidence," he said.

Pérez scowled. "Yeah, I know. Let's see what we can get out of her."

Reid watched on the screen outside the interrogation room as Jonny sat down opposite Bella Montague and her attorney. Bella had composed herself and was now calm and relaxed. Her pale skin shimmered under the harsh lighting, her blue eyes wide and innocent.

Reid thought back to 12 hours ago, when she'd been gyrating on the beach to DJ Snake's particular blend of chaos. He'd been almost convinced she had nothing to do with her ex-friend's murder.

Her lawyer was an eager man with spectacles, who arched forward in his chair, as if he were leaning into his clothes.

"Shall we get started?" said Jonny.

The attorney nodded.

"This interview is being recorded," Jonny said. Reid knew another officer was standing just inside the door in case of trouble, although Bella looked like she was about to step onto a runway, not face a police interrogation. There wouldn't be any trouble—not that kind, anyway.

"Miss Montague, can you explain what your vehicle was doing on Highway Forty-One at eleven minutes past two on the morning of the July sixteenth?" He slid the CCTV photograph across the table towards her.

She glanced down, but her expression didn't change. "I was giving a friend a ride home."

"Into the Glades?"

"Yes, that's where he said he lived."

"*He?* I thought he was a friend. Didn't you know where he lived?"

"No, he was a recent friend."

"How recent?" asked Jonny.

"I met him a few nights before that picture was taken." She nodded at the image.

"Does this friend have a name?"

"Yes, of course. He said his name was Julian."

"Julian."

She nodded.

"Julian Who?"

A shrug. "I don't know. I didn't ask."

"Not such a good friend, then."

She sighed. "Look, I met him at a bar. We hooked up. That's all there is to it."

"What about this night?" Jonny tapped the photo.

"I'd just gotten home from the launch party. I was tired and upset. I was about to go to bed when Julian knocked on my door. He'd been out and thought he could invite himself around for a late-night booty call." She scoffed. "Obviously I said no, but he was pretty drunk, so I offered to take him home."

"That was nice of you, going out of your way like that. Most women would have closed the door in his face."

"I'm a nice girl."

She was smooth, he'd give her that.

Jonny glanced at the file he'd brought in with him. "Earlier that evening, you'd been at a launch party at the Sand Club, is that right?"

"Yes, that's right."

"And at that party, you had an altercation with Natalia Cruz."

Her face hardened. "It was no secret she and I didn't get along, Detective."

"In fact, you got so drunk that night, you had to be taken home by your date."

"Who said I was drunk?"

She'd looked drunk on the security footage they'd seen of the party that night. He remembered her stumbling around the swimming pool, dangerously close to falling in. That must have been an act.

Jonny glanced down at his notes. He frowned. "Your date, Dave said you were—and I quote—pretty out of it. He took you home early."

"Yes, that's right. He took me home early, but not because I was drunk. I was upset by what had happened with Natalia. She used to be my best friend. Did you know she stole my boyfriend out from under me?"

Jonny cleared his throat. "I heard, yes."

"Well, then you know how upsetting it was for me to see them together. I'm afraid I lost my temper, and we had words. Then I asked Dave to take me home."

"That's not the first time that's happened, is it?" Jonny asked.

Reid was impressed. His colleague had come a long way since he'd been a rookie on Reid's team. He was a senior detective now and doing a good job of it.

Ryan was also watching the recording, transfixed.

Bella glared at Jonny, her chin jutting out. Beside her, her attorney tensed. "How is that relevant, Detective?"

"It's relevant because your client has a history of altercations with the murder victim. There was an incident at Ms. Cruz's engagement party, too. You had to be forcibly removed from the premises," Jonny reminded her.

"Like I said, we had our issues."

"And here you are driving your car to the swamp where Natalia Cruz's body was dumped the night she disappeared."

Bella didn't look quite so relaxed now.

"My client has already explained what she was doing there," the lawyer said.

"Oh yes, the friend without a surname. Where did you drop him off?" Jonny asked.

"Outside the Gator Inn," she said.

"That should be easy enough to check," murmured Ryan.

Reid grunted. "The only people who stay there are the kind who don't give their real names and always pay in cash."

Ryan flushed. "Oh, shoot."

"Yeah."

The interview continued. "What time did you get back after dropping your friend off?"

"I don't know. It was late."

"Do you have a number for this Julian?"

"No, I told you. I picked him up in a bar."

"Except he knew where you lived?"

"Yes, we went back to my place the first time we met."

Reid sighed and walked away. That interrogation was going nowhere. They had nothing on Bella. Nothing that would stand up in court. Her explanation, although doubtful, couldn't be disproved.

"Ryan," he called, turning around.

"Yes, sir."

"Do you have a list of staff and students at Natalia Cruz and Bella Montague's school when they were there?"

"Yes, I'll get it for you."

He pulled up the background reports on the first two victims, Sarah Randall and Miranda Hoberman. He'd read them many times but couldn't remember the names of the schools. Getting the details, he called the principals at both and requested a similar list.

They took a couple of hours to come through, but by the time Bella was released, he had a definitive list with which to cross-reference. He hit print and waited for the industrial-sized machine to spit them out. He wanted to tick them off, one by one.

"We can't fucking charge her." Jonny, who never swore, stormed out of the interview room.

Pérez patted him on the back. "You tried. She's tough, and she played us like a fiddle. Had an answer for everything."

"I know she's involved." Jonny clenched his hands into fists. "I feel it in my gut."

Reid glanced up. Yep, he was getting that same feeling, too.

"Where are we with the lab results for Mimi Silverton?" he inquired. "Wasn't there DNA underneath her fingernails?"

"Couldn't find a match," said Ryan. She sounded as deflated as her partner looked. The printer spluttered to life and began churning out Reid's list. Pérez, standing with his legs apart like a cowboy about to draw, glared at everybody.

Reid couldn't blame them. After the high of spotting Bella Montague on the CCTV camera, it was an anticlimax to have her walk out of the precinct without a scratch.

"Did you take DNA from Bella?" asked Reid.

"Yeah, we were in our rights to do that." Jonny managed a small smile. "It's a stretch, but we're hoping it's hers."

"I'll put a rush on it." Pérez spun on his heel and went back to his office.

Reid spent the rest of the afternoon cross-checking the names on his lists. Nothing. No one who'd worked at Radcliffe High had worked or studied at any of the other schools.

"Any luck?" Ryan came over. She had her backpack on and was about to leave for the day.

"Nope. It's another dead end."

She sighed. "Is it always like this?"

"Like what?"

"This frustrating." She waved her arms in the air. "I feel like we almost got her and then she walked out of here. Even though it was obvious she was lying, we couldn't prove it."

Reid pursed his lips. "Yeah, I guess it can be. That's what it boils down to, really. What you can prove in court."

"It sucks."

He could relate. There were plenty of times when they had to let the bad guy go due to lack of evidence. You just had to come back stronger next time.

"We'll just have to dig deeper," he said. "If she's guilty, we need to find a way to prove it."

A flicker reignited in her eyes. A small one, but it was there. "Yes, sir," she whispered.

"Maybe the DNA will give us something." He tried to sound upbeat.

"Maybe."

Reid was packing up when his phone rang. It was Kenzie.

"Hey, how's the patient?" he asked.

"Good, they're letting me go home."

"Already?" He'd thought they'd keep her in for observation overnight. She had been unconscious for a while.

"Yeah, they say I'm good to go. Just thought I'd let you know. No need to come over unless you want to. I'm fine."

"It's not your concussion I'm worried about," he said. "I'm leaving soon. I'll meet you at your place."

"Okay, and Reid?"

"Yeah?"

"Thanks."

30

Kenzie opened the door to find Reid standing there, a sports bag over his shoulder. He suddenly seemed bigger than she remembered, his broad shoulders blocking the porch light.

"Come in."

He gave her a concerned once-over as he walked past. "You sure you should be out of the hospital so soon?"

"Doc gave me the all-clear." She shrugged. "I feel fine, just got a bit of a headache."

"I can imagine." He dropped his bag beside the sofa.

"Do you really think he'll try again?" she asked. For all her bravado earlier, she was feeling a little fragile now. It was a relief having Reid here.

"I don't know, but I'd rather not take any chances. We don't know who hit you yet. It could have been Fernández, his henchman, or someone from the party. Until we're sure, it's best to take precautions."

She knew he was right.

"Can I get you anything? A beer?"

"I'll get it. I'm not here to make more work for you."

She smiled and sank back down into the armchair she'd been curled up in, watching TV. The sound was down low so as not to make her headache any worse.

Reid returned with a beer. "I'd get you one, but I don't think it's wise."

She shook her head. "I'm on painkillers, anyway."

"Have you eaten?" he asked.

She looked sheepish. Truth be told, she'd gotten back and collapsed, and hadn't given a thought to cooking or what she'd have for dinner. The fridge was embarrassingly empty.

"You've got to eat," he said. "I'll make something. I bought some spaghetti and fresh tomatoes on my way here."

"Wow, I'm liking this new side to you. I didn't realize you were so domesticated."

He grinned. "Don't get too excited. This is the only thing I know how to cook to a reasonably high standard."

She laughed. "Well, it sounds great. I forgot all about eating."

"We've got to keep your strength up. There have been some developments in the case I want to run by you."

That piqued her interest. "What developments?"

"I'll tell you after dinner." He ruffled through his sports bag and pulled out a grocery bag.

"I want to know now." She followed him as he walked into the kitchen. "You can tell me while we chop tomatoes."

He snorted. "Deal."

Reid stood in her kitchen, looking around.

"The pans are in that cupboard to your left, and the utensils in that jar on the counter."

He collected what he needed, grabbed a chopping board, and began to slice the tomatoes.

"Let me help," she offered.

He shook his head. "You listen and tell me what you think."

She relented. "Okay."

"Bella Montague was caught on camera the night of Natalia's

disappearance, driving to the Glades. There was a man in the car with her."

Kenzie gaped at him. "Seriously? The same night? After she got home from the launch?"

"Same night."

"Holy crap!"

"I know."

"Who was she with?"

Reid turned the board around and kept chopping. "That's the problem. The passenger's face was dark. Can't make out who it is."

"Could it be Snake?"

He glanced up at her. "What makes you say that?"

She shrugged. "I don't know. There might be something going on between them. I can't shake the feeling there's more to their relationship than meets the eye. When I saw them on the beach, they looked so—together. Even though they weren't." She shook her head. "I know that makes no sense."

"It could have been Snake. I can't say for sure that it was, though. No jury will convict based on that."

"What did Bella say when you questioned her?"

"Unfortunately, I wasn't the one to question her, but she had a perfectly rational explanation. She said he was a guy she'd picked up a few days before, they'd had sex, and the night of the launch he showed up at her door for a late-night booty call. He was drunk, so she gave him a ride home."

"Really?" Kenzie put her hands on her hips. "She gave a ride to a guy looking for a 2:00 am booty call? I doubt that."

"That's what she said. Can't prove or disprove it either way."

"Did she give a name?"

"Julian. No last name. No number. She didn't ask."

Kenzie pursed her lips. "I wonder what Dave would say about that."

"I doubt there's anything to tell. I'm betting Bella made the whole thing up. Julian probably doesn't even exist."

"Which brings us back to my original question," said Kenzie. "Who was in the car with her? Who was her accomplice in Natalia Cruz's murder?"

"Jonny's going to bring in Snake for questioning."

"Wasn't he still at the party?"

"Not at 2:00 am. The party ended around one-thirty. He and his friends searched the hotel for Natalia but as you know, couldn't find her. Snake called the police who told him to wait until she'd been missing for 24 hours to call back."

"So he could have been in the car with her," Kenzie mused. Her brain was working overtime, piecing parts of the puzzle together. "What if Natalia was still alive when he got back from the party? What if he killed her, then Bella picked him up, and they took Natalia's body to the swamp to dump it?"

"Making it look like the Strangler," finished Reid. He swept the chopped tomatoes into the pan.

"No, that doesn't work," Kenzie gnawed on her lip. "Snake got his buddies to help search for her. They would have seen if he had her stashed in one of the wardrobes or something."

"And I checked the CCTV outside the hotel. Bella didn't go back there."

"She may have parked somewhere else," she said, as he turned on the stove. The smell of garlic wafted over, making her stomach rumble.

"It's possible. I couldn't check everywhere."

The pan sizzled. "Who taught you to cook spaghetti?" She wondered at the practiced way in which he stirred the tomatoes, added some water and herbs, and adjusted the heat.

"My mother." A fond smile swept across his face.

"Oh, is she still alive?"

"Yeah, I'm not that old." He laughed.

"Sorry, it's just I've never heard you mention your parents."

"No, well my father died when I was a teenager, but my mother lives in Pennsylvania with my sister."

He had a sister, too. She realized she didn't know much about Reid other than he was a detective. "Do you ever visit them?"

"Once in a while. I spent some time there after Bianca died, licking my wounds, but it got too claustrophobic. I'm not big on talking about my feelings, which my sister loves to do."

Kenzie smiled. "Is that when you bought the place in the Glades?"

"Yeah, got it from a tour company that went bust."

"Why there?" she asked. "It's so isolated and remote."

"Beautiful though," he said, "and I like the solitude."

"Beautiful in a swampy way, I guess."

He chuckled and put another pot of water on the stove to boil. The tomato sauce smelled so good it had given her an appetite when she thought she didn't have one.

"I was 12 when my mother disappeared," she said softly. She didn't know why she suddenly felt the need to mention her mother. Perhaps it was the domestic kitchen scene, the stirring up of old memories. "I remember baking with her. Sifting flour and licking the bowl when we were done."

"It must have been hard to lose your mother at that age," he said.

"It was." She took a deep breath. The panic, the fear, the loss had never fully gone away. "The worst part was nobody knew what had happened to her. At least if there'd been a body," her voice cracked and she swallowed. "I had no closure. I still don't know what happened to her."

Reid had stopped cooking and was watching her closely. "Did you try to find out?"

"There's a reason I'm an investigative journalist."

He gave a knowing grin. "I thought as much. What did you find?"

"Nothing much. I raided my father's files, but it wasn't his case. Too personal. It was handled by Detective Reynolds."

"Captain Reynolds?" asked Reid.

"Yeah, do you know him?"

"He's in charge of my division. He's my boss's boss."

"He was my father's partner for a long time. When my mother disappeared, he headed up the case. My father wouldn't let anyone else work on it."

"I guess I can understand that. He'd trust his partner more than any other cop."

She gave a tiny nod. "He still checks in on me from time to time. He was very sympathetic after I had my accident." She glanced down at her knee.

Reid picked up the spaghetti and lowered it into the boiling water. Steam curled up towards the ceiling.

"That hasn't stopped you from searching for the truth, though," he said softly.

Were they still talking about her mother?

"No, and I haven't given up." She studied his face, so strong and chiseled. A handsome face. It could be hard at times, but now it was relaxed and unguarded. She took a deep breath. "Will you help me?"

31

Reid stared back at her through a plume of steam. "You want me to help you find out what happened to your mother?"

"Why not? You have access to the files. You can look into the police investigation."

"It was a long time ago, Kenzie."

"You have an archive, don't you?"

They did, but he'd need a good reason to dig around in there. Her eyes pleaded with him.

"I'll see what I can do," he said. "But after we tie up these two cases."

She smiled, her dimples flashing. In that moment, he thought how pretty she was, despite her disheveled state. Her blond hair was curling around her face but matted at the back where she'd been hit; her blue eyes were wide and hopeful, and the fine lines she'd acquired from the constant headache gave her a fragility she otherwise wouldn't have had. A vulnerability he found appealing.

"Thank you," she breathed, then she frowned. "Two cases?"

"Yeah, I don't believe they're related. Do you?" She opened her mouth to reply, but before she could, he continued. "If Bella was responsible for dumping Natalia's body, then she's implicit in her murder. And if that's the case, there's no way she's working with a serial killer."

"I agree, it's a ridiculous notion. It's just the school thing—"

"Didn't pan out," he interrupted. "I cross-checked every name on that list."

"Coincidence, then?"

"Must be. It's rare, but it does happen."

Kenzie exhaled. "Well, now we've got a hypothesis, let's try to make sense of it. What was Bella doing on that road? Does it lead anywhere else besides to the Glades?"

"No. The only place she could have been going was the swamp. It tallies with where Natalia's body was found. She'd been moved by gators or the current, but the drop-off point must have been along Highway Forty-One somewhere."

"Have you searched her car?" Kenzie asked.

"We're waiting on a warrant. The judge wasn't forthcoming. Pérez had to argue that the fact her vehicle was caught on camera near the dump site should be enough."

"That and she had two public altercations with the victim where she accused Natalia of stealing her boyfriend."

"As soon as it comes through, we'll get it analyzed."

"What about her apartment?" Kenzie asked.

He scoffed. "That's stretching it."

Kenzie rolled her eyeballs. "What if we go to her house and snoop around?"

"I hope you're not suggesting we break in?"

"No, of course not. You could question her. I could make an excuse and go to the bathroom, poke around. You know how it goes."

He couldn't resist a chuckle. He could see her doing that. "After what she went through at the station, I don't think she'll be too receptive to more questioning."

Kenzie sighed. "You're probably right."

"And anyway, if it's not a sanctioned forensic search, nothing we find is admissible."

She snorted. "Ridiculous."

"Those are the rules." He didn't much like 'em either.

"Didn't stop them ripping our house to shreds when they thought my father had something to do with my mother's disappearance."

Reid focused on stirring the sauce. The pasta was bubbling away like a cauldron. "That's different. He was her spouse. In most homicide cases, the spouse is the prime suspect."

"Not in this case," she said. "No body. No homicide."

Reid had to admit, he was intrigued. When he had more time, he'd retrieve the old case files from the archives and look through them. Perhaps there was something he could do to help Kenzie figure out what had happened to her mother. Or at least find some peace with it.

Reid finished cooking and strained the pasta. Then he put it in two bowls and spooned the sauce over it. "Voila!"

"Impressive. I think I've got some cheese." Kenzie opened the fridge.

They ate their dinner at the dining room table. He was still nursing the same beer, while she'd poured herself a glass of water.

"I was thinking." She twirled spaghetti around her fork. "If Bella and her accomplice did attack Natalia in that hotel room. They would have taken her body out via the beach. Right?"

Reid looked up. "Right. There's no other way without being seen."

"Then her car *must* have been close by. Where would you park if you were carrying a body?"

"I don't know. Close. A body is heavy. Ocean Drive is pedestrian only. The Sand Club has valet, but we checked that out. The only other possibility is Fifteenth Street or one of the parking garages, but again, they'd all have security cameras."

"Fifteenth," she murmured, putting the spaghetti in her mouth. "Damn, this is good."

He grinned. "It's my signature dish."

"Mm." He was glad to see her appetite had returned. She was going to be okay.

"They'd have had to carry the body a long way down the beach to get anywhere else," he said. "Very conspicuous."

"Unless she was still alive," Kenzie murmured.

He paused. "You mean if they'd led her out at gunpoint. In the dark, nobody would know she had a weapon on her. You might have a point there."

"They could have walked along the beach to the waiting car." Kenzie warmed to her idea. "Then strangled her."

Reid picked up her train of thought. "They must have killed her before they drove out to the swamp. There wasn't a third person in the car."

Kenzie shivered. "She could have been lying on the back seat or in the trunk by that stage."

It was possible. It would explain how he hadn't seen Bella's car on any of the security cameras in the area. And how they'd gotten her down to the beach without anyone noticing.

"It's even more imperative we search her vehicle," he muttered.

"Going back to the Strangler, there's something that struck me about how he'd scouted all his victims," Kenzie mused.

"What's that?"

"They were all at the north end of the strip. All within close proximity to the outdoor parking garage behind the Royal Palm hotel."

He put his fork down. "I'm not sure what you're getting at?"

"I'm not either, to be honest, but hear me out. The other day, I checked out all the places the girls had been to on the nights they disappeared. The Ocean Club, Go Social!, and Maxine's. They're all within a short distance of each other. I parked in the 15th Street parking lot. It was the nearest place—the only place, in fact, in that area."

He put his fork down. "Are you saying that the killer may have parked there too?"

Her eyes lit up. "It's a possibility, isn't it? He would have needed transport. There's nowhere to park on Ocean Drive, and if he's anything like me, he'd have used the 15th Street parking lot. It's outdoor, it's dark. Sure, there'll be cameras somewhere, but if his victims went willingly."

"It wouldn't have looked out of place," finished Reid. "Just a couple going home together."

"Exactly."

He took a long stare at her. "I think you might be onto something, Kenzie."

"You do?"

"I do. And first thing tomorrow, I'm going to pull up that security footage. If you're right, we may have caught our serial killer on film."

32

"I know him." Reid faced Pérez across the desk. "Let me interview him."

"The Strangler is Jonny's case," his boss pointed out.

"Snake is not connected to the Strangler," Reid argued. "I'm interviewing him about his wife's murder. That's my case. You put me on it, remember?"

Pérez ran a hand through his hair. "How do you know he isn't the Strangler?"

Reid gave him a look. "Come on. Seriously? With Bella Montague? I don't think so. The Swamp Strangler is a serial offender. He works alone. He rapes and strangles his victims. Bella isn't part of that. This is an isolated case."

Pérez didn't immediately reply.

"This is about Natalia Cruz," Reid insisted. "And no one else."

A sigh. Then Pérez nodded. "Okay. He's yours."

"Thanks."

Reid shot out of the office and into the interrogation room. Snake was slumped in the chair, his skinny legs out in front of him, his one arm draped over the side and his head back. He looked up as Reid entered.

"Jesus, Reid. What's this about, man? Why am I here?"

Reid took a seat and put a manilla folder on the table in front of him. Snake's eyes dropped to it.

"I'll explain in a minute," he said. "Do you want something to drink? Water? Coffee?"

"Nah, I hate police interviews. Tell me what's going on and get me out of here."

"Okay." Reid leaned back, matching Snake's casual style. "But before we start, I must tell you that this interview is being recorded. You're here to answer some questions, but you're not under arrest. You're free to leave at any time."

"I am? That's not what the dude who picked me up said."

"We'd appreciate your cooperation," Reid added. "It won't take long."

Snake's eyes narrowed. "This is about Natalia's murder, isn't it? You've found something."

"We have, and we'd like to run it by you."

Snake pursed his lips, pleased he'd figured out what this was all about. "Sure, anything to help catch her killer."

Reid nodded. He opened the file and took out a photograph, placing it on the table in front of Snake.

He watched as the disc-jockey's eyes flickered over it, but he didn't respond.

"Do you know who that is?" Reid pointed to the driver.

"It looks like Bella, but I could be wrong."

"It is Miss Montague, yes. This photograph was taken at two in the morning, the night Natalia went missing."

Snake frowned. "You're shitting me."

Reid shook his head. "After your launch party at The Sand Club."

"But she was wasted. Her date took her home. I saw them leave."

"That's what we thought," Reid said. "But then she got in her car and drove to the Glades. This image was captured on the traffic cam on Highway Forty-One."

Snake was staring at the photograph as if seeing Bella for the first time. "What was she doing there?"

"That's what I wanted to ask you," Reid said.

He glanced up. "Me? How would I know?"

"There's a man sitting next to her in the passenger seat," Reid pointed out. "Is that you?"

Snake's eyes narrowed to slits. "No, of course it's not me. I was at the hotel looking for Natalia at that time."

"Were you?"

"Yes, I was." He folded his arms across his chest. "I don't like where this is going, Detective. Are you insinuating I had something to do with Natalia's death?"

"Did you?"

"No." His hands curled into fists. "She was my wife and I loved her."

Reid kept a straight face. "In lieu of any children, you also inherited her vast fortune, approximately three million dollars."

He stood up so fast his chair flew back onto the floor. "I don't need to take any more of this shit."

"If you had nothing to do with it, you have nothing to worry about," rationalized Reid. "But storming out of here just makes you look guilty."

Snake glared at him, then picked up his chair and sat down again.

Reid nodded to the photo. "Do you have any idea who this man could be?"

Snake shook his head. "I don't recognize him. It's hard to see, though. It could be anyone."

That was the problem. The mysterious figure was in shadow.

"No one springs to mind?" Reid asked.

"No. She was seeing a firefighter, but that doesn't look like him."

At least they agreed on something.

"Can anyone vouch for you at the hotel at 2:00 am?" Reid studied him. He shifted in his chair.

"I don't know. Maybe. We searched the room and the hotel after the party but couldn't find her. I called her phone throughout the night if that helps. I also called the cops, but they told me to wait till morning."

He knew about the 911 call and they'd already checked his phone's GPS. He, or rather it, had been at the hotel all night. He'd asked Ryan to check Snake's phone records. It wasn't an alibi, but it would help to corroborate his story.

"What time did your friends leave?"

"Some time around then," he said with a sigh. "It was getting late, so we called off the search. It was clear she wasn't there."

"Is that when you discovered her clothes were missing?"

"Yeah. I told you this already when you and Kenzie questioned me. After I got back to the room, I checked the closet for her clothes. Then I noticed her suitcase and a couple of items were missing."

Shit.

Now Pérez was going to ask who Kenzie was. And he'd have to come up with a viable answer. One that didn't get his ass kicked off this case.

"Why did you call the police if you knew her stuff was missing? Didn't you assume she'd left on her own account?"

"No, like I said, we were in love. She'd never walk out on me."

"How do you account for the missing clothes and luggage?"

"Someone obviously made it look like she'd left me, but I knew she hadn't. That's why I called the cops, but no one would listen to me. You all assumed she'd run away." He wagged his finger. "I knew different."

Reid knew his next question was going to get a reaction, but he was going to ask it anyway. "Snake, were you having an affair with Bella Montague? Maybe that's why Natalia left? She found out the night of the party?"

The chair went flying again as Snake leaped to his feet. "What the—? You don't know what the hell you're talking about. An affair with Bella? That bitch almost destroyed our relationship with her spiteful accusations."

"As she sees it, her best friend stole the love of her life," Reid explained, also getting to his feet. He was taller than Snake by an inch, and he had more bulk and cast a bigger shadow. "You."

"I can't help the way it turned out. I met Natalia and fell for her. Hard. When you know, you know, Detective. Haven't you ever felt that way about anyone?"

Reid didn't reply.

Had he felt that way about Bianca? He wasn't sure. They'd had a connection, he knew that much. They couldn't keep their hands off each other, but they never dated. They never had a relationship. He would have liked to, but their jobs and her undercover work prevented it.

Kenzie's face flew into his mind, but he pushed it away. Theirs was a working relationship. Nothing more.

"If you're going to accuse me, then I want a lawyer." Snake put his hands on his snaky hips and did a good impression of a model pout.

Reid sighed. "No, we're not accusing you. Like I said, you're free to go at any time."

"Right then, I'm outa here."

Reid held up his hands. What could he say? He had nothing on Snake. The picture wasn't conclusive evidence. His phone signal had been at the hotel all evening, and there was no proof he had been sleeping with Bella. Kenzie's gut feeling wasn't enough.

"Thanks for your time," he muttered, as Snake stalked past and into the squad room. The officer who'd been standing at the door saw him out.

"I feel like we're going round in circles," Reid told Pérez when he walked out of the interrogation room. "And getting no closer to the truth."

"He's shady as hell." Pérez's gaze followed the musician to the elevator.

"But is he a killer?" murmured Reid.

"That,"—Pérez thumped Reid on the shoulder—"is what you're being paid to find out."

33

"Kenzie, get in here!" bellowed Keith the next day.

She'd just gotten back to work, not wanting to spend any more time recuperating. Her headache had gone and she felt fine, so why not get back to it?

"What do you call this?" He pointed to the article she'd filed, now up on his screen.

"An exclusive." She held her head high. "Nobody else has this information. They all think Natalia Cruz was killed by the Swamp Strangler."

"BEST FRIEND QUESTIONED IN NATALIA'S MURDER?" he read out.

"Yeah, why not? Bella Montague was questioned. So was DJ Snake, but he's a source on this, so I didn't think it would be fair to land him in it."

"But you're happy to drag her name through the mud?"

"I can't help that a camera caught her heading out to the dump site."

His eyebrows shot up. "You're kidding?"

She nodded to his computer screen. "Hence the exclusive. I don't make this stuff up, you know."

"Have you double-sourced?"

"Even better. I saw the camera shot with my own eyes. It's her. Two o'clock in the morning on Highway Forty-One. The only road that goes to the swamp."

Keith whistled under his breath.

"She's looking good for it. They just have to find a way to prove it."

His newsman's nose was twitching. "Okay, Kenzie. Fair enough. This is good work. I just hope it doesn't backfire on us."

"What do you mean?"

"I've just got a letter from DJ Snake's attorney threatening to sue if you print anything about his being a suspect in his wife's murder."

Her eyes widened. "Can he do that?"

"He's taken out an injunction. Unless he's proved to be involved, he doesn't want us to print anything that might implicate him in her murder. He states it will be seen as an attempt to damage his image and negatively impact his career."

"I guess he has a point. I wasn't going to write anything about him anyway." She considered him a friend—sort of. They hung out together. He invited her to his parties. Although, that was likely to stop now.

"What made him write that letter?" She fingered the bump on the back of her head and frowned. "He should know me by now."

"I'd guess it was your friend, Detective Garrett."

"Oh, great. So I'm guilty by association. Snake is only famous because of me. It was my article that landed him his first record deal."

"Perhaps you should remind him of that." Keith leaned back in his chair. "On second thoughts, just stay away from the guy. We can't afford another lawsuit, Kenzie. You know that."

She held up her hands in a gesture of defeat. "I know. I'm not causing waves, I promise. This had nothing to do with me."

"I'll run with the Bella Montague piece because that's big news.

Let's just hope she doesn't have a lawyer waiting to jump down our throats too."

"She doesn't have the money," Kenzie pointed out. "She's not wealthy like Natalia, or successful like Snake. In fact, I think she may have grown up in foster care."

Now where had she heard that? She couldn't quite remember. Perhaps she should look into Bella's background in more detail now that she was a suspect. It would make for a good follow up piece, should Bella ever be charged. She mentioned this to Keith.

"Tread easy," he cautioned, glancing at her head. "You've already had one close call."

"See, I knew you cared." She grinned at him and went back to her desk.

Bella made for interesting reading. She'd been given up for adoption at birth and there was no record of her biological parents. Probably a young, single mother, unable to cope. A prostitute, maybe, or a crack addict.

She'd gone to a couple, the Henderson's. Kenzie frowned. Not Montague. Then how had she gotten her surname?

She dug a little deeper. Phil and Marge Henderson lived in Apalachicola, a small fishing village near Tampa. It was so small Kenzie could hardly find it on Google Maps.

They were poor by the looks of things. Phil was a shrimper. Marge was a receptionist at the local medical center.

It was here that she met Douglas Montague, a visiting salesman from Miami. When Bella was 10, Marge ran off with Douglas, taking her adopted daughter with her. There were no records of Marge marrying Douglas, although Bella took her stepfather's name.

Kenzie called Radcliffe High School and said she was writing a piece about Natalia Cruz. She steered the conversation towards Natalia's best friend, Bella. To her surprise, the principal was more than happy to oblige. Bella was an excellent student. So bright, so hard working. She could have done anything she wanted and been successful at it.

"Really?" Kenzie was surprised. While Bella didn't come across as dumb, she hadn't struck Kenzie as particularly smart. Or perhaps she was very good at hiding it.

Natalia, on the other hand. "A beautiful, sweet, but somewhat vacant girl," the principal had said. "Easily led astray. But don't quote me on that. I don't want to talk ill of the dead."

Easily manipulated by a smarter friend? thought Kenzie.

By five o'clock, she was exhausted. What she needed was to take another painkiller and lie down. A full day at the office had been too much for her.

She texted Reid. "Leaving work now."

He replied a short while later. "Want me to stay at yours tonight?"

She hesitated. It had been nice having him there last night. More than nice. She'd slept well, comfortable knowing she had this great hulking man downstairs in case anyone tried to break in.

They were no closer to finding out who'd attacked her. He might still be out there, waiting for a second chance. She shivered as a chill flowed through her.

"Yes, if you don't mind?" she replied.

He sent a thumbs up emoji in reply.

She smiled, then frowned.

Crap, she'd better stock up the fridge. He'd cooked last night, but she couldn't expect him to do that again. It was her turn tonight.

"How'd the article go?" Reid asked when he arrived. She caught a whiff of his aftershave. He'd gone home and showered and changed before driving out to Bay Harbor Island.

"Good. Keith was excited about the exclusive." She'd run it by

Reid before she'd sent it to her boss. A deal was a deal. He was realistic enough to know that Bella's questioning couldn't be kept secret for long. If Kenzie didn't report on it, someone else would.

"Let's hope it shakes her up," he said, dourly.

"You suspect her, don't you?" Kenzie said, as they moved into the kitchen. She'd opened a bottle of wine. "Want a glass?"

"A small one, thanks."

As she set about pouring, he leaned against the kitchen bar counter and looked at her. "I think she's guilty. I can't explain why. I just do."

"How did Snake appear in his interview?" she asked. "I know you pissed him off."

He grinned. "How'd you know that?"

"His attorney sent a letter to the paper threatening legal action if we published anything that might harm his image."

"He's worried." Reid accepted the glass with a nod.

"He has reason to be," Kenzie mused. "If it got out he'd been questioned, it could affect his career. His record label already wants to drop him. I don't want to be responsible for that, especially if he's not guilty."

"And he's your friend," Reid added.

They took their drinks to the living room. Kenzie sank onto the sofa and rested her head back.

"How are you feeling?" Reid asked.

"I'm just tired. I think I'll go to bed early." She turned to face him. "What happened with the parking garage footage? Did you look into it?"

"I didn't have time," he admitted. "But I gave Ryan the task. She was pouring over the footage all day."

"Does she know what to look for?" asked Kenzie, worried. She trusted Reid to do a thorough job, but she didn't know Ryan.

"She's smart. If there's something to find, she'll find it."

"Okay, good." Then she remembered. "Oh, I did some digging in

Bella Montague's history today. Did you know she got straight A's at school?"

He arched an eyebrow. "Really?"

"Yeah, star pupil apparently."

"She hides it well," he said.

Kenzie laughed. "That's what I thought. A slight anomaly there. We gotta be careful not to underestimate her."

"She sure got the better of us during her interrogation," Reid said. "I couldn't find any reference to that guy Julian at the Gator Inn. The security camera didn't pick up anyone unaccounted for either. She made the whole thing up."

"An A-student," murmured Kenzie.

They chatted more about the case, watched a bit of television, then Kenzie suggested heating up a pizza. "I bought the ingredients to make you my signature dish, but to be honest I'm not sure I'm up for it tonight."

"Pizza is fine. You need to rest." His eyes crinkled.

"Okay." She held his gaze. It was warm, knowing. A flicker of anticipation shot down her spine—or maybe that was just the painkillers kicking in.

"I'll do it." Reid got up and went to the kitchen.

Kenzie lay back and closed her eyes. Had she imagined that, or did they just have a moment?

Once again, he'd come to her rescue. If she wasn't careful, she'd get used to having him around. And that would raise a bunch of questions she wasn't willing to answer just yet.

34

Kenzie woke up on the couch. She must have fallen asleep during the movie they'd been watching. She glanced down to find Reid had covered her with a blanket from her bed. How sweet.

Speaking of, where was he? Then she heard music from the kitchen and Reid's deep voice singing out of tune.

Chuckling to herself, she got up. Her head was still tender but only if she slept on a certain spot. "You should have woken me."

He turned and grinned. "I thought you could do with the extra sleep. Do you like pancakes?"

Her eyes widened. "Who doesn't like pancakes?"

"Great, 'cos I made a bunch of them. Take a seat."

She climbed onto the stool at the breakfast bar and watched as he expertly scooped the pancakes off the pan and onto a plate.

"Another signature recipe?" she asked.

"This one is only for very special occasions," he said.

"What's the occasion?"

"Thanks to your parking garage theory, Detective Ryan was able to identify a man hanging out there, watching single women arrive."

She gasped. "No way! Do you know who he is?"

"We're still trying to identify him, but we have his plates. You were right, he did park there—on all three nights the victims went missing. Now that's a coincidence that I'm not willing to ignore."

"But not the night Natalia was taken?"

He shook his head. "No ma'am. He didn't do it, just as we thought."

Kenzie fist bumped the air. "Yes! I knew it."

"This guy hung around the parking garage waiting for women to arrive. He'd see if they were single, stalk them to the bar or club, then pick them up and walk with them back to the parking lot."

"But how did he get them into his car?" she asked.

"That, we don't know. It was dark when they got back, no lights on the side he parked on. From what Ryan could see, the women didn't look under duress, just a little drunk."

"Maybe he drugged them?"

"That's what I'm thinking. There were no drugs in their system when they were found, but he could have kept them somewhere until it wore off."

She lowered her voice. "When he was raping them."

"Exactly."

She exhaled as she poured maple syrup all over the stack of pancakes Reid had layered on her plate. "What kind of man does that?"

"A demented one, that's for sure."

"He must be pretty twisted." She began cutting into the pile. "How soon after they disappeared were their bodies found?"

Reid didn't need to think about it. "Sarah was found four days after she went missing. Miranda, three weeks. Mimi was also four days."

"He takes his time with them," she whispered, putting down her knife and fork. Suddenly, she'd lost her appetite.

"So it seems, but let's not focus on that. We've got a lead. A real lead. Hopefully this will enable us to identify the Strangler and finally put the bastard behind bars."

"I'll eat to that." She picked up her utensils again.

Reid sat down with a plate piled equally high. "I haven't made these in ages."

"You're pretty good at it," she mumbled, her mouth full.

He laughed. "I messed up the first few, but by the third I had it down pat."

"You know, if you ever decide to leave the force, you could become a chef."

"Nah. Toiling in a hot, sweaty kitchen isn't for me. I much prefer catching bad guys."

So did she, but now she was relegated to writing about them. "Hey, when you catch him, I get the exclusive, remember?"

He hesitated. "Yeah, but this investigation is at a critical stage. Writing anything now would warn him off and we can't have that."

"Don't worry. I've learned my lesson. I'll wait for your go-ahead, but as soon as you have him in cuffs, you let me know."

"Deal."

Reid left Kenzie's right after breakfast and headed to the station. He'd showered and changed last night, so he didn't need to go home first.

"You're in a good mood," said Chris, as Reid walked in. He realized he'd been humming to himself. He hadn't done that in years.

"What's happening?" Reid asked Jonny, after he'd thrown his bag and jacket down on his chair. "Have you got an ID on the perp yet?"

"We've got an address for the vehicle," Jonny said. "We're mobilizing now to pick him up. Want to come along?"

"Hell yeah." He didn't need to think twice. It had been so long since he'd seen any action, he'd almost forgotten what it felt like.

Now, as he geared up with the task force, he felt a familiar buzz as the adrenaline pumped through his system.

"Let's head out," Jonny yelled.

It was weird being part of the task force with Jonny in the lead. A year and a half ago, it was the other way round. Still, it was Reid's choice to leave, and he was glad for his colleague. This was a big career move for him. It could result in a promotion to Sergeant.

Ryan was with them, too. "This is my first real bust," she admitted as they sped away in the police van.

"You'll be fine," Reid told her. "Tactical is going in first, but we'll be right behind them."

Pérez had pulled out all the stops for this one. "The Swamp Strangler has killed three women we know about," he told the detectives before they left. "He'll be armed and dangerous. We can't afford to screw it up."

They got to the vehicle's registered address, a two-story house with a rose-trellis ambling up the wall. It was situated on a wide, leafy avenue in one of Miami's outer suburbs. It was so normal, it was weird, worrying almost.

"He lives here?" asked Ryan, echoing Reid's thoughts.

"Ready?" called Jonny. They all nodded.

"Go!"

The tactical team advanced on the property. The door was painted a welcoming light blue. It matched the shutters over the windows.

The next moment, it was in tatters, hanging off the latch.

Chaos ensued as the armed officers entered. They identified themselves, then searched the house from bottom to top.

"Here," yelled an officer from the main upstairs bedroom.

Jonny glanced at Reid. Perhaps it was habit, perhaps he needed some reinforcement. Reid nodded. "After you, buddy."

They went inside, weapons drawn. First Jonny, then Reid, with Ryan bringing up the rear. They found a man in bed with a young Latina girl. She couldn't have been more than 18.

"Get up!" barked Jonny. The guy was in his mid-thirties. Both sat up, their hands behind their heads. The tactical team trained their weapons on them, but considering they were both butt naked, Reid didn't think they were armed.

"W–What's going on?" stammered the man. He was average height, a little paunchy, with dirty blond hair. Without clothes, he wasn't very impressive.

"You're under arrest on suspicion of the murders of Sarah Randall, Miranda Hoberman, and Mimi Silverton," said Jonny, like he'd been practicing it for some time.

"Who?"

The man looked genuinely confused.

Something wasn't right.

"You know, the three women you raped and strangled," Jonny iterated.

The man's eyes got bigger. "I didn't kill no one."

"Baby? What's going on?" the girl whimpered.

"I got no idea."

Reid, who'd searched through the pile of clothes discarded around the room pulled out a wallet. "Stuart Halston," he read. "That you?"

"Yeah, that's me."

"And that's your Chevrolet Malibu outside?"

"Yeah, what of it?"

Reid looked at Jonny who said, "Put on some clothes. You're coming with us."

"I want a lawyer," the man cried as they cuffed him.

His girlfriend was crying. "You too," said Ryan, throwing her some clothes.

"You'll get one," Jonny replied, as they lead them downstairs accompanied by the tactical team.

"I'm going to search the house." Reid pulled out a pair of forensic gloves. "Ryan, I could use a hand."

She nodded.

"I'll get these two back to the station," said Jonny.

"You don't think it's him, do you?" Ryan said, after they'd left.

He was impressed by how intuitive she was.

"I don't know. He doesn't strike me as a charmer who picks up single girls in bars. Still, that's his car outside." He shrugged. "Why don't you take the upstairs and I'll take down here. Look for any sign of the victims. Remember, he kept them locked up for days before he killed them."

Her eyes clouded over. "Yes, sir."

Reid started in the living room and moved through to the kitchen. The house wasn't a complete mess, but it wasn't in great shape either. He found a couple of wrappers down the back of the sofa, crumbs on the carpet, and two breakfast bowls in the sink. The bathroom was clear. There were no additional rooms downstairs, no basement, and no shed in the garden. Those girls hadn't been kept here.

Ryan came downstairs. "Nothing." She shook her head.

"Let's check the garage." It was the only place left.

They walked from the kitchen into the attached garage holding an assortment of garden equipment and tools. Halston obviously parked his car outside in the drive. Reid took a good look around. He checked the tools for blood stains, searched the cupboards for plastic, duct tape, or anything else the killer would have needed to subdue his victims.

"There's no indication the girls were ever here," Ryan said, after they'd checked every shelf and every cabinet.

"Except for the vehicle," Ryan pointed out.

The CSI team was already loading the Chevrolet Malibu onto a flatbed trailer. It would be taken to the laboratory and analyzed for hair and skin cells from the dead women.

Halston stared at it as if it was an unexploded bomb as he was ushered past into the waiting police vehicle. "I swear to God," he pleaded, his voice breaking. "I didn't kill anyone. I don't even know who those girls are."

His lover was sobbing now. She was being put into a separate police car by a female police officer.

Reid watched as they drove away. Was this guy the Swamp Strangler? All the evidence said he was, but his gut was telling him no.

35

"Who's Kenzie?" Pérez asked once Reid had gotten back to the station.

He sighed. He'd known this was coming.

"She's a journalist. She interviewed me after I found Natalia Cruz's body in the Glades."

"Jesus, you took her with you to question a suspect?" Pérez's face turned a mottled red.

"She was my in." His voice was tight. "I hadn't agreed to take the case at that stage and she knew DJ Snake. Helped make him famous. That's how I got inside the Sand Club and access to video footage."

Pérez studied him from under his bushy eyebrows. "You know we can't risk a leak on this."

"She won't leak it," he said. "I've promised her an exclusive once we catch the guy."

"You know journalists," he grunted. "Can't trust 'em."

Reid knew he was thinking back to the sting operation that had gone so terribly wrong. What would he say if he knew it was the same reporter?

"It's under control," he said.

Commotion came from the interrogation room. "Let's make sure we have the right freakin' guy in custody before you tell her anything. This one's already lawyered up and telling anyone who'll listen that he didn't do it. I have to say, he doesn't look much like a serial killer."

"They never do," muttered Reid, but the lieutenant was right. Halston didn't match the description the first two victims' friends had given. They'd said tall and dark. This guy was average and a messy blond. He might pass for dark in a club, though. Maybe.

Jonny was preparing for the interview.

"If you push him, he'll probably break," Reid said before Jonny went in. The senior detective nodded. "Yeah, that was my plan."

"Garrett, you take the girlfriend," Pérez called. "See if she knows anything about her lover's extracurricular activities."

"Okay with you?" Reid asked.

Jonny gave a stiff nod. He was nervous, Reid could tell. This was a big case, certainly the biggest he'd ever led. "Yeah, go for it. I might be tied up with him for a while. Let me know if you find out anything useful."

"Sure thing." He patted Jonny on the back. "You got this."

Reid went into interrogation room two. The girlfriend, now sweating but clutching herself like she was freezing cold, looked up. "What am I doing here?"

"We're going to have a little talk." Reid sat down. "Do you want some water?"

She nodded.

He glanced to the officer at the door who disappeared to fetch it. Reid fiddled with the folder until the officer returned and handed the woman a bottle of mineral water. She opened it eagerly and drank.

"Right, let's start with your name."

"Monica."

"Do you have a second name, Monica?"

"Cabello."

"And how do you know Stuart Halston?"

Her gaze darted all over the room like she was afraid to look at any one thing for too long. "I met Stu at the local hardware store. I work there, at the register."

"You been together long?"

"A couple of weeks."

"How old are you?"

"What's that got to do with anything? I'm legal, if that's what you mean." She pushed out her chest as if to make a point, but her eyes kept wandering. Sweat glistened on her forehead. Whatever she'd been on was wearing off.

He really shouldn't be interviewing her under the influence of drugs, but she was more vulnerable this way. Hyped up, nervous. And she wasn't so far gone that she didn't know what she was talking about. He guessed a few lines of coke, nothing heavier.

"How often do you see each other?" Reid asked.

"I don't see how that's—"

"Every day? Every night? Once a week?" he asked, cutting her off.

"A couple times a week," she said. "It's pretty casual. What's with all the questions? What did Stu do?"

"What makes you think he did something?" Reid asked.

"Because of what you said back at the house. That he was being arrested on suspicion of strangling those girls."

Reid studied her. She looked very frightened.

"Do you think he's capable of abducting and strangling three women?" he asked.

She shook her head. "Stu? No way. He's a softie. That's what I like about him. He's kinda shy, you know. It took him ages to pluck up the courage to talk to me in the store. Not like his brother."

"His brother?" Reid's head jerked up. "Stu has a brother?"

"Yeah, Pete. He also comes into the store from time to time."

"Did he ever talk to you?" asked Reid.

"Nah, didn't even try. I was disappointed at first 'cos he's really good looking, but he's not kind like Stu."

"What does Pete look like?" He opened the folder.

"Handsome, like I said."

"Tall, short? Dark, blond?"

"Tall and dark. Why are you asking about Pete now?" Her wandering eyes narrowed. "Do you think he murdered those girls?"

"I don't know. Would he be capable of something like that?"

She thought about this for a moment. "Maybe. There's something not quite right about him, you know. He's smooth, that's for sure, but I never felt like he really looked at me. Not like Stu does."

"What do you mean?"

"He kinda looks straight through me. It's weird. I thought it was just because I'm not his type. He doesn't go for Latina girls."

"Who does he go for?" Reid's voice was low.

"Pretty white girls. Cheerleader types. The girls that dated the star quarterback in high school." She rolled her eyes. "*Those* types of girls."

Bingo. She'd just described every one of the Strangler's victims.

Reid took a grainy photograph out of the folder. It was a still taken from the video footage in the parking garage. As he slid it across the table to her, he held his breath. "Is this him?"

She looked down, squinted, bent in closer, then nodded. "Yeah, that's Pete."

36

They had him!

Reid exhaled slowly. The tall, dark, handsome brother would have no problem flirting with girls in a bar and walking them back to their cars, then convincing them he'd give them a ride home himself. He'd spike their drinks. Help them into his car, then take them back to his lair where they were at his mercy.

"Did Pete ever borrow Stu's car?"

"I don't know. He could have, I guess. You'll have to ask Stu."

But Reid was already out of his seat.

"Watch her," he barked to the officer at the door, then ran out of the room.

He knocked on the door of interrogation room one. The conversation stopped, and Jonny opened it. "What's up?"

"Ask him about his brother," hissed Reid. "And whether his brother ever borrowed his car."

"His brother?" Jonny frowned. "Didn't even know he had one."

"The girlfriend identified the brother from the garage pictures," he whispered.

"Holy shit." Jonny's eyes were huge.

"Yeah."

"Okay, I'll see if I can get an address." Jonny slapped him on the shoulder and disappeared back into the room.

Things moved fast after that. They assembled a tactical team, the task force geared up, and they headed out to Pete Halston's house. He lived in the same neighborhood as his brother. Stu, being the eldest, had inherited the family home, but Pete, who was more successful, had bought his own and renovated it. According to Stu, it had been a real tumbledown place, but Pete had done a fantastic job restoring it.

Reid couldn't wait to see.

He was betting there'd be a secret room or hidden basement where he kept the girls. His own personal torture chamber.

The tactical team screeched to a halt outside the property and within a minute had smashed the door down with a battering ram and entered.

Reid waited outside with the rest of the task force for the all-clear. Tactical were in the house a full five minutes before they heard. "Clear."

"There's no one here," the commander said, as they approached the door.

"Set up a perimeter around the house," Reid instructed. He had a strong feeling about this one. The Strangler was here somewhere, and he was going to make a run for it as soon as the coast was clear.

The commander didn't question the order. "Yes, sir."

Jonny seemed content to let Reid take over. "You think he's still here?" Jonny asked.

"He renovated this place himself," Reid said. "You can bet he knows every nook and cranny. Let's do a full search, but stay alert. He could be anywhere, and he'll be armed."

Jonny relayed the message to the rest of the team. Weapons drawn, they went inside. The tactical commander joined them along with two other members of the team, while the rest surrounded the property from the outside.

"Look for hidden compartments, trap doors, fake dry walls, that sort of thing," Reid said.

"Surely he wouldn't be stupid enough to bring them here?" Ryan whispered behind him.

"If he thought he was safe, he might." Most psychopaths were arrogant and overconfident. They didn't feel danger, even though they were aware of it, so they thought they were invincible.

The house was a typical single-story with a red tile roof. There was a patch of lawn out front with a couple of trees and a paved driveway. No car.

They spread out to search. The commander and his two teammates took the bedrooms, while Jonny, Chris, and Jared took the living room and kitchen. Reid stood in the hallway and glanced around.

"What are you looking for?" Ryan asked. She'd stayed with him.

"Where would you put a trap door to a hidden room?" he inquired.

She thought for a moment. "Kitchen, maybe? Or here in the hallway?"

Reid walked up and down, testing the floor. It was terracotta, no way to put in a trap door. He walked through to the kitchen.

"Anything?"

Jonny shook his head. "Nope. You sure about this?"

"No, but let's keep looking." He glanced back toward the hallway. "Hang on a minute."

"What?"

"Does this kitchen look smaller to you on the inside, than it does on the outside?"

Ryan bit her lip. "I don't know. Maybe."

Reid charged outside and surveyed the house from the front. It was symmetrical on both sides, with the door in the middle, but inside, the kitchen was the only room on the right.

"There's a room missing," he hissed. They began knocking against walls and opening cupboards until Reid grunted. "I think I've found it."

At the back of a store cupboard, behind a stack of boxes, was a trap door.

"Oh my gosh," whispered Ryan. "Do you think he's in there?"

Reid tried the door, it was locked. Bolted from the inside.

"Jonny!" he yelled.

His colleague came running. "What's up?"

"I need your help with this." Together, they managed to kick it in. Ryan was covering them with her gun drawn. Once the dust settled, they peered into the darkness.

"See anything?" whispered Ryan, her voice shaky.

"No. I'm going in." He aimed his handgun into the opening. There was no response from inside, so he carefully stepped through. Then he froze.

"Jesus Christ."

"What?" whispered Jonny, stepping in behind him. There were no windows, but enough light fed in from the kitchen for them to make out the layout of the room.

"Jonny, the light."

Jonny turned around and found a light switch. He pressed it and the room lit up.

"Holy shit," he breathed.

They stared at the hidden room. The floor was bare concrete, as were the walls, and a naked bulb hung from the ceiling. There was nothing in it except for a filthy mattress stained with what he could only surmise was blood and God-only-knew what else. Bolted to the floor at all four corners were chains complete with leg and wrist irons.

He'd never seen anything so disturbing.

"It's a real torture chamber," whispered Ryan, who'd followed them in.

"There's a second room." Reid gestured ahead. "He could be in there."

"Easy," warned Jonny, as they took up positions on either side of the door. Ryan got down on one knee and covered them.

Gingerly, Reid turned the handle and opened the door.

A voice said, "Drop the gun."

37

"What happened next?"

Kenzie sat cross-legged on the sofa, watching Reid as he retold the story of how they'd caught the Swamp Strangler.

"I froze, of course," he said, his dark brown eyes intense. "The guy had a 9 millimeter, and he was pointing it right at me. I put my gun on the floor and kept my hands up. I thought he was going to take a shot at me, but he didn't. He was more concerned with getting away."

Kenzie hung on to every word.

"He forced us back out into the kitchen, then ran back into the second room. "It was a sort of den with a desk and a laptop, and an armchair in the corner."

"Do you think he sat there and listened to them beg for their lives?" Kenzie whispered.

"God only knows. That place was appalling. I've never seen anything like it."

She cringed. "Those poor girls. What they must have endured."

Reid scowled. "Yeah, well, he's in custody now."

"How did you get him?" she asked.

"There was a high window that he'd smashed to get out of. He'd moved the desk beneath it and was climbing out when we barged in. Ryan ran outside and called the tactical team surrounding the property and they nabbed him as he wriggled out."

"Thank goodness." Kenzie exhaled under. "That man needs to be locked up for the rest of his life for what he did."

"He will," Reid promised. "We've got enough evidence in that torture chamber to put him away for multiple life sentences. The CSI guys said there was enough DNA to keep them busy for a month."

"That's awful. He could have had countless victims down there. Not just the three girls we know about."

"Exactly, and if he did, we'll go for the maximum charge for all of them."

"That's good." She nodded, then smiled at him. "And I'm glad you're okay. You could have been shot."

"Were you worried about me?"

She flushed. "We should celebrate. You've caught the Swamp Strangler. That deserves a couple of beers at least."

He laughed, letting her off the hook. "Okay, great idea."

She got two cold ones out of the fridge, and Reid opened them.

"Cheers," he said. "Here's to catching the bad guys."

"Cheers."

They each took a swig.

"So, about that article." A smile played on Kenzie's lips.

"Yes." He drew out the word.

"You said as soon as you caught him, I could have an exclusive."

"I remember."

"This qualifies, right? He's definitely the guy."

"It certainly looks that way," Reid said. "Although, I'd prefer it if you waited until the DNA results came back before you went to print. Just in case there's nothing there."

"How could there be nothing there? You said the place was covered in DNA!"

"I know, but I like being sure."

Kenzie couldn't wait any longer. News of the find at Halston's house was going to come out. Questions would be asked. How long would it take before some other savvy journalist linked it to the Swamp Strangler?

"I'll write it up and you can take a look once I'm done. How's that?"

"I can live with that."

"Can I mention your name?"

"I'd rather you didn't."

She studied him for a long moment. "Okay. I won't if you don't want me to. I'll say it was the Miami PD task force led by Jonny Silva."

Reid nodded. "Much better."

"You don't like people praising you, do you?" She tilted her head.

"It was a team effort."

"Fine. Have it your way."

"How's that bump on your head?" he asked. Kenzie knew he was changing the subject, but she allowed it. He wasn't the type of guy who relished being the hero of the hour, even though he usually was.

"Going down." She touched it. "I feel fine now."

"I'm glad. Any sign of anything suspicious?"

"Not a thing. I'm sure the danger's over now."

"We can't be sure of anything," he said. "Natalia's killer is still out there, and you pissed someone off enough for them to take a swing at you. Until we know who it is, I want you to be careful."

"Yes, sir." She gave him a mock salute.

He snorted. "I'm not joking, Kenzie."

"Are you going to camp out on my couch until we catch whoever did it?" she asked, only half-joking.

He gave her a hard look. "Only if you want me to."

Yes, she did.

Having him here made her feel safe, but it was more than that. She liked having him around. But it wasn't fair to keep him here when he had a house of his own. A cabin he hadn't slept in for two nights now.

"I'll be fine." She didn't meet his eye.

He hesitated. "I'm happy to stay if you're unsure."

"No, honestly. I'm fine. I'll lock all the doors and windows."

He grunted. "Okay, well call me if you feel uneasy. I don't mind coming back."

She fiddled with the label on her beer. "Thanks."

He was about to leave when his phone buzzed. "Excuse me. I'd better take this." He turned his back on her and walked to the window. "Garrett."

She saw the muscles in his neck stiffen, then his shoulders slumped. "Okay, thanks for letting me know."

"What's up?" she asked.

He faced her. "Bella Montague's vehicle was spotless."

"What?"

"No sign of Natalia Cruz's DNA. No hair, no fibers, no nothing."

"How can that be? We know she took her body to the Glades in that car and dumped her there."

"If she did, she was very careful," he said. "Forensics didn't detect a thing. They said the car had been freshly cleaned as well."

"Well, that explains it," Kenzie huffed. "She's been one step ahead of us this whole time."

"Maybe it was Bella who attacked you that night at the beach party," Reid said.

Kenzie frowned. She remembered the whoosh and the feeling of hot air before a thud and the fireworks explosion in her head. But there was something else, something she couldn't quite put her finger on.

"Maybe." She stared into the past, trying to nudge the memory.

"Have you remembered something?" Reid came forward. "Kenzie, what is it?"

"I don't know. I think I may have seen something, but I can't remember. It's just out of reach."

"Your brain had a shock. Hopefully it'll come to you as it heals."

She tried to grasp what it was, but the fragment of memory was gone. "No, it's gone."

"We have to release Bella," he said. "We've got nothing to hold her on."

"If she attacked me, she won't try again now the police are on to her."

"I hope you're right," Reid murmured.

He left soon after that. Kenzie stood in her living room, feeling his absence. Part of her wanted to call him back, but she didn't move until she'd heard his car drive off.

She took a deep breath. There was work to be done.

She spent the rest of the evening writing up the article on the Swamp Strangler's arrest, then she called Keith.

"Kenzie, do you know what time it is?"

"I've got something, Keith. It's big."

She told him what had happened, and he forgave her in a heartbeat. "We'll run with it in tomorrow afternoon's edition," he said.

That would give her enough time to clear it with Reid.

It was around one o'clock in the morning when she went to bed. She turned off all the lights and double-checked the locks.

A bang outside made her jump.

Relax. She glanced out of the window. It was only the neighbor coming home after an evening out.

She was on edge. Writing the article had freaked her out, too. That torture chamber, the way Reid had described it. She shuddered and double-checked the lock on the front door.

Eventually, she went to bed.

She was safe. There was no reason for Bella to silence her, not now that the police had her on camera. Any suspicions Kenzie might have had were redundant.

Still, it took her a while to fall asleep. She wished Reid were downstairs. Perhaps she should call him.

No, she wasn't clingy. She was capable of living by herself, of looking after herself. God knows, she'd been doing it long enough.

She eventually settled down and drifted off to sleep.

Kenzie was walking along the sidewalk, waiting for the Uber. She checked her phone. It was a minute away. She felt a whoosh of hot air and smelled something sweet. Heels clicked on the tarmac. Then the pain. Her head exploded in agony. White light flashed behind her eyelids, and she felt herself falling. Then nothing.

She woke up sweating, her heart pounding.

Yes! She'd remembered what it was she couldn't grasp earlier.

The high heels.

She'd heard the sound of high heels on the sidewalk before the whoosh of hot air as her attacker rushed her. Then the sweet smell. Perfume. Exotic, like magnolia.

Bella's perfume.

38

"Are you sure?" Reid asked the next morning when Kenzie called to tell him what she'd remembered.

"Yes, that's what it was. The sound of a woman's heels on the sidewalk. And perfume. I swear it was her perfume. I remember smelling it on her that first time we interviewed her, and then again at the beach party."

"Okay, well that's not enough to file an assault charge, but at least now we have an idea who it was. I've got her under surveillance, anyway."

"For me?"

"Actually no. I wanted to see if she'd lead us to her accomplice."

"Ah. I see."

"But we'll know if she goes anywhere near you."

"That's a relief."

There was a pause.

"I've got to go," Reid said as Pérez marched out of his office, a thunderous expression on his face. "Something's happened."

"Okay, I just wanted to say thanks for okaying the article," Kenzie said.

"No problem. See you later."

He hung up. They'd reached a compromise on the article. She'd agreed to stick to the facts. They'd arrested a man connected to the murders of the three girls who'd been found in the swamp. She'd described the horrific torture chamber in the secret room and the heroic efforts of the police who'd captured him. A forensic team was collecting evidence and hoped to find DNA from the girls. Natalia Cruz's murder was not thought to be connected.

She'd even gone to the house and taken some photographs of the police cordon around it and the white-clad forensic technicians going in and out with their big silver cases and evidence bags.

It wouldn't be long before Pete Halston's name was connected to the crimes, but they should hear back from the CSI team today. Then they'd know for sure.

"Briefing!" yelled the lieutenant.

The entire department filed in.

"What's going on?" Jonny asked.

Reid shrugged. "No idea."

Pérez stood at the front with Ortega. Whatever it was, it wasn't good.

"David Navarro was shot and killed this morning in a raid on the DEA safe house," said Pérez.

There was a shocked murmur.

Ortega looked mutinous.

"Four armed men with automatic rifles stormed the property and killed Navarro, along with the two DEA agents guarding him," continued Pérez.

"The Kings?" asked Reid.

"Most likely. They had the most reason to want him dead. He ratted out their entire organization."

"We can't rule out Federico Lopez and the Morales cartel," said Ortega. "They were supplying them with product."

"They supply the Warriors too," said Reid. "I doubt they had anything to do with it."

"What would you know?" snarled Ortega. "You've been hibernating for the last year."

"That's enough," barked Pérez. "The DEA are looking into it. Matt Garcia is the obvious choice. They've launched a state-wide manhunt for him. It won't be long before he's in custody."

"Good thing he snitched before you handed him over," said Jonny.

"Won't stand up in court," Ortega growled. "Not without Navarro's testimony."

He was right about that. Whatever they had on Matt Garcia and the Kings, it needed to be backed up by witness testimony. It was a bummer, for sure.

Had Lopez been involved? Navarro was no real threat to them. Sure, they supplied the Kings with product, but they supplied several gangs in the Miami area. That was their business. They'd have protocols in place so that the gang bangers never knew more than they needed to. Navarro had admitted he didn't know where they were based. All he had was an untraceable phone number.

Reid was betting the hit was organized by Garcia. Navarro was his fixer. He set up the deals, arranged the drug deliveries, organized executions. He knew everyone in their organization and he could name names. Taking him out would have been a priority.

"Ortega and his team are working with the DEA to interrogate suspects," Pérez continued.

Great. The dickhead would be out of the way for a while.

"We've issued a reward for information," he told them. "There's a dedicated phone line monitored by the DEA, so if anyone calls the station, transfer it to them."

Nods all around.

"Okay, that's it."

. . .

Reid went outside for a breather. He got a coffee from a nearby stall and sat down on a bench overlooking the water. Then he took out his phone.

If Lopez and the cartel had been involved in the shooting, there would have been some activity at the warehouse.

He pulled up the video footage from last night and set it on double speed. The images flew by, blurring into each other. There was nothing until 6:05 am when a car pulled into the warehouse lot. Reid slowed it to real time.

Torres' Audi.

The operations manager got to work early most days. Reid had been monitoring the feed since he'd put it up. It was always the same routine.

Torres arrived around six, parked outside, and went into the office. The trucks rolled in, the workers arrived, and the roller doors went up.

Equipment was loaded onto the trucks, ticked off on a clipboard by a foreman, and driven away to the dockside where it was used to load and unload containers. This was the legitimate side of the business, and it ran like clockwork.

Today was no different.

There were no unscheduled visits, no surprise meetings, and Torres didn't leave the warehouse until after two.

The Morales cartel were not part of the hit on David Navarro. Of that, Reid was sure.

Reid got back to the squad room just as Jonny was about to interrogate Pete Halston, the Swamp Strangler.

"Garrett, you coming?" called Pérez.

"Yeah." He walked over to the screen where they were watching live. Jonny sat opposite Halston and his attorney, a weedy looking man with a hooked nose and glasses.

Jonny started by stating their names for the record. Halston leaned back in his chair, his hands resting on the table in front of him. Loosely clasped. No sign of nerves.

He was good looking in a dark, austere way, with symmetrical features, a strong jawline, and a full head of hair, but his mouth was pulled back in a smirk rather than a smile and his eyes were hard and lacked depth. Reid could see what Stu's girlfriend, Monica, had meant when she'd said he looked straight through her.

"These are photographs of your hidden room." John slid them over the table to the suspect.

He glanced down, then sniffed.

"Can you explain why there's a mattress there?"

"I sleep down there sometimes," he said with a shrug. "It's cooler than the rest of the house."

"You sleep on this soiled mattress?"

"Sometimes."

"And what are these?" Jonny pointed to the constraints chained to the concrete floor.

"I have particular tastes," he said, almost nonchalantly. "Sometimes I like to play games."

"Sex games?"

"Yes, detective."

"And who do you play these games with?" he asked.

Reid narrowed his gaze. Haston's lips turned up at the corners. The bastard was enjoying this.

"Definitely a psycho," muttered Pérez beside him.

"No doubt about it," agreed another officer.

"Occasionally I spend the night with like-minded women," he said carefully. "Everything we do is consensual."

Jonny lay three more photographs in front of him.

"Was it consensual with these women?"

Halston stared at the images for a long moment, then blinked as if coming out of a trance. "I don't know who these women are."

"Sarah Randall. Miranda Hoberman. Mimi Silverton."

Another blank stare.

"Ring any bells?" asked Jonny, unable to keep the disgust out of his voice.

"Sorry, no."

"These women were all abducted, raped, and strangled in the last four months," he said. Reid could hear the strain in his voice. Don't fall apart now, Jonny.

It was hard conducting an interrogation when confronted with such evil. It tested even the strongest detective. Most of the time, Reid wanted to put a fist through their face, but he knew to restrain himself.

"What's that got to do with me?"

"We think you were responsible." Jonny stared at him across the table.

Reid, Pérez, and the rest of the team stared at him on the screen.

Not a flicker. His gaze held steady. "I had nothing to do with these girls' deaths," he said slowly.

"Where were you on the night of March seventeenth?" asked Jonny.

"That was over four months ago."

"It was a Friday night, if that helps," Jonny said.

"I'm sorry. I can't remember that far back. I don't go out much, except to the local bar, so I guess I could've been there."

"What's the bar's name?"

"The Q Bar," he said. "Don't ask me what the Q stands for. I've never found that out."

Pérez shook his head.

He didn't seem at all concerned that he was facing multiple murder charges.

"What would you say if I told you that you were caught on camera in Ocean Drive that evening?"

"I'd say you're probably right," he replied. "Like I said, I can't remember."

"Do you frequent the bars and clubs on Ocean Drive often?" Jonny asked.

"Not really."

"So it's not your stalking ground?"

He laughed. "I don't know what you mean."

Reid glanced at Halston's lawyer, whose face was set in a stiff grimace.

"What about the night of May fourth? Just two months ago."

He pretended to think. "You know, I can't be sure."

"Let me help you. You were once again prowling Ocean Drive."

"Prowling is a strong word, Detective," said his attorney. It was the first time he had spoken.

"What would you call it?" Jonny asked Halston who didn't respond.

"What about the night Mimi Silverton went missing?" Jonny said. "That was less than two weeks ago. You must remember that."

No answer.

"I'll tell you. You were at the parking garage close to Ocean Drive. Do you see the pattern here?"

"What pattern?" He was scowling now, his eyebrows meeting in the middle.

"You were on Ocean Drive every time a girl disappeared. In fact, you were caught on the security camera outside the Ocean Club the night Sarah Randall went missing."

"That's all circumstantial, Detective," the lawyer said.

Halston sat quietly, not saying a word.

"Quite a coincidence, though, isn't it?"

Halston wasn't talking. Jonny would struggle to break him. Perhaps that would change when confronted with the DNA evidence from the torture room.

Jonny hacked away for a while longer, then suspended the interrogation.

"I'm not giving up," he said when he came out, wiping the perspiration off his forehead. "I'll have another go at him later."

They all took a breather. The air needed clearing like it was tainted by the suspect locked in the holding cell.

Later that afternoon, they got the call from forensics. "The lab found evidence of all three girls in the house," Jonny shouted.

A round of clapping and whooping ensued.

"We've got the bastard." Pérez thumped Jonny on the back.

"There's more."

Reid frowned. He'd been afraid of this. "How much more?"

"They found at least six other types of female DNA."

Everybody stared at him.

"Holy shit," muttered Pérez, breaking the silence that followed. "You mean there are six other missing girls out there that we don't know about?"

Reid exhaled. "We do now."

39

Kenzie met Reid at a coffee shop close to the Miami PD building. As promised, he gave her the information she needed for a follow up on the Swamp Strangler. Now that they'd linked him to the three victims, she could go ahead and publish his name.

"This has worked well," she remarked over her latte. "This partnership of ours."

He snorted. "I never thought I'd be friends with a reporter, let alone work with one after what happened before."

"You consider me a friend?" She couldn't help smiling.

He shrugged. "Yeah, well, I've stayed at your house. I made you my infamous spaghetti. I don't do that for just anyone."

She laughed. "I guess we are friends then." A warm feeling flowed over her. "Maybe we can even work together in the future."

"I wouldn't go that far."

"You never know, we might be useful to each other."

"I suppose I could use a press contact." He studied her in that semi-intense more-than-friends way. It made her stomach flutter.

"And I could—" She paused as the door opened and Ortega walked in. His gaze fell on their table. He frowned and strode over.

Uh-oh.

Kenzie forced a smile. "Hi Xavier."

Ortega didn't smile back. "I didn't know you two were friendly?"

Reid's jaw tensed.

"Yes, we met on the Natalia Cruz investigation. Her husband's a friend of mine."

"I see." His dark gaze flickered from Kenzie to Reid and back again. "And now you're meeting for coffee?"

"He's giving me an exclusive." She glanced at Reid. His knuckles had gone white around his coffee mug.

"I see."

"How's your case going?" she asked, desperate to lighten the mood. The animosity between Reid and Xavier was palpable. At any moment, Reid's mug was going to shatter into a hundred pieces and the two of them would go for each other.

"What case? Our chief witness just got taken out by a bunch of gang bangers."

"I'm sorry to hear that." No wonder he was in such a foul mood.

"Yeah, well." he shrugged.

Kenzie tried to wrap it up. "Well, take care of yourself."

He hesitated, then said, "You want to grab a drink sometime? We could catch up properly." His gaze flickered to Reid, who hadn't moved a muscle.

Kenzie wasn't sure what to say. Xavier was a friend, they'd gone through the academy together, and he was a useful source at the department, even if he did sometimes get it wrong. She couldn't afford to burn that bridge. Not even for Reid.

"Yeah, sure. Call me."

He grinned and shot Reid a triumphant look. "I sure will. You take care, Kenz."

Even the shortened form of her name was designed to wind up his colleague. What the hell did these two have against each other?

Xavier ordered a coffee to go and left, making an "I'll call you" signal with his hand as he walked out the door.

The silence wrapped around them. She was almost too scared to look at Reid.

"*That's* your source?" he said eventually, his voice a strangled whisper.

"Yeah. We were at the academy together. He was there when I had my accident."

Reid's eyes glowed with an inner fire. She'd never seen him look so furious. "Is he the one that told you Bianca was out?"

It took a moment for her to register what he was talking about. Then she got it.

Crap.

"Yes. He said she'd been pulled out, but I'm sure it was a misunderstanding. He couldn't have known—"

"He fucking did know," Reid growled. "We all did. Ortega deliberately sabotaged that operation to get back at me."

"Why?" she whispered. "Why would he do that?"

"Because he was in love with Bianca, too. They had a thing, before we—" He left it hanging. Kenzie got the picture.

"I didn't know. Surely he wouldn't have put her life on the line. Not if he had feelings for her."

"He knew, Kenzie." Reid got to his feet. "I told him myself."

Kenzie felt the color drain from her face. "Shit, I'm sorry. I had no idea."

This feud between them obviously went way back.

"Enjoy your catch up," his voice dripped with venom. "You can forget working with me again."

With a sinking heart, she watched him stride out of the shop, leaving his full mug of coffee on the table in front of her.

What the hell?

Kenzie sat motionless, thinking about what had just happened. One moment they were laughing and joking, and the next Reid had stormed out in a rage.

Had Xavier really compromised the operation? Had he put Bianca's life on the line? He could be impulsive, she knew that. Several times on the academy training course she had to reel him in. "*Think, then act,*" she'd told him over and over again. Eventually, he'd listened.

When she'd had her accident, he'd been the first person to visit her at the hospital.

"*You gave us such a scare, Kenzie. Thank God you're okay.*"

He'd come back every day, bringing her flowers and chocolates. Her other colleagues had also come to visit, but not as much as Xavier.

"He's got a crush on you," a female friend had said.

But nothing had happened. She hadn't allowed it to.

Xavier graduated and went into the force. She recovered, wallowing in self-pity until she couldn't stand it anymore. Then she'd dragged her sorry ass out of bed and got a job as a junior reporter for the *Herald*.

The entertainment beat. That was her thing. It was considered frivolous, not real journalism. Still, she'd done it. She'd worked her way up and now she was an investigative reporter on the crime beat. Exactly where she wanted to be.

Well, not exactly. But as good as she was going to get.

She'd cut ties with most of her police trainee friends. It was too hard to see them join police forces all over the state while she was stuck going to movie premiers and chasing B-grade celebs. Xavier had stayed in touch, though. Every now and then they'd meet for a coffee. A friendly catch up.

When she'd been promoted, she'd asked if he'd be a source. Nothing illegal. Just to feed her bits of information from time to time. A favor to a friend. In return, she'd write appeals for information, or spin an article a certain way to draw out a culprit or put on the pressure. It was a useful two-way flow of information.

Then she'd met Reid. He'd barged into her life and taken over that role. They'd worked as a team, on a real case—and Kenzie had never felt more alive. This was her dream, and he'd given her a taste of that.

She didn't want to lose it. Lose him.

What to do?

Her phone beeped. It was Keith.

Where the hell are you?

Coming! she texted back and got to her feet. Time to work.

She had an article to write, and it was a big one. As far as she knew, no other daily had released the Strangler's name yet. Tomorrow, Pete Halston would go down in history as one of Miami's most notorious serial killers. And she'd be the one to break it.

40

For fuck's sake.

Reid stormed into the squad room and made a beeline for Ortega's desk. "It was you, wasn't it?" he hissed. "You told Kenzie that Bianca was extracted, when you knew full well she hadn't been."

"I don't know what you mean." Ortega leaped out of his chair. The two men squared off.

Ryan scurried out of the way. Everybody's eyes turned to the two men.

"You know damn well what I mean. You put her life at risk. She's dead because of you." Reid prodded him in the chest.

"You don't know what you're talking about." He took a step back, but Reid saw the fear in his eyes and knew it was true.

"You bastard! She trusted you. She trusted *us* to keep her safe. How could you betray her like that?"

"I didn't betray anyone. You've got the wrong guy. I'd never do anything to risk Bianca's life."

"You did it to get back at me. You hated that she and I had something. That she rejected you." Reid moved closer as he spoke. He wasn't letting the prick get away with this.

"Don't flatter yourself," he spat. "You meant nothing more to her than I did. Besides, she had feelings for Torres. She told me."

"Bullshit. That bastard put a gun to her head and blew her brains out. Because of what you did. You won't get away with this, Ortega. Her death is on you."

"What's going on?" Pérez stormed out of his office.

"Ortega was the leak," Reid snapped. "He told the press that Bianca was pulled out when she hadn't been. He killed the op."

"Is that true?" asked Pérez.

Ortega didn't reply.

"Murderer," hissed Reid. He clenched his fists. God, he wanted to punch his lights out.

"Garrett, stand down," barked his boss. He sensed Reid was about to lose it. "Ortega, my office. Now!"

Ortega inched around Reid, glaring daggers.

Give me one chance, Reid thought. *One chance and you're history.*

"I'm no more guilty than you are," he snarled. "Are you screwing Kenzie Gilmore now? You like picking up my leftovers, don't you? Perhaps I should warn her you can't protect your women."

That was it.

Reid let out a feral growl and punched Ortega in the face. He flew backward into the photocopier machine, blood spurting from his nose.

"Christ, someone get him out of here!" Pérez roared.

Two detectives took hold of Reid's arms and pulled him back. He was about to beat the living crap out of the little rat.

"Ortega, get in here now!" Pérez yelled, and stormed off to his office.

Reid shrugged free of the men holding him. "Okay. I'm okay. You can let go."

They cautiously released him.

"Easy, brother," Jared said. "It's not worth your career."

Reid thought it just might be.

"I need some air."

They stepped aside to let Reid march out of the squad room and down four flights of stairs to the exit. Once outside, he gulped warm air into his lungs and paced up and down by the water.

Prick.

He ought to have known Ortega was the leak. He just never thought he'd stoop so low as to put another officer's life on the line. All for a petty vendetta. Wounded pride. Jesus.

He clenched his fist. It was beginning to ache. He hoped Ortega's jaw hurt as much. Bianca, dead—because of a police screw up.

And then the jibe about Kenzie. He ground his teeth together as he strode up and down. Had she and Ortega really had a thing? Kenzie had said he'd been there when she had her accident. Was that when it happened? At the academy?

He frowned. The thought bothered him more than it should.

His phone buzzed.

"Get in here!"

Pérez.

The shit was about to hit the fan.

He left thoughts of Kenzie outside and marched back up. When he got there, Ortega was nowhere to be seen. The squad room was ominously quiet, but he felt everybody's eyes on him as he stalked through to the lieutenant's office.

"Sit down," snapped Pérez.

He sat.

"What the hell was that about? You broke Ortega's nose. He's gone to Emergency to get it fixed."

"Good."

"Jesus, Garrett. What were you thinking?"

"Did he confess?" Reid asked. "Did he tell you he leaked information on an active case to a reporter who told the world we had an officer undercover?"

"He said he didn't know she hadn't been pulled out."

"Bullshit," Reid reiterated. "He knew because I told him myself that very morning."

The lieutenant was silent for a moment. "There'll be a formal investigation," he said wearily. "I've already spoken to Internal Affairs."

Reid gave a terse nod. That was something, at least.

"What's this about you and Kenzie Gilmore? That's the same reporter who leaked the story, isn't it? I thought her name sounded familiar."

"Yes, but it wasn't her fault. Ortega was her source. They were at the police academy together. She was going off information *he* gave her."

"So you are sleeping with her."

"I'm not freakin' sleeping with her," he stormed.

Pérez gave him an arched look. "It's not like you to forgive and forget so quickly. Last year, you hated all journalists. You quit your job over this. It effectively put a halt to your career. Now you're happy to work with the same woman?"

It did sound ridiculous when he put it like that.

"She helped out on the Natalia Cruz case," he lowered his voice. The adrenaline was wearing off now. "I told you that. She introduced me to DJ Snake, Natalia's husband, and his whole crew. They're valuable witnesses."

"And suspects," Pérez pointed out.

"Yeah, that too."

"This woman gave you access to them?"

"Exactly. She helped me gain their trust."

"And you're not sleeping with her."

"Jesus." Reid swiped a hand through his hair. "How many times do I have to say it?"

Pérez held up his hands. "Okay. Okay. Calm down. I'm just trying to get the facts straight. I don't want to put IA onto you as well."

"I think they'll have something to say about Ortega's nose, anyway."

Pérez grimaced. "Let's try to limit the damage. I don't want to have to suspend two of my top detectives. Ortega's in the middle of a complex op. Now the DEA are going to have to do without him."

"Sorry about that." It was unfortunate. The last thing he wanted to do was disrupt an op.

"You should be." Pérez wouldn't forgive him in a hurry. "Now, where are we with the Cruz case? I've had her father on the line asking for updates. He's not going to rest until we have a suspect behind bars."

Reid sighed. "Ms. Montague's car was clean. We can't get a warrant to search her house, so we're nowhere."

"Maybe it wasn't her?" the Lieutenant suggested. "I believe we got a complaint about a fraudulent wire scam this morning. Sounded like your guy."

"Antonio Fernández?" His pulse ticked up a notch.

"I don't know. Ryan took the call. She's looking into it."

Reid got up.

"You're on thin ice, Garrett. Watch your step from now on."

"Yes, sir."

He left the office and headed straight to Ryan's desk. She glanced up in surprise. He saw a flash of uncertainty in her gaze. He'd scared her by his outburst. Maybe now she realized he was only human.

"Sorry about earlier," he said. "Temper got the better of me."

"It's understandable."

Was it? For someone on the outside looking in, he wasn't sure. She hadn't been there a year and a half ago. She hadn't lost her friend and colleague.

"Did you take a call earlier about a wire scam?"

"I did. I left a note on your desk."

"Oh, I haven't been back there yet."

"A woman called in and said she'd invested 10 thousand dollars in a trading account in the name of AF Investments. She was checking her balance using an app, and now it's suddenly gone offline. She called the company but got no answer."

That was Fernández alright. "You might get a few more complaints," he said. "They've obviously made off with everyone's money."

Ryan shook her head. "That's so mean. Those poor people. This woman said she'd invested her pension. It was all she had."

"Well, let's try to find this guy." He perched on the end of her desk. "Maybe we can even get some of her money back."

"Okay."

"There's a gym near South Beach called Progressive Overload. Fernández's henchman, Ivan Petrovitch, works out there. They might have an address for him."

"You want me to head over there?" she asked.

"Yeah. You're a detective, aren't you?" Now that he had eyes on Torres, he could afford to bring Fernández in.

"Of course, sir." Her eyes lit up.

"Go on then. Get his details, round up some uniform officers and go pay him a visit. If he's home, bring him in for questioning. Think you can handle that?"

"Yes, sir." She sprung out of her seat. "Thank you, sir."

"You don't have to call me sir," he told her. "Reid is fine, or Garrett, if you prefer." After all, everyone called her Ryan.

She grinned, and grabbing her badge and gun, headed for the elevator.

41

"Garrett, you've got to hear this."

Reid joined Pérez at the screen outside the interrogation room. "What's up?"

Jonny was interviewing Halston again. Armed with evidence, he was going in strong, pushing the serial killer for a confession.

"We have enough to charge you," Jonny was saying. "So if you want to give your side of the story, now's your chance."

There was a pause. Reid saw the gleam in Halston's eye. "He's going to confess," he muttered.

"How do you know?" Pérez asked.

"Look at him. He's preening. He wants people to know what he did."

"Evil son of a bitch," murmured the lieutenant.

He wasn't wrong there.

"She wasn't the first." Halston pointed to the picture of Sarah Randall.

"Fuck me," hissed Pérez. Even Jonny looked shocked. The attorney sat as if turned to stone.

"She wasn't?" Jonny stammered.

"The first was a girl from Jacksonville." He glanced up. "You always remember your first."

A chill went down Reid's spine.

"Do you remember her name?" Jonny asked.

"Felicity Reiner. Sweet Felicity." His eyes hardened. "That's what she wanted people to believe. But she was a slut, prancing around in her little skirt, tempting all the boys. She came into the store once with her dad. Bent down right in front of me. Taunting me." he laughed. "I showed her."

Jonny swallowed. "Where did you hide her body?"

"The Glades, of course. It's the perfect burial ground. If the gators don't eat 'em, the elements get 'em. Those ones you found, those were unfortunate. If you hadn't found them, you'd never have known."

"He's crazy," said Pérez.

They watched with growing horror as the killer listed the other girls and what he'd done to them. Then he paused, looked up at the camera and said, "And then there was Natalia."

Reid blinked. "What did he say?"

"He said Natalia." Pérez looked as shocked as he felt.

"No way. He can't have."

Jonny leaned forward in his chair. "Are you talking about Natalia Cruz?"

"Yeah, who else?"

Jonny studied him. "Tell us about Natalia, then. How did you do her?"

It was a test.

"I found her walking along the beach, all made-up. She wanted men to notice her."

Reid went very still.

"She looked drunk, so I approached her and asked if she needed help. She said she was fine, but I could see she wasn't. She'd been crying."

"Did she have anything with her?" asked Jonny.

"A suitcase. It wasn't very heavy. I don't think there was much in it."

"What did you do with the case?"

"I dumped it. Can't remember where."

Jonny wrote this down, then he glanced up at Halston. "Then what?"

"I offered to give her a ride. She was so grateful, stupid bitch. We were almost back to my place when she suddenly panicked. She wanted to get out of the car."

Reid listened hard.

"We struggled. I tried to stop her, but she opened the car door. I pulled over and she jumped out. I chased her down the road and pulled her into the bushes. She began to scream, so I put my hands around her neck and squeezed."

"Holy crap," muttered Pérez.

Reid didn't know what to think.

"I didn't mean to kill her so soon. It just happened."

Shit.

"I pulled her back into the car and took her to the swamp. I dumped her body." He shook his head. "Such a waste."

Reid gulped. A waste because he hadn't had time to torture her first. To tie her up on that filthy mattress and sexually assault her. What a pig.

"You didn't rape her?" Jonny asked, just for the record.

"No. Not Natalia."

He genuinely looked upset.

"That's it then." Pérez turned to Reid. His eyes were haunted. Reid was sure he looked the same. "He did all four girls."

"Looks that way." Reid frowned. "Although, they didn't find traces of Natalia in his car, did they?"

"Not that I know of," said Pérez. "But what does it matter? We've got a confession."

"It doesn't feel right."

Pérez sighed. "Why would he admit to killing Natalia if he didn't?"

"I don't know." Reid stared at the man in the interrogation room. Halston had a gleam in his eye.

Look what I've done. I'm going to be famous.

"Maybe he wants the attention?" Reid suggested. "Natalia's a celebrity. He gets bonus points for killing her."

"That's demented," said Pérez.

"But what if it's true? What if he's lying?"

"Jesus, Garrett. The guy confessed. Let's close this case and move on. We've got him. Leave it be."

Pérez walked back to his office, shaking his head, but Reid didn't move. He stood staring at the screen. Something about that confession didn't add up.

"I want a shot at him," he told Pérez.

"Why? He's confessed."

"I don't think he did it," Reid said. "He's claiming it, but I don't know why."

"Let it go, Reid, for God's sake. The man's going to prison, regardless."

"Five minutes, Lieutenant. That's all I ask."

Pérez rubbed his forehead. "Okay, fine. But I really don't see the point."

Reid went into the interrogation room where Halston was still sitting. His lawyer was talking to him in a low voice, no doubt going over what would happen next.

"I just have a few questions for the suspect." Reid took a seat.

"You again?" sneered Halston.

"Yeah, me again. I want to talk about Natalia Cruz."

Dark eyes glared back at him. "Sure, why not?"

"Why her? Surely you were taking a risk by targeting someone so famous?"

"I didn't know she was famous at the time," he said. "I saw her walking across the beach and saw an opportunity. So I took it."

"You mentioned she was upset. Did she say why?"

He frowned. "She might have mentioned something about her husband, I can't remember."

"You knew she was married?"

"Yeah, she wore a wedding ring."

"I didn't think you liked married women, judging by all the others. Young, single, sexy. Flaunting their bodies."

His mouth hardened into a thin line. "Whores, all of them. They deserved what they got."

"But Natalia wasn't a whore. She was married."

"She looked like a whore."

"I can see why you might say that. That tight, black dress she was wearing, that would make any man think of sex."

"Exactly. I couldn't help myself."

"Thank you." Reid walked out of the room.

"He didn't do it," Reid told Pérez who was standing by the screen.

"What do you mean? He literally admitted it. Again."

"Natalia was wearing a yellow dress when I found her. It was long, down to her ankles."

Pérez stared at him.

"You said she had on a tight black number."

Reid shot him a pointed look. "Exactly."

42

Kenzie met Xavier in a quiet bar near her apartment. They sat outside, enjoying the breeze that had sprung up during the afternoon. The sun hung like an orange globe over the horizon.

"I'm glad you called." He touched his nose. It was swollen and bruised, and he wasn't wearing cover up on it.

"What happened to you?" she asked.

"Your boyfriend punched me because I told you about Bianca."

"Reid did that?" She didn't know whether to be shocked or amused.

"It's not funny," he retorted, seeing the glimmer in her eye. "The guy's a loose cannon. They should never have brought him back. I don't know what the lieutenant was thinking."

"He's a good cop," Kenzie said quietly.

"He's got anger issues."

That was why she'd called him. She needed to know if he'd done it on purpose or not. If he had, he wasn't the man she thought he was. If he hadn't known, perhaps he deserved a second chance. Either way, she wanted to know.

"Why *did* you tell me the undercover agent was extracted when she hadn't been?"

"I thought she had." His dark eyes met hers. "Honestly, Kenz. I didn't know."

"Reid said he told you." She watched for signs he was lying. She was good at reading people. A hesitation here, a glance there.

There was the slightest flicker in his gaze, so minute, she nearly missed it. But it was there. He *was* lying.

"He's imagining things," Xavier insisted. "Maybe he thought he told me, or he told someone else. I swear, I didn't know. Why would I put Bianca's life at risk?"

"To get back at him," she whispered. "I know you had a thing for her."

"It's true. We went out a couple times, but that was all. Bianca was like that. She didn't want a committed relationship. She loved her job too much. She always said if she ever settled down it wouldn't be with a cop."

"What about Reid?" Kenzie asked.

"They didn't even go out," he scoffed "They just slept together a couple of times. It was nothing."

"Not to him," she said.

"Well, if he fell for her, that's his problem. She had feelings for her target."

Kenzie gasped. "You mean the man she'd seduced to get in with the cartel?"

"Yeah, Alberto Torres. She told me once."

"But he killed her."

"She always had a thing for bad boys."

Kenzie didn't know what to think. Was any of this true?

"If you knew she was in love with Torres, why tell me she was out when she was still undercover?"

The flicker again. That's when she knew he was full of crap.

"She wasn't in love with Torres, was she? You're making that up.

She was in love with Reid, that's what you couldn't stand. That's why you gave her up."

"That's bullshit, Kenz."

But she knew she was right. Now that she'd confronted him, it was written all over his face. "How could you do it, Xav? How could you put her life on the line like that? And make me an accomplice? Do you know how I beat myself up about that?" Not to mention what she'd gotten into at work.

His shoulders stooped. "I didn't know she was going to get killed, did I?"

Kenzie stared at him.

"If I'd known, I would never have told you. I thought the op would go south and Garrett would take the blame. He was gunning for a promotion."

"And you didn't want him to get it."

He shook his head.

Kenzie stood up. That's it. She was done with him.

"What happened to you, Xavier? The guy I knew at the academy would never put a fellow officer's life in danger."

"I didn't know," he whispered.

He was pathetic. She could barely look at him.

"Goodbye, Xavier," she said. "Don't ever call me again."

And she left the bar.

Kenzie got home but couldn't relax. What a mess. Xavier had lied to her. She'd considered him a friend and he'd handed her false information. He'd caused Torres to shoot an innocent woman, all because he was jealous of Reid.

Un-freaking-believable.

He deserved that punch in the nose.

She smirked as she thought about it. Good for Reid. She hoped he wouldn't get into too much trouble because of it.

It was still relatively early. Feeling antsy, she poured herself a glass of wine and took down some old photo albums. Looking at the past always calmed her. Until it didn't.

She paged through her memories, smiling at the old sepia shots of her parents. Her mother, so young and beautiful with her pale blond hair and wispy figure. There was one of her in a long white dress, dancing on the beach. Her eyes glittered with undisclosed joy. She looked happy.

There was another of her mother holding her. They were both laughing. She had a smudge of something on her cheek.

"What happened to you, mom," she whispered into the fading light.

There was a picture of her father with Vic Reynolds. Both looking smart in their Miami PD uniforms. Vic used to call regularly after her father passed away. Now he rarely did.

On a whim, she picked up her phone and scrolled through her contacts until she found his number. His wife had died about 10 years ago. Breast cancer. As far as she knew, he was still by himself.

"Uncle Vic, it's Kenzie. I hope I'm not disturbing you."

"Kenzie, this is a surprise. No, of course not. How are you?"

"I'm good, thanks. I was just looking at some old photographs and I thought I'd give you a call. It's been a while."

"I know, I'm sorry. I've been so busy at the precinct."

"Everything okay?" she asked.

"Better than okay," he said. "We've nabbed the Swamp Strangler. He's confessed to all the murders."

"All the murders?" They must have discovered who the other girls were. That was good news.

"Yeah, even that missing celeb, Natalia Cruz."

Her heart almost stopped.

"He confessed to Natalia's murder?"

"Yeah, isn't that great? That'll make her father happy. He's a friend, you know."

"Did they find Natalia's DNA at his house?" she inquired.

There was a pause. "How do you know about that?"

"I've got the exclusive," she said. "Approved by the department."

"Ah, yes. Well, you know I can't discuss any details of the case."

"Of course. I'm sorry. It's just—I didn't think Natalia's death was related to the other girls."

"Apparently it is. I, for one, am glad the whole thing is over. It's been a major pain in the ass."

Not as much as for the victims or their families, she felt like saying.

"Why don't we get together next week? We'll go out for dinner like old times."

"Sounds great."

Kenzie tried to make sense of it. How could Natalia be one of the Strangler's victims? Had he really confessed, or were they trying to pin her death on him to close the case?

They said goodbye and she sat there, staring at the wall.

Was there any actual evidence? What about the different MOs? The strangulation marks on her neck? That she hadn't been sexually assaulted? How did they explain that?

She tried to call Reid, but it went straight to voicemail.

Damnit. He was avoiding her calls.

She thought about Bella and the way she'd been dancing on the beach.

Some things are worth waiting for.

What a load of crap to throw them off the scent. To throw *her* off the scent because she'd seen Bella and Snake together on the beach.

Then the attack. The heels on the sidewalk. The perfume.

No way had the Strangler killed Natalia.

43

As the sun sank into the Atlantic, Kenzie arrived at the *Herald's* offices. The night concierge greeted her by name. That ought to tell her she needed to get a life.

Still, here she was, unable to let go.

She wasn't even sure what she was looking for, other than something she'd missed. Something to tie Bella to Natalia's murder.

She began by scrolling through the picture archives, looking for all the press shots they had of Snake and Natalia. The engagement party, the wedding, the record launch. There were tons, all filed on the cloud, at a finger's reach should they ever need them for an article or entertainment piece.

She began with the engagement party. Happy smiles, champagne, and laughter. Natalia looked beautiful in a flowing sapphire gown, her dark hair up in a chignon. The party was held at Snake's mansion, and there were plenty of shots of the happy couple on the terrace, by the pool, on the lawn, the palm trees majestic overhead. She saw Bella in the periphery, her eyes glued on Natalia.

Then came the confrontation. Bella screaming at Natalia, her mouth a bright red slash. Natalia looking scared, tears glistening on her face. Snake with his arm around his fiancée, shouting at his ex. Even a fuming Bella being led from the house by a beefy security guard. The photographer had captured it all.

Kenzie could feel the animosity through the screen. There were one or two later shots of a devastated Natalia being comforted by her husband-to-be. Touching photos. They never made it into the press.

Rubbing the grit out of her eyes, she moved on to the next. The wedding. Bella hadn't been invited for obvious reasons, so Kenzie scrolled through these quickly. The wedding dress was exquisite, and Natalia resembled the pampered heiress she was. Her father stood in the shadows, looking over her.

The vows. The guests. Confetti for a beautiful bride.

Then on to the reception. The dinner, the speeches, and finally, the first dance.

They looked blissful. What a shame someone had stolen it all away.

Her vision blurring, Kenzie got up and made herself a pot of coffee. The office was quiet, the big screen television on the wall that usually showed the latest news was off, the air conditioner silent, and only her computer flickered from across the floor.

She liked it like this. Peace in which to work and think. It was easier to switch on when the rest of the world switched off.

Back at her desk, she brought up the photographs of the launch party at the Sand Club. There were quite a few. She started at the beginning, with the guests arriving at the venue. The paparazzi had staked out the place, waiting to see who had been invited.

The guests who were checking into the hotel came first. She recognized several of them. Then Snake and Natalia arrived, leaving Snake's Lamborghini outside the front entrance. They walked in, hand in hand.

She scrolled on. The night of the party. Glamorous guests, more drinking, more laughing. Bella swirled around in her emerald-green dress, her arm linked with Dave's. Except for the moment when she had that altercation with Natalia. Once again, Snake had intervened.

Why the hell did he keep inviting Bella to these things? The woman was a menace.

Dave rushed up, embarrassed. He took Bella's arm. She let him usher her out. Looking at the photographs, Bella certainly appeared drunk. Her cheeks were flushed. She gripped Dave's arm, and she was clearly upset.

Was Dave her accomplice? He was the right height, but was he capable of murder?

Kenzie stared at a picture of him handing Bella a glass of champagne. A smiling face with pale blue eyes. It was possible, she supposed, but she just couldn't see it.

She sighed. This was getting her nowhere.

She scrolled back to the beginning of the night and started again. There *must* be something. What weren't they seeing?

At three in the morning, she found what she was looking for.

"Someone got to him." Reid paced up and down the squad room.

"But who?" Pérez ran a tired hand through his hair.

"I don't know. Bella somehow?"

"Now you're being ridiculous," his boss said. "Bella Montague hasn't been anywhere near the station since she was questioned and released. She had no access to Halston."

"What about his lawyer?" Reid asked. "She could have approached him."

"Look, I know this isn't adding up, but Halston's a sick man. A psychopath. If he's confessed to Natalia's murder, we're going to charge him with that, along with all the others."

"Don't you want to find out what really happened?" Reid scowled at him.

"I know what happened. That man killed her."

"He didn't," Reid argued. "Can't you see he's lying? Someone fed him information about it. The suitcase, the beach, but they didn't tell him about the yellow dress."

Pérez pursed his lips. "Look, it's late. Let's pick this up in the morning."

"Halston will be charged and taken away in the morning," Reid said. "We have to figure this out now."

"Garrett, I've had enough. This has been a long day and I want to go home. Halston is going to be charged with Natalia's murder along with all the others. Do you understand me?"

Reid inhaled. "But Lieutenant—"

"Leave it, Reid. That's an order."

"I thought we were here to uncover the truth," he said, after the lieutenant turned his back. "Since when doesn't that matter anymore?"

Pérez ignored him.

Reid turned and stormed out.

Reid drove home through the breaking dawn. He pulled in beside his cabin and frowned. What was Kenzie doing here?

He walked up to the window of her car and knocked. She was sound asleep in the back seat, curled up like a child. She jerked awake, then sat up, rubbing sleep from her eyes.

He waited as she climbed out.

"Oh, thank goodness you're home. There's something I have to tell you."

He noticed she was shaking.

"You okay?"

"Yeah, yes. It's just too much caffeine. I'm fine."

"Come inside." He noticed her jeans, wrinkled T-shirt, and sandals. "You look like you've been up all night."

"I have." She squinted at him. "Where have you been?"

"At the station. Halston confessed to Natalia's murder."

"I heard."

"You did?" Then he twigged. "Ah, your dickhead source."

"No, not him. You were right about him. He's a liar. I told him I never wanted to see him again. Well done for punching him in the nose, by the way. He deserved it."

Reid spun around. "You told him you never wanted to see him again?" Why did that make him happy?

"Yes. I'm so sorry about that. I'll never trust anything he says ever again."

"Not your fault." He opened the door.

She followed him in. He was still thinking about Ortega when he remembered what she'd said about Halston.

"How did you find out?"

"Vic Reynolds. I called you, but you didn't pick up. I thought you were avoiding me."

"I was."

She snorted. "Anyway, he told me Halston confessed to Natalia's murder. I couldn't believe it. Why confess to a murder you didn't commit?"

"That's what I can't understand," Reid said, going into the kitchen.

Kenzie padded after him.

"He's already going down for at least nine other murders, so I suppose what's one more?"

"Another life sentence," said Kenzie.

Reid put on a pot of coffee.

"Unless he wants the prestige of saying he killed Natalia Cruz," Kenzie said.

"I think someone got to him," Reid admitted.

Kenzie's eyes widened. "You think Bella got him to confess to Natalia's murder?"

He smiled. She'd already known what he was thinking. He liked how she did that.

"I think she spoke to his lawyer, got him to ask Halston to confess. There must have been a payoff. I can't see him doing it for nothing."

"No, but what could she have offered him? Money wouldn't do him any good. He doesn't have family, other than his brother."

"I don't know, but it must be something."

He poured them each a cup of coffee. "Now, what are you doing here? You said you found something?"

"God, yes." She perked up. "I went back to the office last night. I couldn't sleep, so I decided to go through the old photo archives looking for anything we might have missed."

"Kenzie, it's been a long night. If you've found something, please just tell me what it is."

She grinned. "Sorry. I know how they did it. I know how they killed Natalia."

44

"They?" Reid stared at her.

"Bella and Snake." Lack of sleep and too much caffeine made her stumble over her words.

"Hang on." Reid held up a hand. "You're telling me they were in it together?"

"Yes, that's what I'm saying."

"Okay, you've lost me. Can we go through this slowly? I'm not operating on all cylinders right now."

"Sure."

He set the two cups of coffee on the table, then sank into a chair. Kenzie sat opposite him, drumming her fingers on the table. She felt wired.

"So, what did you discover?"

"I went back to the day of the launch party," she said. "There were several paparazzi shots of the guests arriving."

"Okay, and what does this tell us?"

"Natalia and Snake arrived earlier that morning. They were staying in the hotel. Natalia had this massive suitcase with flowers all over it."

"The one they couldn't find after she went missing?"

"That one."

Reid shook his head. "I don't see how—" Then his eyes widened.

Kenzie smiled.

He stared at her. "You're not suggesting—"

She nodded.

"Oh my God."

"It's possible," she said. "The case is that big."

There was a pause as Reid processed what she'd said. She could almost hear his brain ticking over. "He hid her body in the suitcase."

"I think so." She wrapped her hands around the cup, more for warmth than anything else. "Snake spiked his own wife's drink sometime during the night, or even earlier, who knows? She developed a headache, felt sick, and he escorted her back to the room. We saw them on the security camera."

Reid was nodding along as she talked.

"The only time we didn't see them is during those few minutes he was inside their room."

"And that's when he killed her," surmised Reid.

Kenzie gave a tight nod. "I think he strangled her and hid her body in the suitcase, which he stashed in one of the wardrobes. Then he went back to the party. We saw him shout something into the room before he left."

"That was all for show." Reid's gaze was fixed on Kenzie's widened eyes.

"Exactly. He knew the police would check the tape. He went back to the party, socialized, and pretended like nothing had happened."

"Meanwhile, his wife was lying dead in the room."

Kenzie met his gaze. "Yes. Then, after the party, he goes back to the room. Everyone's a little drunk. He pretends to look for Natalia, but she's not there. He calls his buddies, who come up to help him search."

"They look in the bedroom and the bathroom, but they don't check the closet," said Reid.

"Or maybe Snake checks the closet and says she's not in there. None of them were looking for the suitcase at that stage. Snake only told the police about that the next morning when he reported her missing."

"Then they search the rest of the hotel, but of course she's not there either." Reid followed Kenzie in her thought process.

Kenzie continued, "His friends leave. He goes back to the room and takes the suitcase out of the closet. Now this is when it gets tricky. He wheels it down to the beach, which must have been difficult, considering there was a body inside. Bella's parked along the beach somewhere off the radar. They load the case into the car and drive out to the Glades to get rid of it."

"And that's why we didn't find any trace of Natalia's DNA in the car," said Reid. "She was in the suitcase the whole time."

"Correct." Kenzie felt a surge of adrenaline. That and the coffee were what was keeping her going.

"We picked her up on the road camera on her way to the Glades. Eleven minutes past two in the morning, and the guy sitting next to her was none other than her ex-boyfriend, DJ Snake."

They sat and stared at each other.

Reid gave a low whistle. "It makes sense."

"The only thing I haven't figured out, is why," Kenzie said. "From everything I've seen, they were happy together."

"A wise woman once told me appearances could be deceiving," he said.

She couldn't resist smiling.

"How are we going to prove it?" asked Reid.

"We need to find that suitcase," said Kenzie. "It's a pity we can't search Bella's place."

"I might be able to arrange that," he said. "If we can prove she bribed Halston to take the blame for Natalia."

"How are you going to do that?"

"Bring his attorney in. We'll make a big deal of it, put the fear of God into him. I think he'll talk. The attorney won't risk his reputation for a serial killer."

"Will that be enough for you to get a warrant for her apartment?"

"I think so. They won't be able to brush it under the rug then."

Kenzie grinned. "Okay, sounds good." She stifled a yawn. "Do you mind if I crash on your couch for a few hours? I'm way too exhausted to drive home. I'd probably end up in the swamp if I tried."

"Sure, take my bedroom. I've got some calls to make."

"You haven't slept either."

"I'll sleep when this case is over." He winked at her. "I can handle it."

He looked exhausted too. His hair was disheveled, his shirt creased, and his chin covered in stubble.

"Okay, tough guy. Wake me if anything happens."

"Will do."

She went into the bedroom and lay down. God, it felt good to close her eyes. Her head was aching, and she had the shakes from too much caffeine. Just a few hours' sleep was all she needed to see her through the day.

The last thing she heard before she passed out was Reid saying, "Sorry to wake you, Lieutenant, but you're never going to believe this."

45

"Miami PD, Open up!"

There was no answer.

Reid nodded to the team of officers. They battered the door down and charged inside, weapons drawn. In his hand, Reid held the search warrant that had come through only an hour before.

"Clear," shouted one of the officers. "Bella Montague is not here."

"Okay, let's search the property. We're looking for a large floral suitcase, or anything that looks like it might belong to Natalia Cruz."

"Yes, sir."

They spread out and systematically went through each room. It wasn't a big apartment, and it wasn't in the best part of town, although it was tastefully decorated. Like Kenzie had said, Bella Montague didn't come from money. Compared to her wealthy friends, she was a pauper.

There was a photograph of Bella as a child, playing on the beach, bucket and spade in hand. She was smiling, her eyes twinkling in the Miami sun. There was another photograph of her and Snake, presumably when they were dating. It was in a polished silver frame without a smudge on it. This photograph was valuable to her.

He couldn't see any photographs of her foster parents, or any indication of her life before she'd come to Miami.

"I'll take the main bedroom." He headed for the stairs.

Bella's bedroom was sparse and functional. She had a place for everything, and everything served a purpose. No frivolous items, no paintings on the walls, no trinkets.

He searched the dresser and found a box of jewelry. It was all cheap stuff, nothing valuable. He frowned and opened her closet. Again, only the bare minimum.

Something wasn't right.

He took out his phone and called Ryan, back at the station. She answered immediately.

"Ping Bella Montague and Snake's phones. I want to know where they are, right now."

"Yes, sir."

She hung up and he got back to searching. It was in the spare bedroom that he found a trapdoor to the loft. Bella lived on the second floor of a property that had been converted into two apartments. Downstairs got the garden, and she got the loft.

He looked around for the pole, found it behind the door, and pulled down the hatch. It smelled dusty and dank.

He reached for the ladder and extended it down. If that suitcase was anywhere, it was up here. Stupid to keep it in her own home if she had, but it was highly noticeable. Discarding it would be risky. Even cleaned, there was a chance they'd find Natalia's DNA in it. These days, all it took was a tiny drop.

He climbed into the dark room, his pulse increasing with every step. He searched for a light but didn't find one. Improvising, he used the flashlight on his phone. He stumbled around for a full 10 minutes before he found the suitcase, stashed behind some old picture frames.

"Gotcha," he whispered.

His phone rang. It was Ryan.

"Sir, Bella Montague is with Snake at Miami Airport."

"Shit, really?"

"Yes, sir."

"They're making a run for it. Get a team out there now, and call airport security. Do not let them get on a plane."

"Sir!"

Taking out a pair of gloves, he pulled them on and reached for the suitcase. It was one of the largest he'd seen. Kenzie was right, it could hold a body, especially one the size of Natalia Cruz.

Heart thumping, he carried it downstairs. "Get this to the lab," he told one of the officers, then he raced back to his car.

"You found it, didn't you?" Kenzie said, the moment he climbed in. He hadn't let her take part in the search. It made sense now why Bella had met them at a hotel. She didn't want to risk them coming here, where the evidence was hidden.

He nodded. "Yeah, and guess what? Bella and Snake are at the airport."

She paled. "They're escaping. They've got Natalia's money and now they're flying off into the sunset together."

"Not if we can help it."

Reid flicked on the lights and put his foot down. The Ford shot forward, and he drove like a maniac to the airport.

"We can't let them get on that plane," he muttered.

Kenzie, seatbelt securely fastened, sat silently beside him. She let him concentrate on getting them there quickly and in one piece.

His phone rang. He answered and put it on speaker. "Garrett."

"Sir, it's Ryan. I've notified airport security. They're looking for them now. It appears they've already checked in for a flight to Mexico City."

"Crap," Kenzie whispered. "We're going to be too late."

Reid gritted his teeth and kept driving. "Stop them at the boarding gate."

"They're trying. They don't know whether they've boarded or not."

Crap! "We're almost there."

Moments later, they skidded to a halt outside the airport terminal. Reid grabbed his phone, still on speaker, and jumped out of the car, leaving the door open. Kenzie followed. Together, they sprinted to the concourse.

"Which boarding gate?" he shouted.

Ryan's voice echoed back. "Terminal C, Gate Twenty-three."

"This way," called Kenzie, changing direction. Reid flashed his badge at the terminal security checkpoint, and despite some worried glances, they were let through.

Reid took note of the gate numbers as they raced past. "Twenty-three," he called when he saw the sign. "It's still boarding."

They burst into the waiting room for the Mexico City flight. Travelers were queuing to board. Uniformed airport staff were surveying the line. Reid ran up to one of them. "Any luck?"

"No, sir. We don't think they've boarded yet."

"I'll check the restroom," said Kenzie.

She darted into the ladies' before he could stop her. If they weren't in the line, they must be hiding somewhere, waiting for a chance to board. At least they weren't on the flight.

He checked the men's, but it was empty. A short time later, Kenzie re-emerged.

"Nope," she said. "She's not in there."

He raked a hand through his hair. "Where could they be?"

"Could security be mistaken and they did make it onto the flight?"

"I don't know. We'd better check."

They were just making their way to the front of the line when Reid's phone buzzed.

It was Ryan. "Yeah?"

"Sir, they've been spotted in the North Terminal, leaving the airport. They're heading to the bus station."

"Thanks, Ryan," he yelled, taking off again.

"What?" Kenzie raced to keep up.

"They're in the North Terminal," he told her. "They know they're cornered. They're heading for the bus station."

Together, they sprinted out of the boarding area, through airport security and back into the central terminal.

"North is that way." Reid's eye caught a signboard. Kenzie was breathing too hard to reply. They kept running.

"There!" Kenzie pointed, as the two fugitives climbed aboard a shuttle bus. The doors closed and the bus was about to depart. Kenzie stood in front of it and held up her hands.

The driver tooted his horn, but she stood her ground.

Reid pounded on the door and held up his badge.

The doors wheezed open.

"Miami PD," panted Reid, boarding the bus. He looked up the rows until he spotted Bella and Snake. "You two are coming with me."

46

There was a round of applause as Reid led Bella and Snake into the police department for questioning. They'd been read their rights and their hands were cuffed behind their backs.

Snake was complaining profusely, but Bella was silent. She knew the game was up. Kenzie could see it in her eyes.

"She's with me," Reid had said at the front desk, and Kenzie had been waved through. Now she kept to the back of the group, trying to remain inconspicuous.

"Prep them for interrogation." Reid handed them over to a correctional officer.

"They'll both get a chance to lawyer up," he said.

Pérez came out of his office. "Well done." He thumped Reid on the back. "You got 'em."

"Yeah, they were making a quick getaway," he said.

His gaze fell on Kenzie, and he frowned. "What's she doing here?"

"She was instrumental in helping me apprehend the suspects," he said. "Kenzie Gilmore, meet Lieutenant Pérez."

They shook hands, but Kenzie didn't like the distrustful look in Pérez's eyes. "I'm here to observe," she said.

"I said she could watch the interview," Reid explained. "May as well get the facts straight."

Pérez grunted, then pulled Reid aside. "Keep an eye on her, you hear? We can't have her wandering all over the department."

"Yes, sir."

Pérez gave Kenzie a curt nod and disappeared to his office.

Reid gave her a thumbs up. "You're in, for now. But don't push it, okay?"

Her eyes gleamed. "I won't. Thank you."

Finally, she was getting the inside scoop. She glanced around the squad room. The activity, the buzz, the efficient detectives going about their business. This was where she should have been. A pang of regret hit her in the chest, and she caught her breath.

"You okay?"

"Yeah. Just thinking about how different things could have been."

He grimaced sympathetically. "Probably best not to dwell on it."

He was right. She couldn't change what had happened. Couldn't take back the past. At least she was here now, to witness the apprehension of Natalia Cruz's killers.

Snake was put into Interrogation Room 1. The camera on the screen was live, and Kenzie watched as he slumped in his chair, looking more pissed off than scared.

"I can't believe he planned to kill his wife," a young female detective said, coming to stand next to her. "I always thought they were so much in love."

"So did I," murmured Kenzie.

"Detective Ryan, by the way." The detective smiled at her.

They shook hands. "Kenzie Gilmore."

"From the *Herald*. I know, I read your articles."

"Oh." Kenzie took in the young detective. She had dark hair pulled back in a tight bun, her uniform was spotless, and she had ink stains on her fingers. "Reid's mentioned you."

Her eyes lit up. "Really?"

"Yeah, he thinks very highly of you."

Ryan flushed. "He's one of the best detectives I've ever worked with. I'm glad he's back. I guess we have you to thank for that?"

"I didn't persuade him to do anything he didn't want to do," she said.

"Well, you gave him a nudge. That's all he needed." She nodded to the screen. "Here comes Snake's attorney."

The same man as before slid into the chair next to Snake. They put their heads together and talked in low voices. The audio was off so the outsiders couldn't hear their exchange.

Then Bella's camera came online. She sat alone, a forlorn figure in the sparse interview room. "Didn't she want representation?" Kenzie asked.

"No, she declined."

They watched as Reid walked into the room. Lieutenant Pérez joined the crowd at the screen. "Here we go," he mumbled under his breath.

Reid sat down, his long legs stretching under the table. Bella looked pale, her body stiff, her eyes guarded. She was on the defensive.

They got the preliminaries out of the way, then Reid got straight to it.

"What was Natalia Cruz's suitcase doing in your loft?" He slid a photograph of the floral case across the table. She didn't even glance at it.

"Snake asked me to keep it."

"Did you know it contained Natalia Cruz's DNA?"

Kenzie cast a glance at Pérez, but he just shook his head.

"We haven't gotten the lab results back yet," whispered Ryan.

Bella didn't appear shocked. "It is her suitcase."

"Were you aware that it was used to hide her body the night she was killed?"

Her eyes widened, just enough to appear surprised. "No."

"She's lying," Kenzie muttered.

"Why did Snake ask you to keep it? What reason did he give?"

"After her body was discovered in the Glades, he said he wanted to hide it, so the police didn't think he had anything to do with her death."

"Why would we think that?" Reid's gaze was fixed on her face.

"Because he'd told the police it was missing. He knew she'd left him, walked out on their marriage, but he needed a way to prove it. So he hid the suitcase."

"He told you Natalia had walked out on their marriage?"

"Yes, he said things had been tense between them for a while, and she was jealous of his relationship with me, so after our tiff at the launch party, she left."

"What reason did she have to be jealous? She was the one married to him."

Kenzie saw Bella's shoulders stiffen. "Because he was still in love with me. I knew it, and so did she."

"Were you having an affair?"

A pause.

Bella sighed. "No, we weren't. He wouldn't do that to Natalia. But he realized after they were married that he'd made a mistake. They put on a show for their fans, but he didn't love her."

Reid drummed his fingers on the table. "Did Snake actually tell you that Natalia was gone when he got back from the party?"

"Yes, he called me in a panic. Said she'd disappeared and they'd searched everywhere for her."

Reid looked through the folder on the table in front of him. He pulled out a sheet of paper with her call records on. "According to your phone data, you never received a call from Snake that night."

"He must have called from the hotel phone, then."

Reid narrowed his gaze.

"She's so full of it," murmured Kenzie. "Does she expect him to believe she knew nothing about Snake's plan to kill his wife?"

"Evidently," said Ryan.

Kenzie snorted in disgust.

"What happened next?" Reid asked.

"I picked up Snake and we went looking for her. We went to their house, called her father, and eventually went to look for her in the Glades."

"Why there?" Reid jumped on her words.

"Because Snake said she sometimes went out there. I don't know why. You'd have to ask him."

"And you just went along with all this?"

"Yeah, why wouldn't I?"

"Did you want him to take his wife back?"

"I could see he was concerned. She wasn't in her right mind when she left. He said she hadn't been feeling well. She was on antidepressants. She'd been drinking."

"So you acted the concerned friend?"

"Exactly."

Reid slid another photograph across to her. "I take it you'll want to revise your previous statement. The one where you told us you'd given a friend a lift home?"

Her eyes flickered a little, enough for Kenzie to mutter, "She's full of shit."

This time it was Pérez's turn to snort.

"She claims to know nothing about it," Reid said when he emerged from the interview. Despite not having slept for almost 36 hours, he was buzzing with pent-up energy. How he did it, Kenzie had no idea. She was lagging, and she'd managed to get a few hours at his place before they'd received the search warrant.

"She was in on the whole thing," Kenzie said. "I bet she helped plan it. She's the brains, remember?"

"Sir, there's a call for you," Ryan said from her desk. "The lab results are in."

47

Reid sat down opposite Eric Snider, aka DJ Snake. The musician had an arrogant, almost smug look on his face. Reid couldn't wait to wipe it off.

"You're being charged with the suspected murder of your wife, Natalia Cruz," he began. "Do you have anything to say about that?"

He may as well give him a chance to come clean.

"I don't know what you're talking about. My wife disappeared, then a week later, showed up dead."

"Yes, it does appear that way." Reid gave him a hard look. "Except, we know what really happened. Bella talked."

Some of the arrogance disappeared. There was an uncertainty in his eyes now. *Good*, thought Reid. He succeeded at leading Snake on.

"I don't care what Bella thinks. I didn't kill my wife."

"Bella is convinced you're still in love with her. She said you realized your mistake after you got married and that you and Natalia put on a show for your fans. Her words."

His eyes hardened. "She said that?"

"Yeah. Is she wrong?"

His shoulders slumped. "No, she's not wrong. Things went bad after we got married. I think we both knew we'd made a mistake. We rushed into it. Didn't take the time to get to know each other. I don't blame her for leaving me."

"After the launch party?"

"Yes."

"But she didn't leave you, did she? You hid her suitcase at Bella's house to make it look like she'd left you."

There was a pause. His lawyer shifted uncomfortably in his chair.

"Because I couldn't understand why she'd just up and leave without a word. Without taking her belongings. I was hurt, so I decided to make it look like she'd packed her suitcase and left."

"And that's what you told the police the next morning."

"Yes." He glanced at his hands. The smug look was gone now as he fought to make them believe his version of events.

"It's what happened. It's not my fault that serial killer got his hands on her after she walked out."

"He didn't," said Reid.

"What?" Snake frowned, confused. "I thought he confessed."

"He was paid to confess to Natalia's murder. By your ex-girlfriend."

Snake bit his lip. Reid could sense the cogs going round in his brain. How had they found out? Who'd talked? The lawyer? Bella? And how much did they know?

Reid decided to bluff it out. "We know everything, Snake. You planned to murder your wife that night. You spiked her drink, and then you took her back to the hotel room where you strangled her."

"No, it's not true!"

"You killed her right in that hotel room, before putting her body into her own suitcase, and then you went back to the party." Reid glared at him. "You even said something in the corridor to make it look like you were talking to her, when in fact it was all an act. A show for the cameras. Always the performer, right?"

Snake had stopped protesting. He kept his eyes down and refused to look at Reid.

His attorney was decidedly uncomfortable now.

"Your DNA was on that suitcase along with your wife's."

"No comment."

"We found hair and saliva inside the suitcase. Skin cells and fibers from the dress she was wearing at the time."

"Those could have got in there from general handling of the suitcase," the attorney pointed out.

"Try convincing a jury of that," snapped Reid.

When there was no response from Snake, Reid continued. "After the party, you pulled the suitcase down to the beach with Natalia's body in it. Bella picked you up and the two of you took your wife's body to the Glades to dump her. The problem was, you couldn't get rid of the suitcase because it would be found, and your DNA would be all over it, so you dumped her body making it look like she'd been a victim of the Swamp Strangler."

"She was his victim," spat Snake. "I had nothing to do with it."

"This is all conjecture, Detective," said the lawyer.

"You were caught on camera," Reid reminded him. "That's you in the passenger seat, isn't it?"

"No comment."

"It could be anyone," said the lawyer. "We've been through this, Detective."

"There was only one flaw in your plan," Reid said.

Snake looked up.

"The Strangler raped all of his victims. He toyed with them. He tied them up and sexually assaulted them. Sometimes for days. You didn't know that, did you? Because that wasn't made public."

Snake's gaze darkened.

"When we examined her body, it was obvious she wasn't one of the Strangler's victims. And now that Halston's lawyer has confessed to coercion, your denial is worthless. He's willing to testify that Bella offered to pay for a biographer to write a book about the Strangler if he confessed to Natalia's murder."

"I told her it was a bad idea," he muttered.

His attorney gasped.

"Told who?" Reid asked, not a flicker betraying his relief. "Bella?"

"Yeah, I told her we didn't need him. Trying to bribe him was risky."

"It was a brilliant plan," confessed Reid, playing to Snake's ego. Now that he'd broken, he wanted to draw the sucker out. "With the Strangler confessing to her murder, there would have been nothing we could do. The case would have been closed. If only it had paid off."

Snake balled his hands into fists.

"It's over, Snake. You're going down for first degree murder."

"It was all Bella's idea," he said.

Reid relaxed into his chair. "Why don't you tell me about it?"

"She came up with it when we were dating. She never had any money, and my record label was threatening to drop me if I didn't come up with a number one hit."

"The pressure at the top?"

"Yeah. Anyway, Bella had this friend, Natalia. She was beautiful, but simple, you know? She was an heiress, had bundles of money. Bella said if I married Natalia, I'd be set for life."

Reid watched him in silence.

"I didn't want to at first. I said I'd rather be with her, but Bella insisted. She said it would be easy to get Natalia to fall in love with me. She was so gullible, she'd believe anything. Then we could plan it so that she had an accident or something, and I'd inherit her fortune."

"An accident?"

He nodded miserably. "It sounded simple back then. I didn't think it would get so out of hand."

"Murder is never simple," Reid pointed out.

"Anyway, those bodies started popping up in the swamp. Bella said we could make it look like Natalia was another one of his victims."

Another brilliant plan on Bella's part, except she hadn't known about the sexual assault.

"But you had to get rid of the suitcase."

"I asked Bella to keep it. We couldn't dump it, and with police sniffing around, we didn't have time to destroy it."

Reid nodded. That's what he'd thought.

"After Bella was arrested, we decided to leave town. Natalia's estate was going to be all mine. I'm a rich man now." He grimaced. "Or at least I would have been."

He wouldn't get a cent of that money now. Convicted murderers didn't inherit. It was against the law.

"You were going to run off into the sunset together?" To use Kenzie's words.

Snake gave a sad nod. "We almost got away with it too."

Almost.

48

Reid sat outside the warehouse, waiting for Torres to finish work. It was dark already. The manager had been putting in long hours lately, and Reid got a feeling something was about to go down.

He'd kept a close watch on his security cam, still transmitting from the opposite building. He'd been back a few times to change the batteries, and now he had a pretty good idea of Torres's working habits. Yet, he still didn't know much about his personal life.

Tonight, he found out.

Preparing for the trial had occupied most of his days, but this was important and couldn't wait. If the cartel were up to something, he wanted to know.

Torres appeared shortly after eight. He locked the side door, patted the security guard on the back, then left in his Audi. Reid, parked out of sight behind the vacant prefab, eased after him. Since the Morales cartel had reappeared, nobody knew where they were based, or where the top guys lived.

Reid could have enlightened them, but he'd kept the location of the warehouse to himself, even when the DEA had rounded up the Kings, including Matt Garcia, which effectively ended the turf war.

Police had found one of the guns used to kill Navarro in Garcia's house, complete with a fine set of fingerprints, so he was going away for life. First degree murder. He was lucky not to get the death penalty.

For now, the Warriors reigned supreme. But it wouldn't be long before the Kings rose again, or another gang took their place. Until then, Miami could enjoy the relative peace.

He followed Torres to an upscale neighborhood just minutes away from the Miami oceanfront, then pulled over and watched as the Audi drove through a pair of wrought iron security gates.

Reid cut the engine and slipped out of the car. He surveyed the colonial-style villa, complete with columns and an ornate crest. So this was Torres's Miami hideaway. He glanced around for a security guard but didn't spot one. In addition to the Audi, a Mercedes-Benz was parked in the driveway. A second car, or a girlfriend?

Torres was living a relatively normal life. Operating a legitimate business. On paper, he was a model citizen. Except Reid knew better.

Torres got out of the car, opened the front door, and disappeared inside.

Now what?

Did he wait until the cartel manager had gone to bed, then try to break in? Did he come back while he was out?

He was still pondering 10 minutes later, when the front door reopened, and Torres appeared along with an unnatural blond in a bright red dress. They were arguing. "We're late." Her shrill voice rang over the still night air. "The reservation was for eight o'clock. You promised."

"I can't help it," he growled. "I got tied up at work. Did you let them know?"

"Yes, but it's rude. We're always late."

"Get in the car," he barked.

The woman got in and the gates glided open. Reid hid behind a tree a few houses down. Decision time. Follow Torres and see who he was meeting or use the opportunity to have a look around his villa.

Reid stayed put.

Once the Audi's headlights had disappeared down the road, he scaled the wall and dropped soundlessly into the cartel member's property. He hadn't seen Torres set any alarm, perhaps because he'd been in a hurry and his girlfriend was nagging him.

Reid hoped.

He walked around the house, keeping an eye out for cameras. Surprisingly, there weren't any. Then again, what would a legitimate businessman need with security cameras? To be safe, he pulled on a balaclava that he'd stuffed into his pocket at the last minute. He didn't want this coming back to bite him.

Wearing forensic gloves, he forced a window at the back, then held his breath. If the alarm sounded, he could leap over the wall on this side and disappear onto the golf course behind the house. It was a gorgeous spot, tranquil and peaceful. Removed from the manic hustle and bustle of Miami Beach.

All was quiet. Exhaling, he slid open the window and climbed in. A lamp had been left on in the living room, casting a welcoming glow. The house was tastefully decorated with expensive furnishings and fine art on the walls. There were signs of a female touch, so the woman must have lived with him, her Mercedes in the driveway.

Wife? He hadn't thought Torres was married, but a lot could happen in a year and a half.

He searched the downstairs living area, but apart from the framed photographs of Torres with the blond on the mantelpiece, there wasn't much to see.

He ventured upstairs. Three bedrooms and a study. He ignored the bedrooms and headed for the study. If there was anything to find, it would be in there.

The study was as neat as the office in the warehouse. Obviously, Torres was a highly organized individual, but he needed to be to run the cartel's Miami interests as well as his own dock operation.

Reid made sure the blinds were drawn, then turned on the light. Torres wouldn't be back for a while, so he had time. He started with the desk, a large, mahogany piece with three drawers down either side.

He found the usual bits of paper and stationery, a file with the company name on it containing invoices, and personal utility bills. Alberto Torres was now going by the name of Alex Guerra. That was why nothing had flagged on their systems.

Other than the name change, there was nothing to hint of his drug-running sideline. A man like Torres wouldn't be stupid enough to leave anything incriminating in plain sight. Did his wife know what he did for a living? How he afforded this villa in one of Miami's prime real estate areas? If she didn't suspect something, she was a fool. A dock operating equipment company wouldn't support this kind of lifestyle. Or maybe she just didn't care.

The lower drawer on the left side was locked. He searched for a key but couldn't find one. In the end, he took out all the other drawers and went in from the top. No point in locking one if you didn't lock them all.

He rifled through the contents. He found a personal bank statement that he was sure the DEA would give their eyes and teeth to see. This had nothing to do with Regal Holdings. Every month there were eye-watering payments from other shell companies, names that made no sense and probably couldn't be traced. Alberto Torres was a very wealthy man.

Reid took a photograph with his phone, then put them back. He was about to close the drawer when he felt it give a little. He pushed it again and sure enough, it jiggled out.

A false bottom.

He took everything out and laid it on the floor. The last thing he wanted was for Torres to know someone had been through his stuff. Then he removed the flat board bottom and put it aside. There were only two items in the fake compartment.

A handgun and a photograph.

The gun was a Sig Sauer 9mm, loaded. Now that was interesting.

Did Torres keep it here for emergencies? Ready to go in case he was ambushed or had to make a quick getaway?

Reid pulled out the photograph and his breath caught in his throat.

It couldn't be.

He stared at it for a long time, but there was no mistake. The photograph was of Torres and Bianca. They were on a beach somewhere, their arms around each other. That wasn't surprising. Bianca had been undercover as his bit on the side. It was the look on her face that shocked him. Her eyes shone as she laughed up at him. Shone in a way they never had with Reid. The most surprising thing was Torres was smiling back. He was relaxed, tanned, and clearly besotted.

There was obviously more to their relationship than Bianca had let on. Had she fallen for her mark? For the man she was supposed to be betraying?

He stared at the photograph again. How could a man who looked at a woman like that shoot her in the head? Was he that ruthless a bastard?

He worked for the cartel, after all. Perhaps he was a cold-hearted psycho. But why did he keep a picture of the two of them in his desk drawer? This picture? This intimate moment? Was it a macabre keepsake? A memento?

Reid frowned, unsettled. Perhaps he hadn't known Bianca as well as he'd thought he did. He put the photo and gun back, then replaced the contents of the drawer.

What had Bianca got herself into?

One thing was for sure. He needed to do more digging if he was going to get to the bottom of this, but it would have to wait. The trial was coming up and he didn't have the time right now. But he would get to it. It had been a year and a half already.

Alberto Torres, or rather Alex Guerra, wasn't going anywhere.

49

"Congratulations," Kenzie said as Reid got out of his car. As soon as the court case had ended, she'd driven out to his place to wait for him. She hadn't seen much of him in the weeks leading to the trial. He'd been busy preparing evidence and writing reports. They had to make sure both the case against Halston and the case against Snake and Bella were watertight.

She'd attended the proceedings, of course, but in the press section. He'd been in the front row with Pérez. The trial had been drawn out over a week. Reid had been asked to testify, as had the medical examiner. Kenzie had felt proud to have been part of the investigation.

Entry had been restricted for fear of Natalia's fans causing an outburst. As it was, both Snake and Bella were getting death threats. Natalia may have been "simple" and "vacant" but she was loved.

"Thanks," Reid replied. "I'm just glad they're behind bars."

The jury had been unanimous in their decision. Guilty as charged. Snake had been given life without parole, while Bella, who'd been charged with second degree murder, had gotten 10 years.

"Bella should have gotten more," said Kenzie. "She was the mastermind behind it."

"She played everyone," Reid said. "Even Snake, the man she professed to love."

They went inside. As usual, it was stiflingly hot in the cabin. Reid opened the patio doors leading to the deck, but there wasn't much in the way of a breeze.

"Want a beer?" he asked.

"Sure, I think we deserve one."

He got two from the kitchen and they stood on the deck overlooking the grassy river. The sky was strewn with voluminous clouds, but the humidity pressed down on them like a blanket. Kenzie wiped a bead of perspiration off her temple.

"Cheers." She raised her bottle. "To a successful investigation."

"We couldn't have done it without you," he said. "You came up with the parking lot idea, and you figured out how Bella and Snake killed Natalia. I'm sorry you didn't get any of the credit."

"I got my exclusive." The news had broken the day after Halston's arrest. The *Herald* had dedicated a whole two page spread to it.

"You deserved it." He clinked her bottle.

She chuckled. "I think my editor was just relieved nobody filed a lawsuit against us. It had the potential to go that way with Snake being so sensitive about his career."

"It was just a ruse to get you to back off," Reid said. "He was more than happy to give it all up and live in Mexico with Bella."

"Yeah, that's true."

"Anyway, I just wanted to say thank you." His eyes burned steadily into hers. She caught her breath.

"You're welcome. I knew we made a good team."

He grinned, easing the tension. "Ryan did some excellent work tracking Fernández. Thanks to her, we picked up Ivan Petrovitch. Once he heard he'd be deported back to Serbia, he was happy to strike a deal."

She chuckled. "I'm glad. Did you manage to get any of the investors' funds?"

"Some." He shrugged. "But that's not my department. We passed it on to Fraud. They're dealing with it."

"I liked Detective Ryan," Kenzie said.

"Yeah, she's young, but she's a good detective. She's got a great career ahead of her."

Kenzie studied him. "And what about you, Detective Garrett? Are you going back to Miami PD full time?"

"I haven't decided yet."

"Really? I thought for sure you'd go back."

"That place doesn't have very good memories for me. I told Pérez I'd work on this case as a consultant, answering only to him, but I don't think I could run a team again."

"Why not? They all look up to you."

He shrugged. "It wouldn't be the same."

She narrowed her eyes. "Okay. So what are you going to do?"

"For one thing, I thought I'd take a look at your mother's case."

She gasped. "You got the files?"

"I made copies."

She gave a little hop. "Reid, I don't know what to say."

She couldn't believe it. Finally, after all this time, she was going to get a peek at the investigation into her mother's disappearance. Her heart surged with gratitude.

"You're welcome." He grinned at her.

"Can I see them?"

"Sure. They're on my nightstand."

She darted into his bedroom and found two thick manilla folders lying next to his bed. "You didn't tell me you had these," she chastised, coming back outside.

He tilted his head. "I wanted to have a look at them first. I knew as soon as I told you you'd want to see them."

"Is there anything interesting inside? Any leads?" She felt the familiar buzz of anticipation. It was the same feeling she got when she hit on a big case.

"Maybe, I'm not sure yet. There are one or two things we could follow up on, a couple of potential witnesses we could talk to if they're still alive, but other than that, it was carried out pretty much by the book."

"I always thought they gave up too quickly." She hugged the folders against her chest, still unable to believe he'd actually gotten them.

"Yeah, that was a bit odd," he admitted. "But I suppose with no evidence, they couldn't justify the resources."

"Maybe." She wasn't convinced. "Can I take these home?"

"What do you think?"

Unable to help herself, she wrapped an arm around his neck and kissed him on the cheek. "You're the best, you know that?"

He looked away. "Make sure you bring them back, so I've got something to work off."

She grinned up at him. "You didn't think I was going to let you do this alone, did you?"

He smirked. "No, I guess not."

"Do they know you've got these?" she asked.

His eyes flashed. "No, but it was 20 years ago. I didn't think anyone would care."

"I care," she said softly.

"I know you do," he replied.

"Thank you, Reid." She glanced down at the folders. "This means a lot."

"Maybe you can pay me back by cooking for me one night. I'm still waiting."

She laughed. "Oh, yeah. I'd forgotten about that."

"I showed you mine," he teased.

"Okay," she relented. "If you come over tomorrow, I'll show you mine."

His gaze was warm. "It's a date."

The End

The story continues in *Dead Heat*, the next Kenzie Gilmore thriller. Head to the next page for a sneak peek!

Stay up to date with Biba Pearce's new releases:
https://liquidmind.media/biba-pearce-sign-up-1/
You'll receive a **free** copy of *Hard Line: A Kenzie Gilmore Prequel.*

Did you enjoy Afterburn? Leave a review to let us know your thoughts!!

DEAD HEAT: CHAPTER 1

She was at the Christmas market with her friend Bethany. It was a perfect Miami evening—warm, balmy, not a breath of wind. The holiday village sparkled with Christmas cheer. Fairy lights hung from the store fronts; the sound of music filled the air; along with chatter and laughter; and Kenzie could smell roasting chestnuts and the sweet aroma of cotton candy.

An enormous Christmas tree stood in the middle of the square. Green elves with pink cheeks surrounded it and sang carols while Santa sat in his grotto overlooking the square.

Bethany nudged Kenzie. "Look, there's Tom and Christian."

Kenzie glanced over to where Bethany pointed and spotted the two boys from school. They were both cute, with long, tousled hair, torn jeans, and loose-fitting T-shirts.

"Hey, mom. Can we go over to Santa's grotto?" she asked.

Angie, Kenzie's mom, didn't hear her. Angie had linked her arm with her husband's, and Uncle Larry was leading them into the mulled wine tent. Kenzie didn't like mulled wine, or any wine for that matter, and the tent was filled with adults.

She patted her mother on the shoulder. "Bethany and I are going over to Santa's grotto, okay?"

Angie smiled. "Sure, honey. Actually, I'll come with you. I want to look at the other booths. I haven't finished my Christmas shopping yet."

"I'll meet you back here," Angie said to Kenzie's father, giving him a peck on the cheek. Then the three of them walked out of the tent together. "Be good, girls."

Kenzie gave her a half-wave and ran off with Bethany towards the grotto. That was the last time she ever saw her mother.

The girls flirted with Tom and Christian until they left to go to a friend's house. Then Kenzie saw her father standing in the middle of the square looking around. "Have you seen your mother?" he asked as she and Bethany walked up.

"No, she was looking at the booths."

"I can't find her."

Uncle Larry emerged from the mulled wine tent, his cheeks flushed. "She's not in there."

They walked around the market, still busy with festive shoppers, but her mother was nowhere to be seen.

"Could she have gone home?" Larry asked.

"I don't think so. Not without telling me." Bud, Kenzie's father, scratched his head.

"Maybe she felt sick," offered Bethany.

"It's possible." Her father pulled out his cell phone. "I'll call her."

The call went straight to voicemail. He shook his head and hung up. "Her phone's not on."

Kenzie's voice trembled. "Where could she be?"

Her father shrugged. "She must have wandered off. I'm sure there's no reason to worry."

"I'll call Nora," Larry said. "She can check at the house."

"Thanks, Larry."

Her uncle pulled out his phone and spoke to his wife. They lived a few doors down from Kenzie and her parents. Nora had brought them a flower arrangement to welcome them to the neighborhood when they'd first moved in. That's how they'd become friends.

Bethany's phone beeped, and she glanced at it. "That's my mom. She wants me home."

Bud hesitated. He had to get Bethany home, but Kenzie could tell he didn't want to leave the square without his wife.

"I'll walk her back," Larry offered. "I'll let you know when I hear from Nora. Keep your phone on."

"I will. Thanks Larry. We'll wait here in case she comes back."

"No problem."

Larry left with Bethany, while Kenzie stood beside her father under the giant tree's flashing lights, wondering what had happened to her mother. A strange pressure was building inside her chest, which she later recognized as panic.

"I'm going to look again." She took off before her father could stop her. She ran from booth to booth, peering inside, expecting to see her mother's blonde hair as she inspected ornaments or jars of spiced jam. The market was large, and Kenzie was exhausted and overwrought when she got back to her father.

"She's not anywhere." She burst into tears and clung to her father. "Where is she?"

"I don't know. She's not at home. Nora checked." He glanced around helplessly. "I think I'll have to call Vic."

Vic was his partner at the Miami Police Department. A bear of a man, or that's how he seemed to Kenzie. Vic and her father were as close as brothers. Her father always said he'd trust Vic with his life. Bud turned his back on Kenzie and spoke rapidly into the phone for a few minutes. She caught the tension in his voice. It made her worry even more.

Mom, where are you?

A short time later, Vic arrived, followed by two police vehicles. Their blue lights drowned out those from the Christmas tree. People stopped to stare.

"She disappeared." Bud threw his hands up in the air. "Vanished, into thin air."

That's when the nightmare really began.

Kenzie woke up covered in perspiration. She hadn't revisited that awful night for years. It wasn't a nightmare, rather a reliving of the events leading to her mother's disappearance. A lucid dream. And it was always the same. The market, the smells, the grotto, then the overwhelming fear.

She propped herself up in bed and reached for her glass of water. The police file was still open on the bed beside her. She'd fallen asleep reading it. She took a glug and then fell back onto the pillows. Reading the case files was getting to her.

Reid.

She needed to speak to Reid. He'd know what to do.

She showered and dressed, then left the house. The ex-police detective would be at home, in his isolated cabin on the Glades. After his last job consulting for the Miami PD, he'd decided not to go back full time. A pity, Kenzie thought. He was so good at it.

As someone who would give anything to work for the Miami PD, she didn't understand it, but she wasn't him. She hadn't lost a colleague and lover in the line of duty. She didn't carry the burden of that death on her shoulders, though it wasn't his fault.

But that was Reid. He took his responsibilities seriously. He had integrity, and that was a rare trait. It was one of the reasons she trusted him.

Trust. That was huge for her.

Kenzie Gilmore trusted no one. Not until she'd met Reid earlier that year and they'd worked the Swamp Strangler case. Now he was helping her figure out what had happened to her mother almost twenty years ago.

She got into her car and drove out of her condo complex, the manilla folder on the passenger seat.

DEAD HEAT: CHAPTER 1

After a forty-minute drive, she turned off the busy US-27 highway and onto a deserted road to the Everglades Holiday Park. The signpost specified airboat rentals, alligator tours, boat hire, and a general store. It was a muggy, overcast day and the clouds above signified rain–and lots of it. It had been humid as hell for a week now, and they were due a thunderstorm.

Reid's cabin was five miles down this road. Previously an airboat tour company right on the water's edge, he'd converted it into a livable home. It was very rustic, no AC and annoyingly temperamental Wi-Fi, but the view was spectacular, and he enjoyed being away from the chaos of the city.

Kenzie pulled off the road and parked beside his Ford Ranger pickup. He was home. She knocked on the door, but as usual, there was no answer. Not waiting, she made her way around the house, squeezing through the gap in the foliage, her feet squelching on the soggy ground.

He was cleaning his airboat, the water gushing from the hose onto the deck. "You really should get a buzzer." She climbed onto the waterfront wooden deck in front of the house. "You can't hear a thing from out here."

"That's the point." He grinned up at her.

She shook her head. "Can we talk?"

"Sure, just give me a moment." He didn't need to ask what she wanted to discuss. She'd had the case files for a week now. He finished hosing down the boat, then climbed onto the small walkway. He curled the length of the hose around his hand and elbow, then looped it over a low wooden pole.

"Help yourself to a drink." He strode past her into the house, leaving a trail of wet footprints. "I won't be long."

"Sure."

She took a jug of iced tea out of the fridge and poured each of them a glass. When he got back, she was sitting in the living room, the folder on the coffee table in front of her.

"Thanks." He picked up the glass and downed it in one.

Her gaze fell on his unshaven jaw and big hand clutching the glass. "I dreamt about her last night," she whispered.

He sat down opposite her, the wicker chair creaking under his weight.

"Your mom?"

"Yeah. We were in the market square on the night she disappeared. I remembered everything like it was yesterday."

He watched her, waiting for her to continue.

"I haven't had that dream in years, yet it felt so real. I could smell the mulled wine and pinecones."

"Reopening the investigation will bring back those memories," he said softly. "Are you sure you want to do this?"

She didn't hesitate. "Of course I'm sure. I need to find out what happened."

"Okay." He leaned back. "I said I'd help you and I will. You have to realize, though, we might not find anything. It's been a long time and—"

"I know," she cut him off. "But we have to try."

He nodded.

She took a shaky breath. "Should we start with Uncle Larry and his wife Nora? Larry was there. He's not really my uncle, more like a good friend. I just called him that."

"What about Captain Reynolds?" Reid asked. "He was your father's partner. He was the one in charge of the case. We should probably speak to him first."

She liked the way he said 'we'. It helped her recognize she wasn't doing this alone. As a reporter, she was used to investigations, but this one was personal. It felt good having Reid there to bounce ideas off.

"We should speak to him, but it might be a good idea to get some background first. He's a busy man and I don't want to waste his time."

Captain Reynolds headed the Miami PD. He'd come a long way since being Bud Gilmore's partner twenty years ago.

"Sure," agreed Reid. "I'm happy to tackle this however you want. Where is Larry now?"

"We lost touch after my mother's disappearance," Kenzie admitted. "I never saw him or his wife again. They're in Orlando now. I found an address for them in Winter Springs."

"Then, that's where we'll start."

DEAD HEAT: CHAPTER 2

"Maybe I should have called ahead." Kenzie gnawed on her lip as they drove into Winter Springs. It was an attractive suburban area nestled against the blue waters of Lake Jesup. They passed several lush, green parks, a quaint town center, and neatly lined streets with spacious houses set back from the road.

"It's a bit late now," Reid retorted. "Anyway, the element of surprise is always good."

Larry and his wife lived in such a house. It looked new. The garden was well taken care of, and the driveway was swept clean despite the leaves turning a burnished orange above them.

Kenzie remembered Nora had been a florist back in Miami. That's why she hadn't been at the Christmas market. She'd been preparing for a function the following day.

"Nice place." Reid turned off the engine.

The front door opened and a slender woman with gray hair exited. She'd aged, but Kenzie recognized her and was jolted back to afternoon barbecues at their house, helping her mom and Nora in the kitchen.

"You okay?" Reid glanced at her.

"Yeah." She got out of the car and walked toward the woman. "Nora, it's Kenzie Gilmore. Do you remember me?"

Nora stared at her, stunned. "Why Kenzie, yes, of course I remember you. What are you doing here?"

Kenzie gave her a brief hug. It seemed fitting after all these years. Their families had been close, after all.

"I'm sorry to drop by unannounced. I was hoping you'd be able to talk to me about my mother. About the night she disappeared."

Nora sighed, then gave a little nod. "I suspected this day might come." She turned to Reid and held out her hand. "And you are?"

"Oh, I'm sorry." Kenzie flushed. "This is Reid Garrett. He's helping me with her case."

Nora wore a sad little smile, then beckoned them inside. "I'll put some coffee on."

They accumulated in the spacious living room. Wide windows overlooked the front driveway and garden, which was how Nora must have seen them arrive. The floor was tiled, but a large rug covered most of it. A well-used leather sofa and matching armchair were positioned around a deep wooden chest. It was stylish and functional. On a side table stood an arrangement of photographs in silver frames.

Kenzie inspected them. Nora and Larry in their younger days. Larry fishing. A wedding picture of a young couple Kenzie didn't recognize. The Eiffel Tower.

"Have a seat," Nora called from the kitchen. "I'll be right in."

They sat next to each other. Reid was also looking at the photographs. Always observing.

Nora came back with a tray. "I must say, I am surprised to see you after all this time. I was sorry to hear about your father's passing. He was a good man."

"Thank you." Kenzie got up to help her pour the coffee. She handed one to Reid. Black. Then poured one for Nora and herself.

"Thank you, dear." Nora sat herself down in the armchair with a little squeak. "How *are* you, Kenzie? What are you doing with yourself these days?"

"I'm a reporter." She smiled. "For the Miami Herald."

"That is impressive." She glanced at Reid. "And your boyfriend? Reid, was it?"

Reid spluttered on his coffee.

"Oh, he's not my boyfriend. Reid's a–a friend." She hoped he wouldn't notice her pink cheeks. "As I said, he's helping me find out what happened to my mother."

Nora glanced between them, then smiled. "Well, it's lovely to meet you, Reid."

"Likewise, ma'am."

Kenzie kept her gaze fixed on the elderly woman. "Nora, is Larry around?"

Her shoulders slumped. "No, my dear. I'm afraid Larry died several years back. He had a heart attack, like your father. It was very sudden."

"Oh, I'm sorry to hear that."

Damn it.

She'd been hoping to get a first-hand account from him. Nora must have sensed her disappointment, because she said, "But I remember that evening as clear as day."

"You do?"

"Yes. I wasn't there when Angie disappeared, but Larry was in such a state, we talked about nothing else for weeks afterwards."

Kenzie stared at her. "Would you mind refreshing my memory?"

"Of course, dear. I'll tell you what I know." She settled back in her chair, still holding her coffee mug. "I was at home arranging flowers for the Christmas dinner at the Community Center. It was about eight-thirty when Larry called. He asked me to go to your house and see if Angie was there."

Kenzie nodded. She remembered Larry making the call.

"The house was dark. I rang the buzzer and tried the front door, but it was locked. Nobody was home."

"Did you look inside?" Reid inquired.

She shifted her gaze to him and nodded. "Yes, I peered through the windows but couldn't see any movement. I even tried the kitchen door around the back." She shook her head. "Your mother wasn't there."

Kenzie swallowed. "What happened then?"

"Well, I drove into town to help your father and Larry look for her."

Kenzie vaguely remembered a policewoman taking her home and sitting with her until her father got back late that night.

"Didn't Larry take Bethany home?" Bethany. She wondered what had happened to her. After her mother had disappeared, Kenzie had taken time off school, except when she went back, it was a different place. The people were distant. Those she thought were her friends suddenly didn't want to talk to her anymore. Perhaps their parents had warned them off. A mysterious disappearance. A father under suspicion. It didn't make for comfortable friendships.

"Yes, he did. But he came back again. We had quite a search party. That detective Vic Reynolds was there, along with a few of his officers. There was also a group of locals, mostly stall owners. We looked everywhere." She shrugged. What more could she say? Angie had vanished.

"What about the residents?" Reid asked. "I didn't read anything in the report about door-to-door inquiries."

"We did that ourselves," Nora confirmed. "I remember taking several streets and walking up and down, asking if anyone had seen Angie. The others helped. We even had a photo of her, but no one had seen a thing. It was as if she was never there."

"How can that be?" Kenzie muttered. "How can she disappear like that?"

"It's a mystery. And after all these years, no one ever found her body?"

Kenzie gripped her mug. "No. Not that we know of."

"It's most bizarre. It's almost as if…as if…" She paused, her gaze faltering.

"As if what?" prompted Reid.

"Well, as if she left on her own accord."

Kenzie opened her mouth to refute that claim when Nora held up a hand. "I'm sorry, Kenzie, Angie would never have left on her own volition. It's just that there was no trace of her. There were no reports of a kidnapping, no struggles or screams, nothing. It was like she walked out of that market square, climbed into a car, and drove away."

"Did they put out an alert at the airport?" Reid asked.

"I believe so, but that was some time after she disappeared. If someone had picked her up and driven her straight to the airport, she could have gotten away before anyone noticed."

"Her name didn't appear on any passenger lists," Kenzie insisted.

"That doesn't mean anything," Reid muttered.

It was true. False passports were possible to get hold of. If she'd left by boat, she may not even have needed one.

Kenzie shook her head. "I can't see her running away. Why would she do that? Why would she leave me? Leave her husband?" She looked at Nora. "She was happy, wasn't she?" Was there something she wasn't aware of, something her father hadn't told her?

"Yes, dear. Your parents were thrilled. In fact, they were celebrating because they'd just found out about the baby."

"The baby?" Kenzie went cold. "What baby?"

"Oh, I assumed you knew." Nora's hand fluttered to her mouth. "Oh, gosh. I'm so sorry to be the one to tell you, Kenzie. Your mother was expecting."

DEAD HEAT: CHAPTER 3

"She was pregnant!" Kenzie exploded once they got back to Reid's car. "How did I not know this?"

"I'm surprised Captain Reynolds didn't tell you," Reid said. He could understand her father not wanting to mention it, not after her mother had gone missing. It would have been too raw, too painful.

If Kenzie's father hadn't told her, he'd wanted to leave it that way. As the years passed, he probably thought it best if she didn't know. It would lessen the heartache from losing a little sister or brother, along with her mother.

"He didn't say a word. How could he keep this from me?" Her chest rose and fell as she ranted. Heat emanated off her.

"They probably didn't want to upset you," he said reasonably, but that was no excuse. She'd deserved to know.

"Maybe he didn't know," she blurted. "Captain Reynolds, I mean. Perhaps my father didn't tell him."

"It's possible, although unlikely. They were partners, right?" Partners usually knew everything about each other's lives.

Her face fell. "If Larry and Nora knew, Vic must have known. He was like a brother to my father."

"On the other hand, none of the police reports mentioned it," Reid pointed out.

"Hmm." She paused as he backed out of the driveway. "Don't you think that's strange?"

He frowned as he sped down the street. "Yeah. If your father had told the police she was pregnant, the report would have shown she had no reason to run away. Wasn't that the theory they eventually came to?"

Kenzie bit her lip. "It was a ridiculous theory. They were happy. You heard Nora say as much. They were expecting a baby. Why on earth would she run away?"

He shook his head. "I don't know, Kenzie, but we need to speak to Captain Reynolds."

She gave an eager nod. "Agreed."

The sun was a thin, orange slit on the horizon when they got back to Miami. The dense cloud cover prevented it from putting on a show, but the sea below shimmered with a peachy glow. It still hadn't rained, but it would. Soon.

Reid dropped Kenzie off, then drove back to the Glades. He was almost home when his phone rang.

He glanced at the screen. Lieutenant Pérez. Now what did he want?

"LT, how's it going?"

Pérez worked for the Miami PD and used to be Reid's boss. They'd always had a mutual respect, and Reid might say they were becoming friends.

"I'm in the neighborhood. Wanna meet at Smiley's for a drink?"

"Sure." He was only going home to an empty cabin.

"See you in ten."

Reid passed his house and drove on to a small village deeper in the swamp. If you could even call it a village. It had a bar, a motel, and a convenience store, along with a couple of fishing companies and a gator farm. The local community were not the friendliest types, and it had taken Reid six months for them to accept him. He wasn't sure if they knew he was a cop, or had been a cop, but no one had said anything about it.

He drank at Smiley's, minded his own business, and bought a few supplies at the store from time to time. That was about it.

He'd just sat down at the bar when Pérez walked in. A few locals glanced up, then went back to their beers. Rock n roll music played in the background, and four rowdy men were competing at darts in the corner. They'd probably be beating each other up by the end of the night. It was that kind of place.

"Hey, how you doing?" Pérez shook his hand.

"Good to see you," Reid said. "What can I get you?"

"Bud Light. I'm watching my weight."

Reid chuckled. "Fair enough." He ordered, then turned to Pérez. "What brings you out this way?"

"I had an errand to run. Nothing important. Thought I'd check in and find out what you're doing with yourself."

"You mean am I bored yet?"

Pérez shrugged, but his eyes twinkled. "There's a job at Miami PD if you want it."

"I told you, I'm not coming back."

"I know, but I had this feeling you were going to change your mind."

Reid shrugged. "Hasn't happened yet."

The barman put their drinks down and Reid paid.

"Fine, have it your way." Pérez glanced around. "This place gets worse every time I come here."

"Yep. There are fights every night. The cops don't even venture out here anymore."

A leggy blonde stalked past and gave Reid the once over. He didn't respond, and she kept walking.

"Why do you come here?"

"It's close. I can walk home if I have to."

"Quite a walk."

"It sobers me up."

Pérez laughed. "So, what are you going to do now? Give airboat tours?"

"Maybe. I haven't decided yet. I'm working a case for Kenzie Gilmore at the *Herald*."

"Investigation work?"

"Yeah." He didn't say what. It was best that Pérez didn't know he had that file. Maria, manager of archives at the station, wouldn't tell. He'd gotten her husband off a DUI charge a couple of years back. She owed him.

"I see how this is going. Private dick, eh?"

He shrugged. "What do you want, LT? I know you didn't come all this way to see how I was doing."

Pérez reached for his beer. "We're having trouble finding qualified detectives to work cases," he admitted. "Jonny's good, but he's young and now that Ortega's on suspension, we're a man down. We need someone with experience to run the department. We need you, Reid."

"How's his nose?" Reid asked. The last time he'd been at the Miami PD, he'd punched his fellow detective, Xavier Ortega in the face, and broken the lying shit's nose.

Pérez rolled his eyes. "Fine, thankfully. You're lucky he didn't sue you."

"It was his fault," began Reid, getting riled.

Pérez lifted a hand. "Yeah, I know. Let's not go there. He's off for six months. Lesson learned."

Except it wouldn't bring Bianca back. Ortega blew her cover and the cartelman had executed her before they could get to her. Before *he* could get to her.

He took an angry pull on his bottle.

"I take that as a no?"

Reid almost felt sorry for Pérez. He was doing his best under difficult circumstances. Crime rates were skyrocketing, the drug gangs were regrouping after last month's bust, but they'd be back. Domestic violence was out of control. And as Lieutenant, Pérez had the public to answer to, quotas to live up to. No matter how you tried, you couldn't make those stats look pretty.

"Look, I wish I could help you out, but–" He broke off as a bottle smashed behind them. They spun around to find a man clutching his head. Blood dripped through his fingers onto the floor.

"Here we go," muttered Reid.

"Bastard," growled the injured man, launching himself at his attacker. The two men went sprawling backwards into a table. The occupants scrambled out of the way, but not before their drinks went flying.

"Hey!" The barman leaped over the bar.

The overweight bouncer lumbered over. He tried to wrestle one of the men off, but they flung him aside like he was nothing more than an irritating mosquito.

Reid glanced at Pérez, who nodded.

They got up to break up the fight. Reid took the guy with the head wound, still bleeding profusely, and tried to pull him off the other guy. He got an elbow in the eye for his efforts. He grunted, then got the guy in a headlock.

"Easy," he growled, wrestling him into submission.

Pérez helped the guy on the floor to his feet. Both were panting.

"Okay, calm down you two," Pérez snapped. The brawling men stood down, catching their breath.

Reid released his guy. Freaking hell, his eye stung. He blinked several times to clear it. The injured guy was bleeding all over the floor.

"Here, hold this against your head." Reid reached over and grabbed his drink napkin from the bar.

The man did as instructed. The blood had left a dirty, red smudge down his cheek. He was a mess.

"You need a doctor?" Reid asked.

The man shook his head.

"Okay, then. You'd better get out of here. Go home and get washed up."

"Yeah." The man stumbled out of the bar, shooting a last penetrating look at his adversary.

"What the hell you do that for?" Pérez asked the guy who'd smashed the bottle on the other guy's head. "He could have pressed charges."

"Bastard deserved it," was all he said before he too stormed out of the bar.

"I'm going to call it a night." Reid grimaced at his shirt. It was smeared with the injured man's blood, sweat, and God knows what else. Plus, he wanted to ice his eye.

Pérez went back to the bar and drained his beer. "Yeah, good idea. We'll pick this up another time."

Reid hoped not. He didn't know how much longer he could keep saying no.

Loving *Dead Heat*? Follow the link below to purchase now!

https://links.withoutwarrant.ink/DeadHeatAFF

ALSO BY BIBA PEARCE

The Kenzie Gilmore Series

Afterburn

Dead Heat

Heatwave

Burnout

Deep Heat

Fever Pitch

Storm Surge (Coming Soon)

Detective Rob Miller Mysteries

The Thames Path Killer

The West London Murders

The Bisley Wood Murders

The Box Hill Killer

Follow the link for your free **copy of *Hard Line: A Kenzie Gilmore Prequel.***

https://liquidmind.media/biba-pearce-sign-up-1/

ALSO BY WITHOUT WARRANT

More Thriller Series from Without Warrant Authors

Dana Gray Mysteries by C.J. Cross

Girl Left Behind

Girl on the Hill

Girl in the Grave

The Kenzie Gilmore Series by Biba Pearce

Afterburn

Dead Heat

Heatwave

Burnout

Deep Heat

Fever Pitch

Storm Surge (Coming Soon)

Willow Grace FBI Thrillers by Anya Mora

Shadow of Grace

Condition of Grace (Coming Soon)

ABOUT THE AUTHOR

Biba Pearce is a British crime writer and author of the Kenzie Gilmore series and the DCI Rob Miller series.

Biba grew up in post-apartheid Southern Africa. As a child, she lived on the wild eastern coast and explored the sub-tropical forests and surfed in shark-infested waters.

Now a full-time writer, Biba lives in leafy Surrey and when she isn't writing, can be found walking through the countryside or kayaking on the river Thames.

Visit her at bibapearce.com and join her mailing list at https://liquidmind.media/biba-pearce-sign-up-1/ to be notified about new releases, updates and special subscriber-only deals.

Made in the USA
Monee, IL
02 July 2023

e7c4a341-d041-4c9a-b265-aca4b5279bd2R01